D0512506

WHERE
the
WORLD
turns
WILD

STRIPES PUBLISHING LIMITED
An imprint of the Little Tiger Group
1 Coda Studios, 189 Munster Road,
London SW6 6AW

www.littletiger.co.uk

First published in Great Britain by Stripes Publishing Limited in 2020
Text copyright © Nicola Penfold, 2020
Cover image © Kate Forrester, 2020

Quote from *Oak and Ash and Thorn: The Ancient Woods and New Forests of Britain*
by Peter Fiennes, published by Oneworld Publications, 2017

ISBN: 978-1-78895-152-4

MIX
Paper from
responsible sources
FSC® C020471

The Forest Stewardship Council® (FSC®) is a global, not-for-profit organization dedicated to
the promotion of responsible forest management worldwide. FSC defines standards based on
agreed principles for responsible forest stewardship that are supported by environmental, social,
and economic stakeholders. To learn more, visit www.fsc.org

10 9 8 7 6 5 4 3 2 1

WHERE the WORLD turns WILD

Nicola Penfold

Stripes

PRAISE FOR
WHERE THE WORLD TURNS WILD

"Some books are excellent story telling, and some books broaden your knowledge and mind, and some just ought to be written and this book is all three. I loved it."
Hilary McKay, author of *The Skylarks' War*

★

"A brilliant adventure that pulls you headlong into Juniper and Bear's world, where survival depends upon finding the wild."
Gill Lewis, author of *Sky Hawk*

★

"I've raced through *Where the World Turns Wild*… I think it truly is a fabulous debut with a powerful ecological message that could not be more timely. The plot and characters kept me gripped […] and I can't wait to see what Nicola writes next!"
AM Howell, author of *The Garden of Lost Secrets*

★

"Nicola Penfold's *Where the World Turns Wild* is a journey between extremes of grey and green, propelled by a bold and timely concept, and written with sharp, intelligent prose. A truly heartfelt and very striking novel."
Darren Simpson, author of *Scavengers*

★

"A beautiful, memorable story about all the important things – love, family, loyalty, and courage – contained inside a brilliant adventure, *Where the World Turns Wild* can't fail to enthrall any reader lucky enough to encounter it."
Sinéad O'Hart, author of *The Eye of the North*

For Matilda, Daisy, Freddie and Beatrice,
and the wild in all of you.

I wonder what would happen if every human on the planet were to fall asleep for one hundred years like the princess and her courtiers in Sleeping Beauty. *The mass extinctions would end. The forests would return... Will [the trees] miss us when we're gone? And who would tell them how beautiful they are?*

From *Oak and Ash and Thorn: The Ancient Woods and New Forests of Britain* by Peter Fiennes

PART

I

City

1

Once upon a time, almost fifty years ago, climate change and deforestation and humans ransacking everything good and beautiful, had driven our planet to breaking point. Nature was dying – plants and trees, animals, birds, insects – new species disappeared every day. But then the ReWilders created the disease.

It was grown in a lab by their best scientists and let loose in a population of ticks – eight-legged little creatures that hide in the undergrowth.

The beauty of the disease was no animal or bird ever got sick, only humans did. Humans got so sick they died. Lots of them. And the disease was so complex, so shifting, it was impossible to treat and impossible to vaccinate against. The only way for humans to survive was to live enclosed in cities, shut away from all other living things. And that, of course, had been the ReWilders' plan all along. For in the abandoned

*wastelands outside the cities, nature could regrow, and it grew
wilder and wilder. Wilder than ever.*

*It was humans or the Wild and the ReWilders chose the
Wild. I would have chosen it too.*

The glass tank is slippery in my hands and my cheeks burn
red as I walk down the corridor from Ms Endo's room.
Stick insects. One of the city's few concessions. Therapy
for wayward kids. For us to concentrate on, to control our
out-of-control imaginations. The Sticks are the last remedy
in this place.

Before you're sent to the Institute. That's the next step.
The cliff edge. There's no going back from that.

There's a whisper around me. Kids in my year and
Etienne too, though he's calling my real name – "Juniper!
Juniper!"

They're not going to forget this in a hurry. Juniper Green,
getting the Sticks. But if I concentrate hard enough I can
shut them out. I can shut them all out.

I grab my bag and storm past everyone – through the
door and the playground, and across the road that separates
Secondary from Primary. Bear will be glad of the insects at
least.

But my brother's not in the surge of bodies rushing out of
his Year Two classroom. I catch the teacher's eye quizzically

and she beckons me over. "I'm sorry, Juniper. He's in with Mr Abbott. You'll need to go and collect him."

I gulp and my eyes sting with held-back tears. Not Bear too.

Ms Jester looks at the tank. "Your turn for the stick insects, huh?"

She puts a hand on my shoulder. She was my teacher once. One of the good ones.

I nod vacantly and make my way down the corridor, keeping my gaze straight ahead. There are fractals on the walls either side – repeating patterns that are meant to be good for your brain. Soothing or something. Usually the fractals are OK, but today the grey geometric patterns leading to Abbott's room make my eyes hurt.

The head teacher's room is right at the top of the school – a glass observatory from where he can survey not just Primary and Secondary but the whole of the city almost. I take a deep breath, but even before I knock Abbott's voice rings out from behind the door. "Enter!"

I go in, leaving the stick insects outside so he doesn't have another reason to gloat. The Sticks are Ms Endo's thing. Abbott wouldn't allow them if he had his way. They're not meant as punishment – Ms Endo's our pastoral support worker and she's not like that – but still everyone knows. I'm on my final warning. One more slip up and I'll be sent to the Institute.

Bear's curled in a plastic chair – his eyes rimmed red, his cheeks blotchy and swollen. I rush over. "Bear! What's happened?"

"Your family is surpassing itself, June. Twice in one day," Abbott chimes, signalling an empty chair. But Bear's not going to let me disentangle myself now, so I sit on the same chair and Bear folds himself into me, his head pressed against my chest. He's shaking.

"I'm afraid it was another disruptive day for your brother," Abbott says, frowning at Bear, who's completely turned away from him, his hands over his ears.

"OK," I say, wary, stroking Bear's long dark locks. The curls the other kids rib him for.

"I've made several attempts to contact your grandmother."

"She'll be in the glasshouse. She never hears the phone in there."

Abbott glares at me – his porcelain face cracked, like the vases you get in the Emporium, the old junk store just around the corner from our block. "Then make sure she checks her messages. We have to come up with a plan. Your brother's becoming increasingly difficult to control."

Use his name, I shout silently at Abbott. It's because he hates it, the same way he hates mine. Animals, trees, flowers – our city forbids them all, so I'm always June to Abbott. Plain, ordinary June.

"What happened?" I ask instead.

4

"Your brother threw a chair. It could have hit another child."

"It didn't?"

"That's not the point. He's wild." Abbott leans in closer and I can smell the carbolic. It's coming right out of his pores.

"He'd like to be," I say, nervous, wishing Annie Rose was here. She wouldn't hold back. Not when it comes to Bear. Well, of course he won't sit at a table all day and be quiet. He's a child. He needs to be outside more!

Abbott looks astonished. To him any defence is just impertinence. "I think we've heard enough on that subject for one day!"

The whispered hiss of the other kids comes back to me.

It's coming up to fifty years since the city declared itself tick free and our citizenship class had been asked for essays. 'Reasons to be proud'. The best ones were to be read out before the whole of Secondary. I should have known Abbott would get involved. Get involved and twist everything around.

What was I even thinking? 'The beauty of the disease'. 'Choosing the Wild'. I gave Abbott a plate of gold when I handed in that essay.

"Bear wouldn't want to hurt anyone," I go on, quieter now. If you knew him, I think. If you could see him with the plants in our glasshouse.

"Perhaps you'd care to see a clip of him this afternoon."

"No," I say quickly. "I don't need to."

But it's already playing. On the white screen Abbott has waiting on his desk for the ritual shaming, the humiliating rerun of misdemeanours.

Bear's a different person on that screen. Like a caged animal, if we even knew what that looked like any more.

"I'd really rather not watch," I say. I can feel Bear's heart racing – fast, fast, too fast. His fingers are pale from holding them against his ears so tightly that not one decibel goes in. I want to pick him up and carry him away, but I've had enough warnings today about where rebellions lead.

I wish I could shut my eyes, like Bear has, but Abbott's gaze doesn't leave my face. He's watching my reaction. He's enjoying this.

On screen, Bear's thrown a pot of crayons across the floor – scattered them, like a broken rainbow. Ms Jester's come over, smiling, but cautiously. The other children have formed an arc. Leering around him, they're laughing, expectant.

"Why did he do that?" I ask. "Bear loves drawing. Something must have upset him."

Abbott remains silent. I can hear the chant through the speakers.

"Through the city storms an angry bear."

The on-screen Bear is bristling. If he was a bear, all the

hairs on his body would be raised.

"Shall we pick these up?" Ms Jester's saying. She's kneeling down to help him, but the chant's getting louder.

"*An angry bear*
With his long brown hair.
Send him back! Send him back!
Send him back to the forest!"

"Class, please! Quiet!" Ms Jester's begging them but Bear's already starting to shriek. Hands over his ears, he's opened his mouth as wide as he can and he's screaming.

The children explode into laughter – they're pointing and coming closer. It's not an arc any more, it's a circle and Bear's in the middle of it – screaming, lashing out.

"Please turn it off," I say to Abbott. My tears are coming now.

"This is the part, here," he says dispassionately.

That's when Bear breaks free of me. He runs out of the room and down the stairs, and I go after him, I have to, only just remembering to pick up the Sticks on my way. So I never see Bear picking up that chair. I never see whether he meant to hurt anyone. I wouldn't blame him if he had.

2

"Bear! Wait! Slow down!"

He's fast, my little brother. In a couple of years he's going to be way faster than me. He's over the playground already, hurtling across the Astro to the school gate.

"Wait, Bear! I've got the phasmids! I'm bringing them home." Despite himself, Bear starts to slow at that. "The phasmids, Bear! Like you wanted!"

He turns around, his eyes on the tank in my hands. The vivarium.

"Wow, Ju. What did you do?" he asks breathlessly. There's a gleam in his eye.

"I wrote something they didn't like."

"I drew something they didn't like," Bear says, proudly now.

"What did you draw?"

"Trees. In the city. What did you write?"

"Something about the ReWild. I tried to defend it."

"Ju!" Bear's look jolts me. I've gone too far even for him. You can't say the things I wrote in that essay – you can't have those views. The ReWilders can't be anything but bad. Terrorists. Traitors to their own species. Only sometimes you have to stand up for what you believe in. Last night, something had turned in my brain and I just couldn't write an essay of lies.

"But you got the Sticks, Ju!" Bear says, peering into the vent. "How many are there?"

"Five, Ms Endo said. But I've only seen two so far."

"What will you call them, Juniper?"

"You can help me choose."

"Can I?" He looks at me, completely grateful and excited. I love him so much it scares me.

"Let's get out of this place, Bear."

"Skedaddle?" he says.

"Scarper," I join in, and we ping back all the words we can for leaving as we wind our way through the estates to the south edge of the city where our apartment is.

Bear's amazing for six. He knows as many words as me, he just won't write them down. The only mark-making he'll do at school are his drawings and then he always gets into trouble for drawing the wrong things.

Trees in the city. Make-believe.

By the time our leave-takings are all used up – the fleeing

and the bolting and the bunking and the disappearing – we're almost there.

You can spot our building a mile off because of the tall glass dome at the back. We call it the Palm House. That's what it was once, for the old Victorian mansion block where we live. We have a tiny apartment on the ground floor where the entrance to the Palm House is. There are no palms now. They're banned species. They need too much water. It's just cacti and sedums. Succulents. The plants that require least water of all and could leach nutrients out of a stone if they needed to. Still, they're the best things about this city.

My grandmother's a licensed Plant Keeper. People need to see green things. It's a medical fact. So the Keepers are tasked with growing safe species – plants adapted for dry, desert conditions, plants the ticks would never go for – to be distributed through all the estates. Into the schools and workplaces and hospitals. A fix of green for people's windowsills.

"Annie Rose!" I call as we go into the Palm House. She doesn't stand for being called Grandma or Nanny or anything like that – she's always just wanted to be Annie Rose. "We're home!"

"Juniper berry! Bear cub!" Annie Rose's voice sings out. "Come find me!"

I'm thirteen now but I still love this game. This must be

10

the best place in the city for hide-and-seek. Old towering cacti, dense mats of sedums, we creep through them. Bear runs ahead silently. He's learned to pad.

I know from Annie Rose's squeal when he's found her. I see his tousle of hair lifted up, triumphant – black against her beautiful silver-grey. "How was your day, Bear?"

Bear grunts and pulls away, and a shadow falls across Annie Rose's face though her eyes stare blankly ahead like always. "Not good, huh?" she asks.

"I hate school," Bear growls.

"You're home now." She reaches out to find him.

"I'm going to be sick tomorrow."

"No, Bear!" I say, pleading. "It just makes it worse." He's had too many days off already. Any more and we'll have Educational Welfare coming round, asking questions.

"Come into the kitchen," Annie Rose says gently. "Let's make tea."

"No," Bear says. "Never!" And he's off through the plants – howling, squawking, screeching. Every animal noise he knows.

"You come then, Juniper." Annie Rose sighs and puts her arm out for me to take. I try and manoeuvre the tank to one side so she doesn't notice, but it's wide and the edge clangs against her. "What's that?" she asks, feeling the smooth surface with her hands.

There's no point lying. The school always leaves a

message when anyone gets the Sticks. The beeping on our answer machine will be furious today if Annie Rose hasn't already silenced it.

"Ms Endo gave me the phasmids," I say quietly.

"Oh, Juniper." Annie Rose sounds sad but there's not a hint of anger. This is what I love about her most. She's always on our side.

3

"How could a piece of writing get you in so much trouble?" Annie Rose asks, when I tell her about Abbott's reaction to my essay. "You write so well. All those words you know."

"It was about the ReWild."

I watch the confusion in Annie Rose's face change to something else. Fear, I think.

"He made me read it out in assembly, Annie Rose. In front of the whole of Secondary. Only not all of it. Not the things I most wanted to say."

It was the first part I wanted them to hear. Where I wrote about what the world had been like once – the magnificence of it, the beauty. I'd stayed up for hours working on that bit – crafting it, re-crafting. Pulling words from the thin yellowing pages of our old dictionary, looking them up again in the thesaurus section at the back, changing them for other words. I needed to get it right. To do it justice. If they could imagine it. If, just for once, the kids in my school could be allowed to hear about it, to know about it, then they'd see things differently. They'd know why the natural world had to be saved. At any cost.

But Abbott hadn't let me read that part. Or the next, where I named all the things humans were doing back then. The long list of ecological disasters. The burning of fossil fuels. Greenhouse gases. Deforestation. The oceans filled with plastic. Overfishing. Toxic waste. Pesticides. Overflowing landfill. Rivers of oil and chemicals. Fracking. Etc., etc., on and on, ad infinitum. And the one common factor in all those things. The one undeniable culprit. Us.

Someone had to stop people from ruining everything.

Annie Rose sounds nervous. "What did you write, Juniper?"

"I said the ReWilders chose the Wild over humans."

"And?"

I say the next words quickly. "I said I would choose it too. I would choose the Wild. Over people."

"And Abbott made you read that out?"

"Yes. He said I would condemn everyone to the disease. To the ticks."

He did worse than that. He brought up a montage of old film on the screen at the front of the hall. A hospital corridor lined with metal trolleys and writhing, desperate

14

people. A young mother cradling her dead child and herself sweating with fever. A mass grave. A crowd of mourners.

I'd stood there in front of the moving pictures, the sadness spilling out from the crackly old speakers, and Abbott had, in his finest preacher voice, listed the symptoms that followed a tick bite. The circular weals on the skin. The fever. The shakes. The vomiting. The diarrhoea. The bleeding that signified the final collapse of your internal organs. Young and old it was the same. The disease didn't discriminate.

Then still with the mass grave behind him and the keening of the mourners through the speakers, Abbott had pointed to me and calmly said, "This. This is what you would choose. This is what you find beautiful, June Green?"

"No," I'd said. "No." And I hadn't cried in front of them, even though I'd wanted to. I'd tried to explain. "That's not what I meant. There was just no other way. We were killing ourselves already. The Earth's our home. We need it as much as any other species."

Abbott had shut me down and ordered me into the central aisle of kids, who bent away in a wave like I was diseased, like I was dangerous. And they began their chorus. Their whispered words. *Freak. Feral. Wilding.* Which I'm used to by now. Same as Bear. But today there were other words. *Traitor. Terrorist. Murderer.*

I'd walked down the aisle to my class and stood trying to

15

find where my space had been as my classmates bunched together and looked up at me with scared, accusing eyes. *Traitor. Terrorist. Murderer.*

I don't tell Annie Rose all this. Of course I don't. "The whole school hates me now." That's what I say.

"I'm sure they don't actually hate you."

"They do, Annie Rose!"

Annie Rose sighs. "Sit down, Juniper." She takes my hair – the two long plaits I weave each morning to keep my hair out of my eyes when I paint – and she twirls it round her hand like it's precious silk. "Abbott deliberately took your words out of context!"

"Maybe they weren't out of context. Maybe most people deserved to die!"

"Juniper!"

"What, Annie Rose? We had our chance. We pretty much killed everything. We were killing ourselves too. The disease gave nature a chance to recover and that's good, isn't it? That's a good thing."

Annie Rose's face is contorted, like she wants to nod and shake her head at the same time. "Not to Abbott. Not to Portia Steel."

I roll my eyes. "Didn't it give Steel exactly what she wanted? The chance to swoop in and save everyone? Our president protector?"

Annie Rose smiles, despite herself. "Oh, Juniper! Things

16

were different when the disease first came. Steel was different. Cities were collapsing everywhere. Armageddon really had come. Portia Steel stepped up to save us."

"I know, I know!" I drawl. "The Buffer Zone. Glyphosate Patrol. Burying the rivers underground." That was what our citizenship essays were meant to be. Ovations to our acclaimed leader, Portia Steel. We're meant to be proud of her because she made it all happen. Other cities didn't fare so well, but ours triumphed. We eliminated the disease entirely.

But power corrupts. Annie Rose says that's one of the oldest stories of all.

She laughs softly. "The venom in you, sometimes, Juniper. You remind me so much of your mum." Then she sighs again. "You have to be careful. You have to be more careful than anyone else."

"I know that."

"Do you?" she asks, turning her face towards to me like she really can see.

"Yes. Of course I know."

"You have to try and fit in. You and Bear both."

"But we don't, Annie Rose."

I look at the picture on our kitchen wall. It's a hut by a lake surrounded by mountains. I drew it when I was little and anyone who saw it would think I conjured up the whole thing from my head, from a child's outlandish imagination. But it's real. It's where Bear and I were born.

A faraway valley called Ennerdale in a land of lakes and mountains.

So maybe we are freaks and we'll certainly never fit in here. We're transients, visitors, imposters. We came from the Wild and one day we'll go back there.

"No one would have listened to my stupid essay anyway. I don't know why I bothered," I say.

Annie Rose's voice is tired. She's been through this so many times before. "Juniper, you've got to give the other children a chance. They're not to blame. They don't know any different. When I was young…"

"You went on marches to save the world," I cut in. "I know, Annie Rose."

Annie Rose looks sad. "The kids at your school have never known what nature is. It's not their fault. Don't be so hard on them, Juniper. You're as prickly as the cacti sometimes!"

I scowl, but Annie Rose can't see scowls. The lenses in her eyes are clouded over like frosted glass. I get this sudden gush of love – love and guilt and sadness, everything mixed up together like the colours in my paint palette. "I'll try, Annie Rose."

She squeezes my hand. "You're a good girl, Juniper. Don't let them tell you any different. Now come on. Scoot! I have to call that ridiculous head teacher about your brother."

4

Bear's peering over the Sticks. Ms Endo was right. There are five. Only two of any significant size though. I make Bear leave the small ones in the tank. It's not that I think he'll hurt them – years of plant-tending have taught us both how to be careful. It's because I'm worried we'll lose them. That they'll slip away and I'll have failed from the start at my redemptive project.

"Look at this one, Ju!" Bear says, excited, as the largest insect climbs on to his hand. "Who shall he be?"

"How do you know it's a boy, Bear?" I ask, rolling my eyes.

"Cause he's so fierce!"

"I think she's Queen of the Sticks. Queen Lady Jane Grey," I pronounce in a solemn voice, remembering an old history lesson.

Bear nods approvingly, repeating my words. "Queen Lady Jane Grey. Who's the other big one then?"

"He's for you to name."

"I'm going to call him Phantom. Cause they're ghosts, aren't they, the Sticks?"

"Yes. Phasmids, that's what it means. Ghosts. They're so good at camouflaging themselves they can disappear. What about the little ones?"

Bear's nose wrinkles, the way it does when he's thinking. "I don't know, Ju. I don't reckon they look much like anyone yet."

"Let's call them Stick, Twig and Leaf for now."

"You're funny, Ju." Bear sits down next to me, Queen Lady Jane Grey still walking herself slowly up his arm. "I'm sorry about school," he says in a quiet voice.

"No, Bear," I say, stroking his hair, looping it round my fingers. "You just had a bad day. I had a bad day too. Some days are like that."

"The kids in my class say I'm wild. They say I should be sent back."

I pull a face. "They don't know what they're talking about. They don't have the slightest idea about the Wild."

"We do."

"A little. But we can't talk about it at school, can we?"

Bear shakes his head. "It's our secret, Ju. Yours and mine and Annie Rose's."

"And Mum and Dad's," I whisper. Tears have spilled into my eyes and there's a pain all around my heart. Our parents sent us here to keep us safe. We're here for our benefit – it wasn't that they didn't want us. Only none of that stops you feeling abandoned.

"When will they come for us?" Bear asks.

"One of these days," I say looking away, out into the green sea of plants.

"I'm fed up of waiting."

I squeeze him tight. "Me too, Bear."

"Careful, Ju. You'll crush Lady Jane! I'm going to show her round. This can be her kingdom!" He gets up and spins away from me.

5

I walk through the Palm House row by row, checking for signs of disease. At the furthest end from the house, the tallest plants are stacked together. Too close really – it can make them prone to blight and mildew to be so confined. But they're our screen. We don't want to see what they're hiding.

Most places in the city there's a wall, but where there's a building they don't bother. Our building is made of glass so we can see right out to the three-mile-wide stretch of rocks and gravel that rings our city, drenched in herbicide and insecticide to keep the ticks away. The Buffer Zone.

There's a space at the back of the plants. A little space, where you can be right up against the glass. I push the plants aside, ignoring the prickling on my arms.

I don't look at the Buffer, I never do – it sends a chill right down my neck. I only look beyond. Right to the horizon where I swear I see the beginning of green. That's where the Wild begins.

I was there four whole years before Mum brought me to the city. Even though I'd stayed healthy all that time, Mum and Dad were still worried about the disease. That's what Annie Rose says.

Sometimes I wonder if that's true. Maybe they were just fed up of having a kid to look after. But maybe not, or maybe afterwards they regretted sending me away, because a few years later they had Bear.

Then they gave him up too. Bear was only two years old. We never saw who brought him. A knock on the door at night, footsteps scurrying away and a small child in the doorway, clutching a crumpled note. Crying.

Dear Annie Rose. This is Bear. He's for Juniper. Take care of him, and our Juniper Berry. Marian and Gael xx

Gael's our dad, but I don't remember him at all.

Annie Rose has photos hanging around of Mum. Her Marian. Only they're all blurred and faded, and you can't really know someone from a photo.

It's Emily that makes me feel closest to Mum. This old rag doll with starry eyes and a cotton dress that looks like a meadow. Her face isn't happy but it isn't sad either. It's kind of thoughtful. Wistful. Like she's remembering something. Something worth remembering.

I keep Emily on my bed and even though I'm way past

doll age, sometimes I still talk to her. Tell her things. About how wound up and trapped I always feel. About all the things I'm forgetting from out there. How I'm worried one day inside my head will be as grey and concrete as the city.

The doll's the most precious thing I own, apart from Bear of course. And he's not really mine. Bear doesn't belong to anyone. He's as wild as they come.

That's why Annie Rose and I both ignore so much of what school tells us when they say he won't sit down to be taught, that he won't form letters or write numbers or even draw anything they want him to draw. We don't want him taming.

Babies develop according to their environment. That's one of the most incredible things about being human – how adaptable we are when we're small. Those first formative months. That's why all the other kids can stand living here. Nature has been banned from the cities, and they hardly mind at all because they grew up in this grey concrete metropolis.

And that's why Bear and I hate it so much. Because when we were little our brains got used to trees and flowers and animals, and even though we can't really remember much of all that, this whole city is a cage for us.

I don't think our parents are really coming back for us. Not now. I think it's too risky. But that's OK. As soon as Bear's old enough for the journey, we're breaking out of the city ourselves.

6

"Juniper!" Annie Rose calls and I slink back into the kitchen. "Can you get me down a jar of Rainbow Mix?"

Our kitchen is the most impractical food preparation space ever. Most of it is taken up with this old wooden table, then around the edges are shelves. Only the lower ones are full of books, not food. Our kitchen's a library really.

Most of the books are forbidden now. There's too much nature in them. A few years ago, Portia Steel, in her wisdom, outlawed even 'descriptions and depictions' of the Wild.

I scrape our wooden stool along the floor deliberately and stand on tiptoes to reach the Rainbow Mix. It's right up by the ceiling.

I place the jar on the work surface with a thud. "Yummy! My favourite!"

The label shows carrots and sweetcorn and beetroot cut

improbably into stars, but when you open it up, when you actually see what's inside, the colours are muted and the shapes are mushy and don't hold together. "You wouldn't eat it if you could see it," Bear tells Annie Rose every time she tries to get him to try some.

"Thanks, Juniper," Annie Rose says, ignoring my sarcasm.

She's buttering bread – a layer of grease on a solid square of congealed mycoproteins.

"I got through to Abbott," she says.

"And?" I prompt.

"He said Bear overreacted to some harmless rhyme at school."

"Harmless?" I boil. "How dare he? If you had heard it! If you had seen Bear on that screen. How scared he was."

"Abbott gave me a rundown of your essay too. He enjoyed that."

I flush. Of course he would.

Annie Rose opens her mouth to speak, then stops. When she talks her voice is measured. "There was something else too. He was talking about your blood. Yours and Bear's. *Maybe they can't help it, if it's in their blood. Maybe that's what we should be doing something about.*"

I laugh. "Do something about? You can't change what we are. As much as Abbott would want to."

Pretty much everyone who ever came into contact

with the disease died, but there were a few miraculous exceptions. People who had resistance to it. We learned about it in biology. Some freak sequence of amino acids that gave you immunity. Scientists had tried to replicate it in the lab but they couldn't. You have to be born with resistance. Like Bear and I were.

Annie Rose frowns. "Abbott was hiding something, Juniper. And taunting me with it. The man's draconian."

A little voice pipes up behind us. "Is tea ready? I'm starving!"

Annie Rose smiles. "We were waiting for you, Bear cub! This table's missing its knives and forks. Where were you?"

"Draconian. Like a dragon, Annie Rose?" Bear asks.

"Oh, much worse than a dragon," Annie Rose says, and Bear starts parroting 'draconian' round the kitchen as he lines up the cutlery.

"What would I do without you two?" Annie Rose laughs, but her face crumples as she realizes what she's said.

Annie Rose had a blood test right after the ReWild. She's always known she doesn't have resistance to the tick disease. She knows Bear and I will leave one day and she's gathered the things we'll need for the journey, but she'll never be able to come with us. When Bear and I go back to the Wild, we're leaving Annie Rose for good.

7

We do the bedtime ritual together, Annie Rose and I. Pyjamas, teeth, hair – tousling Bear's curls into some kind of shimmery order – and though we barely fit any more, all three of us, we squeeze into Bear's room.

When he came to us, Bear wouldn't settle in a bed. Every night he rolled off and woke crying, so instead Annie Rose made this little nest in the smallest room of all, a cupboard really, with a mattress on the floor and painted stars on the ceiling.

I was a different person then. My behaviour record was immaculate. Exemplary. But the real me was hiding. When Bear came, he brought me back to life. His energy and spirit, they woke mine back up. I could smell the Wild on him. I could hear it in his voice.

Annie Rose gave me paints and brushes and asked for the stars, but I didn't stop at that. I got out Annie Rose's old wildflower book and painted them around the walls so Bear could see them – ferns and forget-me-nots, cow parsley, harebells and foxgloves, poppies and cornflowers. His own meadow.

I did it for him. For Bear – this tiny brother, this creature who had miraculously been brought to me, with his big open heart and all that energy coursing through him.

I was out in the Wild twice as long as Bear but Bear kept hold of it better, like he kept hold of his curls. Like the curls are his wildness.

Bear thrusts a book into my arms. "It's Kingfisher tonight, Ju!"

Birds of the World. I look down at the amazing winged creatures on the cover. It's Bear's favourite book, even though he knows every single bird already. But then Bear knows most nature things. Acorn, buttercup, conker, daisy. That's Bear's alphabet. The only one he's ever bothered learning.

He points to the kingfisher on his wall, flying over the meadow. "It's on its way to the river, Ju. Remember? For fish."

"Yes," I say and I stare at it, all blue and orange and cyan. I painted all kinds of birds, but it's the kingfisher I'm most proud of. Tears mist up my eyes. "I'm going out. Annie Rose can read tonight, Bear."

Bear sits bolt upright. "Ju! You love kingfishers!"

"I'm going out," I repeat flatly.

Annie Rose places her hands on Bear's shoulders. "Let your sister go. I'll tell you all about kingfishers. I saw one once, when I was very little. It must have been one of the last of all."

"Did it have a fish, Annie Rose?" Bear asks, wide-eyed, lying down to listen, even though he's heard it a thousand times before.

Annie Rose's voice floats after me as I go to the kitchen table to pick up my sketchbook and pencil. "You do just mean the Palm House, Juniper?"

"Of course," I say. "I know the rules."

8

In the night, Bear comes into my bed. He's half asleep, rubbing his eyes. Usually I go straight back to my dreams but tonight I can't. I'm worried about Bear, but I'm worried about me too. I'm lying awake, listening to the generators and the city sirens that call out above everything whenever there's any kind of alert. Someone breaking Curfew. Disturbance at the Buffer. Trouble in the Warren. You never really find out.

"Camouflage," Ms Endo said, when she put the tank of phasmids in my arms. "That's what you could learn from them. You've got to keep your head down, Juniper. Blend in a bit. Has something happened you want to talk about?"

"No," I'd said, but I'd stopped there because how could I explain? It's not one thing – it's everything. Everything's just gone on too long. Each long day at school like the one before and the one before that. Everything regulation.

Everything the same.

When it's cold, they turn the heating up. When it's hot, they put the air-con on. When it's dark, all the city lights illuminate to make it exactly as bright as the day before, for the exact same period of time. Until switch-off. 8pm. Curfew. That's when our days end. When the wail of the siren sounds. The klaxon.

I know it's autumn because it's the end of October and I'm eight weeks into Year Eight, but there are no leaves to colour and fall and in our crowded, clean city the cold never really penetrates too much. The breaks go up if it's windy, the canopies if it rains.

And every morning I'm waking from my dreams of an altogether different kind of canopy of branches and leaves, and I think I can't stand it any more. Another day in this city.

Then I think of Annie Rose and the hard place inside me softens a little.

When the Buffer went up, it was the Plant Keepers who kept a link to the outside. Most of the ReWilders had left the city by then. They'd taken their chances out there and most had already died. Not just from the disease. Hunger. Cold. Annie Rose said humans had forgotten what it was like to survive off-grid.

A few of them found Ennerdale though and for a while the ReWilders kept up communication with the Plant Keepers.

Supplies came in, supplies went out. Messages. And, in our case, children.

But all that was a long time ago. Almost all the Plant Houses have closed now – there's just ours on the South Edge and another one in the north. And you can't bring things into the city these days. Barely even messages, but certainly not people. Everyone's too scared.

Over each district there looms the tallest building in the city. All grey and shiny, like the suits worn by Portia Steel's officers. The City Institute.

Annie Rose said Portia Steel opened it in person, in the days when she was still seen around, when she wasn't just a photo on everyone's walls. There was a big fancy ceremony and Steel cut the bow on a red ribbon. She said the Institute was her gift to our city.

It's a mental health hospital. A facility for people who've gone off the rails. People who are too angry, or too unpredictable, or just too sad. Adults mostly, but children too. The Institute is meant to help people get better, so they can better manage life in this place. Only that's a big fat lie because no one comes out. No one ever comes out.

Bear's stirring beside me, tossing, turning. "No! Go away! Leave me alone!"

"Shush," I murmur. "Shush." Like the wind, whispering to him.

These are the dreams he comes into my bed to banish.

He never talks about them. I don't know whether they're a rerun of his school day. I don't know what he's trying to push away as he kicks his legs and hits out with his hands.

If I wake him, he's more afraid than ever, so I put my arms round him and whisper him back to a better place. To when he was little, out there with Mum. She would have known what to do.

9

Bear drags his feet all the way to school.

"Come on, Bear, you're faster than this. You can run like the wind, remember?"

"I won't go, Ju!"

"You have to, Bear. Every kid has to go to school. It's the rules."

"It's a stupid rule. I won't. I won't go!"

He's shouting loudly. We're only a block away from school and the pavements are full of kids.

"Come on, Bear, it's just a few hours. And it's Friday. It's the weekend tomorrow. Maybe you can tell Ms Jester about the Sticks. Maybe she'll let you draw one. You'd like that, wouldn't you?"

"No, I wouldn't," Bear says, defiant. "I won't go, Ju."

"Please, Bear," I say, changing tactics. "Do it for me. I need you to, Bear."

I can hear the whispering around us. I think I even hear the chant – that hateful verse they've made up about him. There was one about me too, once.

"Juniper Green, Juniper Green.
She's so crazy, I think she's going to
Scream."

They don't say it any more – I think they've forgotten it – but sometimes I recite the words in my head. Like they've become this truth. This suppressed scream that one of these days is going to leak out of me.

"Please, Bear."

He hates it when I plead with him. He doesn't want to make me sad. Tears well in his eyes and another rhyme starts around him.

"Cry baby Bear,
Crying for his lair."

I flash my head, angry – but the kids who were singing look away, or break into a run. Only a few older ones hold my gaze – curious, amused.

"Shall we show them how fast we can run?" I say, making my voice loud so the challenge is public.

Bear wipes his sleeve against his face and a spark of defiance dances into his eyes. "Sprint?" he says.

"Tear," I answer, and we hold hands and run past them, fastest of all. No late marks today.

I'm called to Ms Endo's office right after assembly. There

are about a dozen other kids there. There's just one other Year Eight – a girl, Britta.

Etienne's here too, and it's seeing him that makes me realize what everyone has in common. We've all been given the Sticks. I'm just the latest recruit.

Ms Endo smiles at me. "We have a treat in store for you today, Juniper. We're going to get leaves for the stick insects."

The atmosphere in the room is kind of gleeful. On a table is a box and the other students are fingering its items – shells and fossils, pinecones and dried seed heads, feathers and animal bones. It's all contraband. Bear's talked about it. He says Ms Endo calls them her treasures.

"The minibus will be here in ten minutes," Ms Endo says. "I've just got to check something at the Infants, then we're good to go. Please make Juniper feel welcome."

The other kids glance at me, disinterested. Only Etienne looks up. Etienne who spoke my name for the first time in months yesterday.

He hands me a skull, like some kind of silent greeting. I know from the books Bear pores over at home that it's a bird skull. A bird of prey. A raptor, Bear would say. I love the idea of these creatures dancing in the sky, scouring the earth, ready to swoop. For the kill. But the bone in my hand only makes me sad. The deep round sockets where the eyes would have been and the hooked beak, blunted now, that could once tear through flesh.

"Hi," I say awkwardly.

Etienne lives upstairs in our block. He used to come down to play in our glasshouse but stopped when he went up to secondary school a year before me. Something changed. He started saying our games were kids' stuff.

Plus he got into trouble at school. He beat up a boy in his class. He beat him really bad. Hospital bad. Everyone thought that was it for Etienne – exclusion, the Institute – but he's still here, kicking around. It's probably because of his mum. She's high up in the city design department, programming the fractals they plaster the city with. The never-ending patterns, which are the same whether you're looking at one tiny section or a whole wall.

Etienne gives a low whistle. "That was some essay, Juniper Green."

I pull a face. "I didn't think you were allowed in assembly?"

"They let me in for that one. A Juniper special."

My cheeks rash. "Yeah, well. You heard it. You can hate me now too."

"Hate you?" Etienne actually looks surprised. "Nah. That's just Abbott."

"You heard what the other kids were saying."

"Not all of them." Etienne shrugs. "You know how Abbott stokes them up. Anyway, you'll be all right with us.

The Remedials. There're no big Abbott fans here."

Everyone's listening now. A couple of the others pull faces and groan, and one girl, Serena from Year Ten, sticks two fingers down her throat and pretends to gag. Then with the same two fingers she points up to where Abbott's office would be. "Bang, bang," she says all slow and deliberate. She winks at me.

My eyes flit up to the corners of the room and Etienne laughs. "Don't worry. There aren't any cameras here. Ms Endo makes sure of it."

"So where do we go for the leaves?" I ask, switching subject.

Etienne's face lights up. "The North Edge."

"The Plant House?" I say, surprised, and something stirs inside me because it's all the way across the city where I've never been before.

Etienne nods. "They have a special licence to grow leaves for phasmids. Actually, I guess it's not only for the phasmids, it's some Future Science thing. Stick leaves are why Ms Endo got us in there. But it's weird we're going today. It wasn't meant to be for a couple of weeks. How's your glasshouse doing, Juniper?"

I shrug. "It keeps me almost sane."

"Does it?" Etienne asks, a weird longing in his voice.

"Annie Rose says the North Edge is like a palace!"

Etienne grins. "Oh, it's way better than that."

39

On the bus, everyone takes a double seat for themselves so they can be by the window. It's a novelty. For us kids anyway.

The grown-ups are probably all fed up of the daily commute across the city – the routes to the Farms or the Park. They sound like nice places to work – farms, park – but they're not.

The Farms are pesticide and fertilizer central and farmhands spend their whole day in Hazmat suits, trying to get fruit and vegetables and cereals to grow in the worn-out soil they have left. The Eco Park is the city dump, where all the rubbish gets sent for sorting. We don't have the raw materials to be fussy any more. If something can be melted down and used again, that's what happens.

You can see the Park workers now, scurrying along the pavement, one after another after another, like the ant trails we read about in one of our books.

"Mum," a wavering voice calls. It's Britta. She's pressing her fingers against the window of the bus, staring at a woman at the back of one of the lines.

The kids clamour on the glass to get her mum's attention. Britta doesn't. She just watches. Her mum's head hanging low, her back all stooped.

I went to Britta's flat once. Before Bear came and reminded everyone where I came from and all the kids started keeping their distance. It was Britta's eighth birthday. Her mum and dad had arranged a treasure hunt and laid clues through all the rooms of their flat. I found the treasure at the end and it was a box of chocolates for us to share.

Britta's mum wasn't stooped then. I remember her throwing back her head, laughing at the chocolate round our faces. "You've all got extra smiles today. You must be extra happy!" She looked extra happy too.

I guess the Eco Park takes happiness away pretty fast. Plus Britta's dad isn't around any more. He got admitted to the Institute. It was the talk of the school, until another person was admitted. Someone else's parent.

"Oi! Tick truck," one of the boys calls, and I grab on to the seat in front as everyone moves to the other side of the bus and starts banging against the windows again, only louder this time.

It's Glyphosate Patrol day. The trucks are out.

No place to hide! That's their motto and the vans have this ugly great tick on the side. Just so we remember what we're scared of. They hunt down every single bit of green – each stray blade of grass or seedling that's somehow resisted the defences and taken root in the city's streets – and they spray, in their unwieldy white suits and boots. Like misplaced moon men.

Etienne's on the seat in front of me, his forehead pressed against the glass. He's so still I'd figured he was sleeping, but occasionally a noise erupts from him. A shudder. For one awful moment I think he's crying, but then it hits me. It's laughter. He's laughing at them. At the Glyphosate Patrol. Why would he do that?

10

The North Edge glasshouse must be five times the size of our Palm House. Everyone goes quiet as we enter and I go quietest of all. It's like my dreams made real. There are way more plants than we grow and they're wilder, rampant. Leaves like hearts spread up the walls and they're wet – covered in tiny drops of water that glisten in the sunlight that's spilling in from the domed glass roof.

The others know the drill already. They've each brought with them a small plastic box and they disappear off in different directions, a skip in their step.

The Keeper heads over to introduce himself. He's called Sam and he looks as old as Annie Rose. Older. What wisps of hair he has left are pure white.

"So who's our new recruit?" he asks and Ms Endo says my name. My full name. Juniper Berry Green.

Sam starts at this. I know I'm not imagining it as there's

something about Ms Endo's manner too, something expectant. She's prompting him. "Juniper's grandmother, Annie Rose Green, tends the old Palm House on the South Edge."

"Annie Rose Green," Sam says, his forehead furrowed. "We used to know each other. You're her granddaughter? But Marian left?"

"Yes." I shift on my feet at Mum's name and Sam's scrutiny, and because Etienne is standing nearby, listening. "She ran away."

"I remember. Her and that boy. Sebastian wasn't it?"

I nod, my cheeks flushing. Everyone knows that bit. Mum ran off with a boy, only Mum got all the blame because the boy, Sebastian, was the son of one of Steel's favourite henchmen. People said Mum corrupted Sebastian, that she led him astray. They said she preyed on him because she found out what his blood test had shown.

Sam's staring at me strangely. "Marian made it then? She survived out there?"

I nod, proud suddenly. Because Mum did survive and I'm proof of it.

"She sent you back?" Sam looks puzzled and like he's about to ask something else, but Etienne gets in first.

"Can I show Juniper round?"

"You won't forget anything?"

"Of course not," Etienne says, pulling a face.

44

"Don't forget your box," Sam says, still looking at me curiously but handing me the same white box the others have. "Pick wisely. You have a good guide there."

Etienne blushes. "This way, Juniper!"

11

"The heart-shaped leaves are ivy. The Sticks love it," Etienne tells me as I watch his fingers prise off a leaf. "Glyphosate Patrol would have a fit wouldn't they, if they could see all this?"

I look at him and we burst into a fit of giggles.

It feels wrong at first, to break off leaves, but there's no shortage here. The ivy is twined round metal pillars that support the roof, and there are strands twisting all the way to the top and at our feet too – stretching out along the walkways.

"It's like a jungle. Bear would love this."

"You haven't seen the best bit yet," Etienne says and leads me on, leads me deeper. Where the leaves tangle together and some kind of fruit hangs from the stems.

My hands reach out but something pierces my finger and there's a bright speck of blood. "Ouch!"

Etienne pulls me back. "Careful! I should've warned you. There are thorns." He's right. The plant is armed – ribbed with needles or spikes.

I look around to see if anyone else saw, embarrassed to have been got by a plant. I grew up with cacti. I know how to be careful. But no one's about.

"It's a berry?" I ask, thinking of the pictures on the jam pots in our kitchen. We barely ever see fresh fruit. It's grown out in the Farms, but by the time we see it it's so heavily processed it barely resembles the thing that actually grew.

"They're blackberries," Etienne says and now it's him looking around surreptitiously. "Try one."

I know instinctively which to take. There are firm, tight green ones and red ones like blood, but my hand reaches for the darkest of all. I tease it from its stem and it explodes in my mouth, all sweet and tart together.

"Good, huh?" Etienne says.

"It's amazing! I want another! I want them all!"

"OK, Juniper! But you have to pick some leaves too, OK? Not the bright green ones – the young leaves are poisonous. The Sticks want the older, darker ones." He pulls stems aside to show me, his fingers finding a path between the thorns.

"You've got the knack," I say, impressed.

"Ha!" Etienne grins and then says, almost shyly, "Sam's teaching me. He lets me come at weekends. He says I can be his apprentice. When I'm done with school."

"A Plant Keeper?"

Etienne looks embarrassed. "Someone's got to take over eventually."

"I guess."

"I suppose you're one already."

"I guess," I say again, and suddenly I feel sad. Plant Keeper. The greatest aspiration Etienne can have and it's still inside the city.

For ages, Etienne and I wander through the rows. We don't say anything of consequence, and we don't mention all the time he's been ignoring me, but it's nice somehow. Etienne chattering on about the plants, like no one else would.

In one corner there's a fluorescent line like police tape, like a crime's happened right here in the glasshouse although that's ridiculous. It's just tape and it's low and flimsy. I'm thinking about crossing it, just to see, when Etienne pulls me back. "Don't, Juniper. Sam would be livid."

"Is that where he breeds the Sticks?" I ask, for past the tape a few metres in, there's a fine mesh wall. A gauze like on the top of the vivarium.

"I don't think so. The Sticks don't come from here. It's some medical thing. We'd contaminate it if we went near."

"Yeah?"

"Yes," Etienne says firmly.

"OK," I say, straining my eyes past the mesh. But Ms Endo's calling out our names. Rounding us up for the glyphosate tray on the way out to drench the soles of our shoes before we head back to school.

"Juniper, you've got to remove the evidence!" Etienne points to one of the mirrors that hang throughout the glasshouse, bouncing back light. My lips and face are smudged red like war paint. I wipe it off and smile.

12

We get back to school just as the tannoy is belting out the tone for home time and I go straight to Bear's classroom. I breathe a sigh of relief. He's on the carpet, staring through the doors.

"Has he been OK today?" I ask.

"Yes," Ms Jester says, but her eyes don't meet mine.

Bear doesn't bound across the room to me like he usually does. He walks over slowly, stopping at his peg to pick up his school bag.

"Hi, Bear," I say, pulling him out from the flow of kids to button up the coat that's hanging off him, half dragging across the floor. "I've got a surprise for you!"

Bear raises his eyebrows hopefully. "More Sticks?"

"No. But I went on an adventure today. I got them more leaves. Something else too. But we can't stop till we get home. It's secret."

"OK, Ju," Bear says, but he winces like he's in pain and that's when I notice. The white bandage on his left arm, just below the sleeve of his T-shirt, where I'm bending his elbow to try and force it into his coat.

"What's that?"

Bear's eyes well up. "She stabbed me!"

"Who did?"

"I dunno. Some woman in a white coat."

"Wait there!" I charge back to Ms Jester. "What happened to Bear's arm?"

"Nothing serious, Juniper," she says, trying to sound breezy. "He had a blood test."

"A blood test!"

Ms Jester's face falls a little. "Mr Abbott said he'd got the necessary permissions. Maybe he spoke to your grandmother?"

"No. No!" My heart is pounding in my ribcage and I can feel sweat breaking out on the back of my neck.

"I saw your name on the list too. They didn't come over to Secondary?"

"I wasn't there…" My voice trails off and Etienne's words come back to me – *It's weird we're going today. It wasn't meant to be for a couple of weeks.* And Abbott too. What was it he said on the phone last night to Annie Rose? *Maybe it was our blood they should be doing something about?*

51

Suddenly Ms Endo's here and she's angry. "The phlebotomist came? For Bear? It was to be Secondary only. Primary are too small. Abbott promised me!"

"I couldn't do anything. Abbott insisted," Ms Jester splutters. Her neck's red and she's breathing fast. "And the lady, the phlebotomist, was nice. She would have been gentle, only he struggled."

"I bet he struggled!" Ms Endo says, fuming.

"It was just one vial!"

"But what's the point if they don't intend…" Ms Endo stops. She looks at me and then at Bear, who's still holding out his arm like it's not part of him any more.

"Intend what?" I say quietly.

Ms Jester jumps like she'd forgotten I was even there. She backs away from me to start passing kids out again. Kid, school bag, lunchbox, like packages on a factory conveyor belt.

Ms Endo pats my arm. "I'll sort it out. It's an error. An oversight."

"I was meant to be tested too, wasn't I? That's why we went today? To the North Edge?"

"Juniper," Ms Endo says carefully. "Leave this. It's not your battle. I'll sort it. You take Bear home."

"We have a right to know!"

"Juniper," Ms Endo says again, nodding in the reassuring way she always does when she's dealing with Bear.

"I promise you I'll go and see Abbott now. You two go home to your grandmother." She ruffles Bear's hair. "You'll feel better soon, sweetheart. None of that bounding about for a while, OK?" She winks at me. "Don't worry. I'll see you both on Monday."

I nod, watching as she heads towards the staircase for Abbott's office. Somehow walking to Abbott's room like that, head down, Ms Endo looks just like a child.

"Will it be OK, Ju?" Bear tugs at my hand.

"Of course it will," I say, keeping my voice light. "Let's get home. We can tell Annie Rose all about it."

13

Annie Rose is pacing round our kitchen. She sent Bear into the glasshouse to play, but not before she unwound his bandage. The inside of his elbow is black and blue, showing the marks of his struggle. There are five separate pinpricks, where the needle has breached his skin. I had to describe it out loud as Annie Rose's fingertips felt gently, searching for answers.

Bear cried when he looked, and when Annie Rose took a warm cloth and wiped away the congealed blood.

"I don't understand," I say now. "I don't understand why they want his blood."

"Juniper, sit down."

"Annie Rose!" I say, my heart tripping. "You're scaring me!"

"Sit down, Juniper. Please."

Annie Rose sits next to me. "That must be what Abbott

was talking about. The blood test. They must want to confirm Bear's disease resistance. Yours too no doubt, if you'd been there."

"What's it to them? Why would they care?"

Annie Rose traces her fingers along the tabletop. The flecks of paint and indentations from all our words and pictures, Bear's and mine. And Mum's before us. "They must want to use your blood somehow. Make the vaccine they always said was impossible. Maybe they've found the science to make it work."

"Why would they bother?"

"So they can go back into the Wild."

"They hate the Wild!"

Annie Rose nods. "But it's useful to them. Steel needs it more than ever now, to regain her popularity."

I snort. "What? She doesn't need more popularity. Portia Steel's our saviour. Everyone says!"

"That's propaganda, Juniper!" Annie Rose says gently. "Surely you can see that. You of all people. You hear the sirens? And the drones, every night now? The city's starving."

"Yes," I say quietly. I hear the sirens. The sirens and the drones and the marching feet too. Steel's Street Patrol, marching with a new urgency.

"People are getting angry, Juniper. Steel's talked about sending out hunting parties for years. To get food. Fuel.

Materials. Medicines. Why do you think no one ever sees her any more? She hides in her bunker because she knows what might happen if she comes out. Only she's running out of time. She doesn't want the city's fiftieth birthday party to be an uprising. She has to find a way back into the Wild."

"She can't. She'll wreck it."

Annie Rose nods but stays silent.

"We can't let her, Annie Rose!" I cry. "Things would be worse than ever."

Portia Steel's hatred for the Wild runs deep. As if the Wild is some rival leader. Some rival god. When I think of Steel out in the Wild, it's with an axe in her hand.

"We have to think about what this could mean for you, Juniper," Annie Rose says. "For you and Bear."

"I won't let them take my blood. I won't, Annie Rose."

"Abbott," Annie Rose says fearfully.

"Abbott can go to hell. I'll—"

Annie Rose cuts me off. Her voice is stern. "Juniper, you will not do anything. You know what he'd do."

Annie Rose doesn't say the word out loud and I don't say it either. We're both thinking it though. The Institute.

"We should check the things tonight," Annie Rose says softly. "After Bear's gone to bed."

"The things?" I ask, confused.

"The journey things."

56

"No, Annie Rose!" I cry, shocked, because suddenly I realize what she means. The things for our journey, mine and Bear's. Our journey back to the Wild. To Ennerdale. But it's not time yet. It's not time and we're not ready. My words come out in a torrent. "I'll keep my head down from now on. I'll toe the line. I'll get Bear to as well…"

Annie Rose shakes her head. "It's not about that, not any longer. Not if they're coming for your blood."

"Bear's not old enough to travel out there. And it'll be winter soon. You said we'd go in spring and that we'd find someone to help. Annie Rose!" I want to take her hand like Bear does when he wants you to listen. I want to take her hand and tug it hard.

It's not that I don't want to go. It's that we can't go now.

We're not ready to go and we're not ready to say goodbye.

But there's a cry coming from the Palm House and then Bear's at the kitchen door, demanding our attention. "I'm hungry, Annie Rose!" and "Ju, shall we get the Sticks out?"

14

"Juniper, where's my surprise?" Bear says after tea.

He's got his Jungle spread out over the table. His menagerie. Little plastic animals that are his favourite things in all the world.

The blackberries. I'd forgotten all about them.

I find the white box in my school bag and hand it over. Bear eyes it suspiciously. The blackberries are squashed and bleeding, the leaves around them stained black.

"I'm not eating that," he says.

"They're blackberries, Bear." I wanted them to be a gift, but they just look damaged. Dangerous.

"Blackberries, Juniper?" Annie Rose says, feeling the soft, rounded segments. "Wherever did you find them?"

"We went to the North Edge," I say quietly. "To collect leaves for the phasmids."

"Sam's place?" she asks, surprised.

"Yes. He said he knew you."

"Once," Annie Rose says, her cheeks dimpling a little, like the beginning of a smile. "He knew you were Marian's daughter?"

"Yes."

Bear's opening his mouth to say something, but Annie Rose deftly slips a blackberry into his hand. "Sam gave you the berries?"

"I took them. I wasn't meant to but I did anyway. It was stupid. I should have known they wouldn't keep."

"Being a bit squashed won't change their taste. Come on, Bear. I'm definitely eating mine." She places the fruit in her mouth. "Oh my word, that's delicious! It's a long time since I tasted anything that good."

Bear's staring at the little fruit, turning it over in his fingers.

"It's what they eat in the Wild," Annie Rose says, lowering her voice.

"What does it taste of?" he asks.

"Like the jam pots, only fresher."

Bear brings the berry to his nose and sniffs, then he puts out his tongue to touch its surface. "It's sweet?"

"You'll love it," Annie Rose says.

Bear looks at me for confirmation.

"It grew, Bear. It grew on a bramble. I picked it with Etienne."

"Etienne?"

Bear hero worships Etienne, he always has. Even when Etienne started ignoring us. Bear moves the berry round his mouth approvingly. "You got any more?"

15

I'm too agitated to help with Bear's bedtime routine. Annie Rose does it all and comes to find me after. I'm in the hidden space, looking out across the Buffer. I don't why. This time of night there's only darkness.

"Penny for them?" she asks softly, but I don't say anything.

She stands next to me and I watch our faces beside each other in the glass. I can never see myself in the photos of Mum, she looks like a stranger, but I know when I'm old I'll look just like Annie Rose.

"Was it my essay?" I ask finally, my voice trembling.

Annie Rose's voice is fierce. "No, Juniper. No! Don't ever think that! Abbott's had his eye on our family for years. Your mum got him into trouble when she left. Letting two of his students slip away, and one of them from Steel's inner circle. Abbott's always had it in for us."

"But what does it mean? The blood test? What will happen?"

Annie Rose shakes her head. "I don't know. But I have a bad feeling. Come inside, Juniper. I can't manage that chest on my own. Not any more."

I follow her into the kitchen, my footsteps heavy on the Palm House tiles.

The chest is where we store my grandfather's things. He was a potter. He made bowls and vases in a time when there were still flowers to buy. He died when Mum was my age but Annie Rose kept all his tools. There's even a bag of clay, though it's hard as rock now and falls away like dust when you touch it.

"Take one side, Juniper," Annie Rose says. For the things we need aren't in the chest itself. They're beneath it, deep under our kitchen floor.

Annie Rose only ever showed me once. Just after Bear came, when everyone was talking about us all over again.

The slate flagstone underneath the chest is loose. Annie Rose uses one of the tools – a file – to get into the groove around the slate square and prise it up. "It's a while since this was lifted."

"Let me do it," I say, frightened suddenly at how pale she looks. How old.

It takes a few attempts but I manage to raise it a fraction and then somehow manoeuvre off the whole flagstone so

I can see right down to the timber joists holding up our kitchen floor. On the earthen surface an arm's length under that there's a plastic crate with three letters on its lid.

I read them out slowly. "S. O. S. What does it mean, Annie Rose?"

"It was a distress code. A radio signal. For ships out at sea."

"Yes, but what does it actually *mean*?"

"Save our souls," Annie Rose answers, and I gulp.

There are two red ropes wrapped around the crate. They slip through my hands and burn into my skin, but I don't let go until the crate is up on our kitchen floor.

Another time, another circumstance, and the things we unpack would be wondrous. We have this book, *Campcraft*. It's one of my favourites, even though it's over a hundred years old and the pages are yellow and the binding's all broken. It tells you how to prepare for sleeping outside. Camping. People used to do it for fun, for holidays. They used to go away for a week or so, somewhere nice, somewhere different, just for the fun of it.

The book tells you how to keep warm and dry. It tells you how to find food and find your way using a compass and the stars, which out of the city's glare are bright and guiding. It's got a list in the back – essential kit – and the box contains some of the things on that list.

There are two thick waxy plastic sheets called tarpaulins.

One's a groundsheet, the other a roof to make a tent. There are pans for cooking and two bottles for carrying water, and a small tube of test strips to check that water's safe to drink.

There's a sleeping bag and a metallic sheet called a space blanket, all shiny to reflect your own body heat back at you. There are torches and a round golden compass – a clock that shows direction not time. North, East, South, West.

In a waxy pouch are small boxes with elegant, long-necked white birds on their lids. Swans. Annie Rose hands me a box. "Strike one, Juniper. Let's check they're still OK."

The stick inside has gunpowder on the end and you rub it against the gritty surface of the box and some kind of chemical reaction takes place. You get fire. Only I don't. My palms are sweaty, my fingers clumsy.

"Faster, Juniper. Firmer."

I try again but the stick breaks.

"Juniper, come on," Annie Rose says, and I realize she's laughing. "Anyone can light a match."

Angry now at how she can laugh at a moment like this, I take out another stick and strike it all the way down the side of the box, and there it is. A flame. Warm and golden and alive.

You're not allowed fire in the city. The buildings are too close together, fire is forbidden. But here it is – one flickering flame, getting ever closer to my hand.

"Don't let it burn your fingers, Juniper! Blow!"

I blow. I blow hard, like kids in stories when it's their birthday and they're blowing out candles on a cake.

The pairs of boots make me go cold. They're adult size and it's fine for me because my feet are big. Annie Rose always says how tall I am, that I must get that from my dad. But the boots would dwarf Bear's feet. He'd slip right out of them.

"The boots, Annie Rose," I say, my voice wavering. "Bear…"

Annie Rose just nods. "We'll get some. The Emporium or something. We'll sort it, Juniper, don't worry," and she signals for me to keep on unpacking.

There are knives in another of the pouches. One is small, like our pruning knife in the glasshouse. One's bigger. Sharper. I touch the blade with my finger. "What are the knives for, Annie Rose?"

"You won't be able to carry enough food to keep you going you all that time. Ennerdale's three hundred miles away, Juniper. You'll be walking for weeks. You'll need to hunt. Rabbits. Birds." Annie Rose pauses for a moment. "When your mum went, she had a gun."

"A gun?"

"An air rifle."

I shake my head. "No, Annie Rose. I'm not taking a gun!"

Annie Rose's face is like stone, all fixed and hard. "Do you hear the wolves at night?"

Of course I do. We all do. The city has noises of its own – the sirens, the hum of the generators, the wailing of the Curfew. The mechanical parts of the city, always working, but the sound of the wolves carries above it all and Bear and I weave it into our stories. The call of the wild. "I couldn't, Annie Rose."

"You'll need something."

"No," I say again, panicked now. "I mean, I just couldn't." I look at the items spread round our table – relics from another world. "I can't do any of this!"

"You can, Juniper," Annie Rose says firmly. "Just like your mum did."

"I'm nothing like my mum."

"You are," Annie Rose says, serious but with this ghost of a smile flashing up on to her cheekbones. "More than you know."

"I won't have a clue out there."

"Look, Juniper." Annie Rose puts her hand out to the shelves running round our kitchen. She recites the titles to me. The bedtime stories when I was young. The odd kinds that you'd never find at school. *Wild Flowers and Edible Plants* and *Navigate with the Stars* and *First Aid Naturally.* The fairy tales too, with their big, unending forests. *Sleeping Beauty. Red Riding Hood. Hansel and Gretel.*

Some Annie Rose and Grandpa Edward had kept hold of from their own childhoods. Others turned up in the Emporium, on the dusty shelves at the back of the store where barely anyone goes. Maybe we're not the only ones who don't want good books pulping.

I'm shaking my head. "I barely look at them any more."

Annie Rose doesn't let me falter. "The books you read when you're young, they become part of you. And Bear can help too. He's good at this." She's right. Annie Rose has given him the same stories, even though she can no longer see the pages. Bear describes the pictures and she fills in the words from memory.

"I need to go the Warren," Annie Rose says calmly.

"The Warren?" I baulk.

"You need that gun, Juniper. You need to be able to hunt."

"But not the Warren, Annie Rose! You can't possibly go there." Maybe you'd find an air rifle, you'd probably get most things there, but the Warren's the most dangerous area of the city. It's practically the reason Curfew was invented.

"It's not such a terrible place, Juniper. Not everyone there is out to get you."

"No, just some of them," I say, exasperated. "Honestly, you can't see any more, Annie Rose! You never go out!"

She used to go out. Even with her failing eyesight, she used to go places. But as soon as I was old enough to take

Bear to school and go shopping and stuff like that, she stopped. She hasn't left the house for over a year.

"There was a man there. He was a ReWilder. Silvan. He helped your mum. I've got my stick. I remember the roads. I know where to go."

"No, Annie Rose. It's changed," I plead. My brave, belligerent grandmother. There's nothing she wouldn't do for us. "Sam!" I cry, because even though the trip to the North Edge already feels an age away, his face is suddenly clear in my head. "Sam could help us get one. He's a Plant Keeper."

Annie Rose sighs. "No, Juniper."

"Sam knew your name right away. And Mum's. He asked after her."

Annie Rose nods slowly. "Marian went to him. He helped her, but that was a long time ago."

"It's worth asking, isn't it? It's better than the Warren. Etienne goes to the North Edge at weekends. He's helping out there. He'll take me."

"Juniper, you can't tell Etienne!" Annie Rose says, and there's a flash of anger.

"I won't tell him anything. But he'll take me. I know he will."

"You're not to breathe a word about any of this when Etienne's around!"

"I won't."

"For his sake as much as yours."

"I won't, Annie Rose. I promise."

Then we're putting the box back under the flagstone and I'm heaving a sigh of relief, hoping I don't see it again for a long time yet.

It's just the map I keep out and for ages I stare at it, running my finger over the orange line Mum drew on by hand. The roads and rivers that are meant to guide us back to Ennerdale. There's barely any more sense to them than the fractals. How on earth am I meant to find our way home?

16

Saturday morning is compulsory fitness. Every under-sixteen in the city has to engage in physical activity from nine till midday and today is no different. No one can see any change in our behaviour or routines, no one can be allowed to suspect anything. Least of all Bear. You can't trust a six-year-old not to blab.

Bear and I go to the climbing centre. His 'Infant Frame', my 'Teen Terror'.

Bear bounces in, smiling. He loves this. The adrenaline rush. The thrill of climbing.

I'm always scared, always expecting to fall. I triple check my harness each time I go up and I go slowly, carefully, feeling for each foot hole, each fake rock to grab with my hand.

I don't know why I do it. Sometimes I wimp out and go to the treadmills instead, where I can just run. No need to think. Easy. But today I need to test myself, prove myself – find my limit and then go further. Plus I need to speak with Etienne and this is his second home.

The climbing centre is in this old Victorian water-pumping station called the Castle, and at the top, in the turrets, some of the windows are still uncovered. I've never got to them. I've no idea what you can see from up there, but I figure that you've got to be able to see past the Buffer.

If I don't look down, I can carry on going upwards. It's just one more hold, one more grip, then pull my rope up, pull out the slack, find the next foothold. Then repeat. Just don't look down.

I'm going vertically up the tower into one of the turrets. This is way further than I've ever been. The windows are just a few metres above. Someone's up there already, taking a breather, before they loosen their belay and walk themselves back down. It's Etienne. He's gazing out of the window, waiting for me.

Find the hold, grip with my chalked-up fingers, then find the footholds, right foot, left foot, pull out the slack and keep breathing. And don't look down.

Before long I'm level with him and with the windows too. They're stuck in this half-open position and I can feel the change in the air. It's different to the stagnant city air – cooler, fresher. Like it's come from the Wild. You can taste the oxygen.

I gulp it in and move sideways one step, so my head's level with the glass. Only you can't see out, not properly. You can't see the Wild. The view is obstructed by these angled-down sheets of metal. You can gaze down at the grey of the city, marvel at it – the housing blocks, the schools and hospitals and the Institute – but you can only see to where the Buffer Zone begins.

I start to cry. Stupidly stupid tears, running down my face. I daren't even use my hand to wipe them away, for fear of making my fingers too wet to grip the wall.

"Juniper," Etienne says softly, bringing his body closer so he's right next to me and we're looking out of the same window.

"I thought I would be able to see further. I just wanted to see it. Just a glimpse of it."

"It's torture, isn't it, this city?" Etienne says.

"But why doesn't anyone else think that?"

Etienne sneers. "They don't know what they're missing. How can they, when all the views are like this? Listen, I should have done this yesterday. Apologized. For last year. I was an idiot."

"You don't need to," I say. "It doesn't matter."

Though it had mattered. It had hurt. Stung. Etienne was the big brother Bear never had and he was my friend. Then he had grown up and cast us off.

"I told you I was fed up of the glasshouse. I said I didn't

want to hang out with you any more."

"You outgrew playing with a five-year-old and a girl. It's not a crime."

"No, Juniper. Honestly. Your glasshouse was the best thing in my life and I loved being with you and Bear. It's just…" His eyes glaze over.

"You don't have to explain."

"I want to."

I nod, silently.

"You heard what I did?" Etienne looks sad or angry, or both.

"To Jack?" I say, even though it's obvious that's what he means. Jack's the boy Etienne beat up and everyone knows what Etienne did to him. Jack was off school for days and still came back with bruises.

"I should've walked away. I should've left it. But I couldn't. I couldn't even see straight. Jack was baiting me." I look at Etienne's fist and it's coiled into a knot. Trembling. His voice is trembling too. "Do you ever feel like that? So angry you could tear someone apart?"

I think of Portia Steel, controlling the whole city from deep inside her bunker, and Abbott, getting Bear's blood tested to punish Mum for running away fifteen years ago, and I nod.

"Well," Etienne says, like that explains everything. And maybe I should stop there but I can't help myself. Jack's an idiot. An idiot and a sneak and a name-caller, everyone knows that, but he wouldn't deliberately start a fight. No one in their right mind would. Not with the Institute looming over us.

"Why though? What had he done?"

Etienne looks awkward. "There was a book I was reading. It wasn't approved."

"What book? I read unapproved books all the time!"

"Not at school you don't. And it was stupid of me, stupid because it wasn't my book to be flaunting around."

"Huh?" I say, totally confused now.

"It was yours, Juniper."

I know straight away which book he's talking about. "*The Secret Garden*!" I say.

We've lent Etienne loads of books. Heaps. But that was the last one, about a girl, Mary Lennox, who finds this garden that's been locked up for years, and Colin – sickly, spoilt Colin – who goes outside, after spending his whole childhood hidden away indoors.

I couldn't ask for the book back. Not after Etienne started ignoring us. Not after he said those things. Only sometimes I imagined him with it and thought, *Well, he might not have our Palm House any more, but at least he has that.* The Secret Garden. *It's better than nothing.*

"Jack took it off me. He was laughing, holding it out of reach, saying he should send it for pulping because it had garden in the title and a robin on the cover. He didn't even bother reading any of the words inside it. I couldn't help myself!"

Etienne's eyes fix on mine.

"What happened to the book?" I whisper.

"Abbott took it."

"Abbott?" I ask, and something is slow inside me. Slow and thick, and I think it's the blood in my veins.

"He was on a witch-hunt, Juniper. He wanted to know where it had come from. Who it had come from. I wouldn't say. So he started watching everything I did, every person I hung out with. He said he'd report the culprit to Steel herself. That was why, Juniper."

"Steel?" I think of our books back home. The shelves and shelves of them. None of them approved.

"I had to make you stay away from me, Juniper. And Bear. Because of Abbott."

"Do you think he pulped it? *The Secret Garden*?" I think of the book, with the key and the door and robin on the front. Mushed down into pulp and remade as something new and regulation like the grey-lined exercise books we use at school.

Etienne shakes his head. "Nah. It's still there, in his office. Top shelf. He won't destroy it until he finds out who it came from."

"So why are you talking to me now?"

"Your essay. I figured you already did a good enough job

75

of getting Abbott's attention."

I'm filled with this complete hopelessness. This sudden despair. "How can he get so angry about a book? It's just words."

Etienne's voice is bitter. "It's what it represents. How can people ever be satisfied in this city if they know what's out there?"

"Etienne," I say in a sudden rush. "You know you go to the North Edge at weekends? For your apprenticeship."

"Yes?"

"I wanted to ask you—"

But there's a shrill whistle from below. We've lingered way too long. We let out our belays and abseil down in parallel, silently now.

17

Bear and I wait outside the climbing centre and Etienne gives a huge smile when he sees us. I get this pang because I know I'm using him. Using him and putting his apprenticeship at risk.

Bear shows off about how high he went today, then changes tack, saying he's tired, that his legs won't work. Etienne hoists him up on to his back. "Is that better, Bear cub?"

"I'm not a baby any more!" Bear says. "I had a birthday. I'm six now."

"Six, wow! That's why you're so heavy," Etienne groans, pretending to flail. "You're big enough to walk then, Bear man."

"No, I like it up here!" Bear says quickly. "I can see everything from here!"

"Everything?"

"Yes. Everything."

Etienne shoots a smile at me.

Bear whistles and chatters to himself. He's a bird – the first in his book. An albatross – this huge seabird with a wingspan as long, longer than a fully grown person. Arms outstretched, soaring. This is one of Bear's favourite imaginings, but he doesn't normally get to be this high.

"Whoa! Careful!" Etienne laughs as Bear leans back. "You've got to hold on!"

Bear shrieks with joy.

I laugh. "You're good with him."

"He's a good kid."

"I wish school thought so."

"What do they know?"

I shrug. "Etienne, I want to come with you this weekend. To the North Edge."

Etienne stares as me. "Why? You've got the Palm House already."

"The North Edge is different. You know that."

He's shaking his head and his face has fallen. I shouldn't have asked. It's not fair. "You can't, Juniper. Sam forbade it. I'm not to bring anyone."

"Why not?"

He laughs. "Rules are rules, Juniper! What's got into you?"

I pull a face like I'm all put out. Envious. "So when do you go on your little jaunt?"

"After lunch. I get the Metro."

"They let you on the Metro?" It's not that you can't, it's not exactly forbidden, but it arouses suspicion. Travelling to the other side of the city is just not a desire they would understand. Why would anyone want to? We're meant to have everything we need on our doorstep.

Etienne's looking at me strangely. "I have a permit. Why are you so bothered anyway?"

"Oh, nothing. Forget it."

We're at the Emporium now. Bear's jumped down from Etienne's back and has his face pressed against the window. The display changes all the time. All the things they're not allowed to make any more, or can't. Hardly anyone cares about this stuff now, but we do, Bear and I. We're like magpies.

"Can we show Etienne the snow globe, Ju?" Bear asks. "With the lions and the horse and the Christmas tree?"

The globe turned up weeks ago and Bear hasn't shut up about it. It's a city square enclosed in a glass dome and when you shake it, these white flakes swirl around. It has *Trafalgar Square* written around the base.

I can't think about snow globes today though. I've got other things to look for.

I leave Bear and Etienne rooting around the old toy section and go straight to Footwear.

There are ballet shoes and football boots and bowling shoes. There's even an ancient pair of ice skates with rusty metal blades. But there's nothing small enough for Bear's feet.

"Juniper," says a cheerful voice and I jump. It's Barney, the storekeeper. "I don't normally see you in this section!"

Barney's looked out for me ever since I came to the city. And Bear. Barney knows just what we like. Plastic animal figurines for Bear's Jungle. Paints and brushes and old art paper for me. And books for both of us. Barney gives us first pass on any new kids' books that come in, always winking at us in the same way, putting his finger up against his lips to show it's secret, like we didn't already know. Old books are hidden at the very back of the store – the dark, dusty bit that looks like storage, but has some of the best treasure of all if you know where to look.

Barney calls the things he sells anachronisms because they're out of time and out of place. He knows we are too. I think that's why he's kind to us.

"I was looking for shoes. Bear's are wearing out," I say. "Only he's got another six months on them yet."

Barney whistles. "He's growing fast, your brother. You must be watering him too much in that Plant House."

I smile thinly. "So this is all of Footwear? You don't have anything else in child sizes?"

"Sorry, Miss Juniper. Anything useful never makes it this far. You know that."

I nod. Barney's right. There are never enough shoes, or clothes, or anything any more.

"Barney," I say in a rush. "You know out there before, in the olden days. People used to hunt, didn't they? Rabbits and birds and things."

"Game," Barney pronounces.

"Pardon?"

"That was the word. Game. Hunting animals – for food, or sport."

"Game. Exactly," I say, relieved that he's following me. "And they'd use some kind of gun, wouldn't they? An air rifle, I think."

Barney nods noncommittaly.

"Well, what if I wanted one of those?"

His face crumples. "I've never allowed anything like that!"

"It's not what you think," I say quickly. "It's not for here."

"There are too many guns in this city!"

"It's not for the city," I say firmly, though I'm cold inside. This could be the most stupid thing I've done yet.

"Juniper, what are you thinking? This isn't the place." He's shaking his head.

"No." I turn away. I can't bear to see the look on his face. The disappointment. "I'm sorry," I say, kicking myself for even asking.

I can hear Bear baying with laughter, and Etienne too, and I trail towards them through the shelves of forgotten things. I know where they are from the creaking of the rocking horse. They're in Pets.

A patchy old fox with glass beads for eyes makes me jump, even though it's long dead. Stuffed and put in a transparent box with no blood left for ticks to feed off.

Barney doesn't mind breaking a few rules – the plastic animals and the books and the horse. But not a gun. Not an air rifle. I should have known that.

Bear's swinging to and fro on the old painted pony, his arms wrapped round its neck.

Etienne's next to him, clinking through a basket of silver and gold medallions. "What are these?"

"Pet tags!" Bear says. "Rufus, Jamie, Leo. Smoky, Poppy, Bo. Goldie. Spot." Bear sings out the names. He knows all of them by heart.

"Come on, Bear," I say in a dull voice. "Annie Rose will be waiting."

"Ju! We haven't found the snow globe yet!"

"Bear!"

"It's OK, Ju. I know where it is." He leaps off the rocking horse and runs ahead into Miscellaneous. He reaches to the back of the bottom shelf, where the snow globe is hidden behind old tin jugs and kitchen utensils. His little fingers stretch around the glass sphere, and the three of us peer in together to watch the snow fall, turning everything magic.

18

After lunch I wait for Etienne outside the old warehouse, a couple of streets away from the Palm House. They're turning it into flats, but there's been some delay and it's been an empty shell for months now. The exterior is painted with fractals. Green ones that remind me of our succulents. I'm staring into the coils – the precision of them, the absolute perfection – when I hear Etienne's footsteps. His face falls when he sees me.

"Juniper! What are you doing?"

"I'm coming with you. To the North Edge."

"Juniper," Etienne says again. "You don't have a permit. Sometimes the guards check."

"Sometimes?"

"Yeah."

"Maybe today they won't."

"And if they do?"

"Then I'll bluff it."

He stares at me, curious.

"Please, Etienne."

He doesn't look happy about it but he nods.

The Metro station is just a few minutes from our block. Etienne goes first and I follow. I'm not sure if it's deliberate on his part, this separation, so that we stand out less, or whether he's just annoyed at me for risking one of the few good things he's got going.

We go through the brick arches of the station and the train's already waiting on the platform. I don't need Etienne to tell me to run, I just do – straight past the train guard and into the carriage.

If the carriages had seats once, they've all been ripped out. You hold on to straps in the metal ceiling as the train lurches from side to side, swinging wildly on the tracks.

I look at Etienne, alarmed.

"It hasn't broken yet!" He winks at me.

The city passes in a blur. It was a university town once and though the colleges are long gone, sometimes you catch the odd glimpse – spires and steeples, golden stone arches, angels and gargoyles. It was meant to have been one of the most beautiful cities in the world.

It's just a few minutes' hanging on and we're there. North station is all aluminium and sparkling glass. Sort of dazzling, but unsettling too for it's right on the edge.

The Buffer's just the other side of the glass for everyone to see. To make it clear that this really is the end of the line.

"This way," Etienne says, brushing past me. I follow, dodging the Eco Park workers on their way for a shift and a group of kids who have somehow found space for a game of football. Then Etienne grabs my hand to pull me away down a quieter street.

It's only once we've left everyone else behind that he starts talking. "Sam can write a permit for the way back. Don't forget to ask." That's all he says. He doesn't ask why I've come.

Sam's there when we go in, watering a row of plants. "You've got company?" he says to Etienne, his voice gruff in a way I didn't notice yesterday.

"I thought Juniper could help."

"Of course," Sam says, but there's a distinct coolness. "If you supervise her. I've got work to do." He disappears off, abandoning the watering can in the middle of the walkway.

"This way," Etienne says. "You can help with the weeding."

For a while I work in step with him. There's a different quality to the earth here. It's denser, wetter than the Palm House. We're picking out seedlings – new little sproutings, pairs of leaves that have sprung up in the wrong places. We put them all in a blue plastic bucket.

85

"Shouldn't we start repotting them?" I ask. "Before they dry out?"

"These? There's nowhere for them to go. Sam just composts them down. You can't save everything, Juniper."

"I guess," I say, throwing another seedling into the bucket. "Sam wasn't exactly pleased to see me."

"He's just busy."

"I need to talk to him."

"Juniper? What's going on?"

"Don't, OK?" I say quickly. "Please. Don't." I can't answer his questions and I don't want to lie.

Etienne shrugs. "He'll be in the Potting Shed."

"The Potting Shed?" I raise my eyebrows. "That sounds like something from a hundred years ago."

Etienne laughs. "It's what he calls his office. That way. Look up. You can't miss it."

19

There's a cylindrical staircase to the top of the glasshouse and then a long walkway just below the ceiling with a birdcage bit at the end. Looking at it makes me queasy, but that's where Sam is – I can see his silhouette.

The steps are tight and narrow, circling round to the centre – a spiral, going higher. I have to focus on my feet so I don't look over the banister, which is low, so low that I feel top heavy. Like my own weight might drag me down to the floor. Vertiginous, that's the word.

I used to think vertigo was a fear of heights. It's not the fear itself though, it's the feeling it gives you – things spinning, tilting. The dizziness. The sickness. Acrophobia – that's a fear of heights. But this morning I climbed to the top of the climbing wall and if I can do that – scale a vertical tower – I can walk along a horizontal walkway.

There's no door at the end, but Sam hasn't heard me

coming and it feels awkward to just start speaking. I knock on the metal frame.

"Juniper!" Sam's voice is heavy, unsurprised. Like he's been expecting me.

Potting Shed? The name's misleading. There are no plants at all, just a computer and stacked empty plant pots and on the wall, Portia Steel's official photo. Her yellow hair, all straight and perfect; her face, like white stone or porcelain, untouched by sun or laughter or age. It's been the same photo for as long as I can remember. Surely Portia Steel has aged like her city?

I deliberately turn my back on it. "You knew my mum?" I say.

"Not really." Sam's eyes are glazed over like he's not actually looking at me.

"But you met her?"

"She came here once."

"Are you still in touch?"

"No," he says quickly.

"I need to find someone who can help me. Me and my brother. I think we might be in trouble."

Sam laughs – this low, bitter laugh. "And you think I can help?"

"Yes," I say, undeterred. "You helped our mum."

"Juniper," Sam says, angry now. "You can't talk like this. You don't know who might be listening." His eyes flick to

Portia Steel's photo.

If Sam's warning me, I call his bluff. There's a camera in the corner, but barely any of them work any more. Our city's all out of electronic parts.

"You're listening and you're a Plant Keeper. We need to find a way out of the city. And things we need for our journey."

Sam sits on a high stool, his shoulders drooped. He hands me one of the pots with black letters emblazoned around the rim.

"Future Science," I read aloud. "That's why you can keep all the plants. That's why this place still exists."

"You'd think it was a benevolent enough kind of existence."

"It's science, isn't it? You're growing the plants we might need one day, for food, and medicines. Someone has to. It's important."

Sam shrugs.

"You have to help us! They took my brother's blood!" I say, desperate now. "They would have taken mine too, if I'd been there. If I hadn't been here instead."

Sam nods but stays silent.

"Annie Rose says they're trying to make a vaccine, to go into the Wild."

"No," Sam says in this low flat tone that frightens me. "A vaccine won't work. Not with that disease. You need to be born with immunity. You need to inherit it. Or…"

"Or?" I prod, though I'm not sure I want to hear the answer.

"You need a live supply. Of antibodies. Steel finally thinks they've got the science to make it work. They're going to do transfusions – pass immunity from one person to another. Your blood into theirs."

I gasp. "We have to stop them!"

"We?" Sam laughs and my skin crawls. "This place is a test zone now."

"A test zone?" I look down to that meshed corner with the fluorescent tape. Like a crime scene. "The ticks are here, aren't they?"

"Steel's people are already recruiting," Sam says, still in this detached tone. Robotic. "For volunteers. For blood, like your brother's, and trial participants to test out their theory. Imagine volunteering for that!"

"My brother wasn't a volunteer," I say caustically.

"That's what they'll call him. That's what they call me."

"You made a deal with them. They pay you and you get to do the best job in the city. Bear's a kid – he didn't get anything for his blood."

"He'll get something soon enough. You both will. A bed with your name on in one of their hospitals."

"How can you?"

"How can I not?" Sam's gaze sears into me. Of course

90

he's looking at me. He always was. It's just the light is gone from his eyes.

A door slams below and there's heavy footfall on the concrete, ricocheting up to us. Sam looks startled. He's about to head down the stairs but turns back to the desk instead to scrawl words on a small card. "You'll need this. Your permit."

"I won't need it," I snap. "I'm not coming back. And you shouldn't let Etienne either, or any of the others." I picture us all yesterday – the Remedials, running through the plants like it was a big playground.

"You'll need it," Sam says again, forcing the card into my hand. "Stick to what I've written."

Etienne's waiting at the bottom. "You've got guests," he says to Sam and his eyes flit to the card.

A woman and a man are walking in our direction, both in the grey-sheen suits of the regime. They're city officials, coming to police their project.

"We'd best get back," Etienne says loudly, casually.

The officers stand across the walkway, blocking it.

"This site is restricted entry," the woman says. "We're going to need identification. For the minors."

Sam's voice is friendly. "The kids? Ah, you don't need to worry about them. It's one of those therapy things the schools are trying. These two are harmless enough."

"It's the weekend," the woman says, her face unchanged.

"Why are they here now? We'll need verification."

"Show them," Sam says, and Etienne and I hand over our cards with our full names printed on. Except it isn't my name.

"Mary Lennox," the woman reads out loud.

I stare at Sam. Mary Lennox from *The Secret Garden*. Is this his idea of a joke? I keep on smiling, even though my insides feel like they're being squeezed by a huge great fist.

The female officer nods. The name clearly doesn't mean anything to her. "You're on the wrong side of the city," she says, pointing to the bottom of the card where Sam has printed SOUTH. "You better get a move on. Curfew's coming."

20

I walk to the station in a daze and don't notice anything until Etienne hisses my name. "Ju! Your permit!"

There's a guard at the door of the train. She glances down at our cards and we both jump on board.

"Did Sam help you? Did you get what you needed?" Etienne asks as the train rattles off. The carriage is virtually empty and we're in a corner by ourselves, clinging to the straps. "Aren't you going to tell me anything? I got you into the North Edge. You owe me!" He smiles to show he's at least half joking.

I should thank him for letting me tag along, but I just shake my head. The train's fitted with cameras and even if it is all phony, I can't take risks. Not now. Not after what Sam said.

"Did you tell Sam about *The Secret Garden*?" I ask.

Etienne looks surprised. "No. Why would I?"

"I dunno. Why would he write Mary Lennox on my permit?"

Etienne shrugs. "Maybe he read it once. He's old enough to have had a copy. And you're the girl with the garden. The glasshouse garden anyway. Sam likes to kid around."

"Does he?" I frown and turn away to gaze out at the city as the train lurches us home.

Annie Rose was right. Bear and I have to leave. We have to leave before the labs open on Monday.

Between our platelets and our plasma, there's this thing other people lack. This specificity. The right kind of white blood cell – fast, shifting. Theirs can't keep up with the disease, but ours can. The Wild's in our blood. It's in our blood and Steel will want every last drop.

The train doesn't go through the Warren but I'm there in my head already, retracing Mum's footsteps. Silvan, Annie Rose said. If he was an actual ReWilder, surely he'll help? Is it too much to hope he's still there?

The Curfew siren's wailing as we make it home and Annie Rose is in the doorway of the Palm House, waiting. "Juniper! What on earth were you thinking?"

"I'm sorry," I pant. "Can Etienne go through the kitchen?"

"He better had. The drones are out. Can you not hear?"

I listen for the low moan in the distance. Annie Rose is right, the drones are circling, but that's the same every night – it's background noise and I've tuned it out. I barely hear them.

21

I set out early Sunday morning with my empty school bag. Annie Rose hands me leaves of money at the door.

"Our rainy-day money, Annie Rose!" I exclaim. "I can't take that! What if you need it? After we've gone?"

Annie Rose presses the notes into my hand. "When's it ever going to rain in the city, Juniper? You get what you can and be careful."

I nod. I looked up Silvan in a book of names we have on our kitchen shelves. The omens are good. It means *of the forest.*

It's dark in the Warren. Shadowy. It's not that the buildings are taller, they're just closer together. It's dirty too. I bet Street Patrol don't linger here. At least that means I'm unlikely to run into them.

I turn into the first street like it's familiar and walk at average pace, holding myself tall but not too tall. I want to look like I'm from around here. Then I turn a corner and jump.

Pairs of orange eyes stare back at me. Strokes of black and grey with shards of sunlight flecked in their fur. Wolves. Poised. Ready. Circling round their heads are black birds. Crows, ravens, jackdaws? Bear would know. Birds that were portents of doom, or stole bright shiny things.

The girl drops her spray can and it clatters on the stone pavement.

She turns, ready to run. Maybe it's the way I'm looking at her wolves and birds that stops her. She laughs. "Your face! They scared you!"

"They're beautiful. They're so…" I'm not sure what word to pick. I've never seen anything like them before, not this big, this brazen, out on the street for everyone to see, where it would usually just be fractals.

"I get enough practice!" the girl says.

"Yes?"

"Yeah. Sometimes they come, early in the morning, like you," she says, suspicious.

"They?"

"Street Patrol. To whitewash them."

"No!" I shudder. I don't know if it's the thought of Steel's Street Patrol being here after all or imagining a can of white paint blotting out her work in one go. Real. That's the right word for her paintings. They're so real. "What if they caught you?"

"They never would," the girl says. "I know this place. I'd run. Fast. Like my wolves."

"Yes?" I say and I blush because she's caught me staring at her legs. They're held in a kind of frame. Metal on the outside, so her trousers bunch up above her thighs and you can see where metal pins enter her legs, just above her knees. The skin's purple and rubbery.

"Yeah! Course!" The girl looks defiant. "I'm waiting to have them out," she says, gesturing at the frames. "Mum's saving up. Anyway, they don't slow me. Get aways, see?"

I look around. The girl didn't pick this place for nothing. There are seven separate paths you could take from this one spot.

"What you doing round here?" the girl asks, lowering her voice. "You looking for something? Food? Medicine? Clothes?"

I blush again. My clothes may be old and worn, but they're nothing compared to the girl's. She's pretty much in rags. "Not something. Someone," I say. "An old family friend."

"They live here?"

"Used to. We lost touch."

The girl rolls her eyes. "You going to ask me or what?"

"Silvan."

For a moment, I swear the girl looks disappointed. Then she flicks her hair out from over her face. "I know Old Silver."

"Silvan," I correct.

The girl giggles. "Yeah, if you insist."

"He's still here?"

"He's nowhere to go, has he? Course he's still here. Silver's got a way of hanging on."

"Will you take me to him?" I ask hesitantly, because I've got nothing to offer her. What could I have brought anyway? Pot plants? That's the only currency our family has – that and the blood in our veins.

The girl doesn't seem to care. "Haven't anything better to do, have I? This way."

The girl's light-footed and fast, despite her legs, and I struggle to keep up. There's an unevenness to her walk, almost a bound or a leap, that makes me think of Bear. She doesn't take the main streets, if you could call them that. We go through alleyways and up steps and all the way into buildings and out the other side. Sometimes I think we're intruding, that we've walked into someone's apartment, but we haven't. It's communal space, access ways, corridors. Each individual dwelling is just so small that people's belongings spill outside. Humming fridges. Tables. Kids' toys. Clothes horses with hanging laundry.

The damp from the laundry, the smells of cooking, the sticky cloying scent of people on top of people on top of people, it gets into my mouth and into my nostrils. And the noises spin round my head – water moving through pipes; cisterns emptying and refilling; the whistle of an old-fashioned kettle on some stove somewhere.

There are voices too – shouting, crying, laughing, and a hacking cough that hacks and hacks and hacks.

"Do you live near here?" I ask, gripped with this desire to know more about this girl who can paint wolves and birds so anatomically perfect, even though she's never seen them. And never will.

"Somewhere near here," the girl says, shrugging again, like a shrug is as natural a movement as her limp.

We're going over a stone walkway that's almost a bridge, enclosed in ornate stone archways filled in with a lattice of iron bars. I wonder what you used to see through those arches. Now it's just sheets of corrugated metal.

"Have you always lived here…?" I start to ask but my voice breaks off into a cough.

"It's the air," the girl says, glancing back at the walkway. "Miasmas. Coming up from the river. It runs right under the Warren."

I nod because I know all about this. Everyone does. After the ticks came, health officials got paranoid about mosquitoes – these little flies that could bite like the ticks did, suck your blood. If the disease got into the mosquito population, it'd travel way faster. So any place the mosquitoes could breed, any standing water, was disallowed and city officials dug down deep instead. They built these vast subterranean reservoirs that were easier to mesh.

I cough some more and the girl stops. "You need to breathe more slowly. In. Out. See?" The girl demonstrates. "Only not too deeply! You don't want Warren air going too deep." She delves into her paint-stained satchel and hands me a bottle of water. She must see me hesitate, even though I don't mean to. "It's clean, promise. I boiled it for ages."

She starts off again, round more turns, down steps and up steps, and then into a kind of alley where she stops. "Through there," she whispers, pointing across a broken cobbled street to an old building with a crack across its front. "Silver's always in there."

"Silvan," I correct under my breath. Words are important. Names especially. Silver is wrong. It's a pirate name. Long John Silver. It makes you think of money. Greed. That's not what the ReWilders were about.

The sign over the doorway fits though. The Eagle. I feel this deep-down tingle.

"What is that place?" All these thoughts spill into my head. Maybe it's a secret club, or society. Some link to the outside. Maybe there will be someone who can tell me about Ennerdale and how to get there – outside, where eagles still fly.

The girl's laugh is shrill. "Don't you know a pub when you see one?"

"A public house?"

The girl shrieks. "A public house! Some of the stuff you come out with! Are you even from this city?"

"Will it be open?" I mutter, flushing at my ignorance and my quaint words from too many old stories.

"This place is always open. You really don't know very much, do you?"

"Well, thank you for showing me the way," I say aloofly.

The girl looks sad. "Oh, don't sulk. I didn't mean to tease. What's your name?"

"Ju—" But then I remember how even if we can escape, Annie Rose will still be here and I can't leave any trails back to her. And for this bounding, laughing girl too, it's better for our paths never to have crossed. "June," I say, parroting Abbott. "Like the month."

"You're kidding?" The girl's face lights up. "I'm a month too. I'm May. And my sister's April."

There's real glee on her face and I smile. "Maybe one day I'll meet her," I say. "Three months in a row. We can be the whole of spring."

May's smile disappears like someone snatched it away. "April's not here any more."

"Where is she?" My breath catches in my throat.

May points to the tallest building there is, shining in the distance, towering over everything, all concrete and metal. The Institute.

"I'm sorry," I mumble. "I'm really, really sorry."

May nods at me. She knows there's nothing I can say. "Whatever you want old Silver for, I hope you get it."

"Me too. Thank you, May."

"See ya, June!" She bounds off round a corner and is gone.

22

The red door of the Eagle is ajar. I push it open. If I don't go in straight away, I'll lose my nerve.

It's dark inside and the air's thick with something that isn't just vaporized river water. Something thick and sickly that scratches at my lungs. For a moment I think the room's empty, but it's just my eyes adjusting to the smoky air as I go in. There are tables and chairs, and at a wooden counter, people sit on high stools. Two men are talking in low, blurry voices, but most are slumped over, staring into the bottom of their drinks.

In old books, public houses are bustling, noisy places with roaring fires, where travellers swap tales from the road. This place just feels quiet. Unhappy.

Behind the countertop – the bar, I remember the word now – there's a woman gazing off into space. She must feel my eyes on her as she moves her head to look at me.

She curls her index finger to beckon me forwards. "You're underage."

"Sorry?"

The woman points to a sign. No Under 18s. "You are, aren't you?" Her nails are long and curved and black, like talons.

"I'm looking for someone," I say, deliberately avoiding her question.

"Well, are they here?"

"The thing is," I stammer. "I-I don't know what he looks like. But someone told me he's often here, so…" My voice trails off.

"And have you got a name?" She seems half bored, half amused.

"Silvan."

"Never heard of him."

"He might go by the name of Silver now."

The woman sneers. "Old Silver? You don't want to be messing around with him. He's one of our best customers, if you know what I mean."

"I have to speak to him. It's important."

She leans across the bar and I see inside her mouth – tarnished gold where her teeth used to be. "Well, he ain't here. He does come in, most days." Then she sniggers. "What am I talking about? Most days! Silver comes in every day."

"I could wait."

"You've forgotten my sign," the woman says, pointing.

"I can wait outside. If you tell me what he looks like. Please!"

The door swings open behind me and a man rushes in. "Watch it! Street Patrol!" Sounds from the street fly in – shouts, running footsteps, things being packed away.

The woman's gaze cuts right into me and I freeze. I can't be found here, but I can't very well run right out into the grasp of Street Patrol either. Her eyes flit to a door behind her and I'm already climbing on one of the stools to clamber over the bar and get to it.

Through the door there's a hallway and then another door that must lead outside, except it's padlocked. There isn't anywhere else to go. Then I spot the steps leading below, to the cellars.

I scurry down into the gloom. The smell is overpowering – damp and mould mixed with the oversweet smell of the pub upstairs. There's a strange muffled sound.

The room's full of boxes and metal canisters and I creep round them, trying not to knock into anything. There are footsteps in the hallway above now. The metal toecaps of Steel's patrol.

I squeeze behind a tower of crates and bend down low. If I don't move, maybe they won't see me. And that sound – I know what it is now. It's the river, just like May said.

Then I hear the creaking of the steps. Someone's coming. Or two people. One's a patrol officer – I recognize the tread. The other's the woman from the bar.

"Caw!" The man's retching loudly. "It stinks! How can you stand it?"

"You get used to it! And it comes in handy, for keeping folks away."

"It's a stash all right!" The man sounds impressed.

"It is. You wouldn't be doing yourself any favours removing it."

"And why would I do that when you're going to reward me for my discretion?"

"So is it liquid or flesh you're wanting?" I take a sharp intake of breath and the man's eyes dart across to my hiding spot.

The woman sniggers. "You're lucky. Some fresh cuts came in last night." She kicks her foot against one of the boxes.

Cuts? Flesh? I shrivel right down to where the floor's wet and sticky and I can hear the river deep beneath me. A glugging. Like drains emptying. Like our stomachs when they're empty.

Boxes are scraped across the floor and opened and there's the man's awful laugh, all greedy and sly, and the woman's too. I wonder if she's guessed I'm here, or if she even cares.

"And they've been checked, right?" the man's asking.

"Why do you think they're skinned? You think I'd allow them in if there was a chance of ticks? I've got my reputation to think about."

"There were feathers last time. My wife didn't like that."

"I bet she enjoyed the meat though, and those kiddies of yours. I've heard Portia Steel's cutting rations again next month. Her farms aren't performing. The cultures are failing. And still you come, wearing her shiny suits."

"It pays though, doesn't it? More ways than one." The man sniggers. As he looks through the rest of the boxes, I breathe in more and more of the river. The miasmas May talked about.

Eventually though he makes his selection, and I listen to their footsteps back up to the bar.

Ages pass, or minutes, and I still don't dare move, even though there's a cramp in my legs and I could pass out from lack of air. When I finally stumble up from behind the crates there's a man standing at the top of the cellar steps. I gasp. But he's not wearing the sheen suit, his boots don't have those metal toecaps and he's old with silver hair.

"The landlady said I had a visitor." The man hoicks up his sleeves and holds out his arms, which are all drawn over with ink. Leaves, feathers, fish. He's showing me. This is who he is. Or who he was.

"Silvan," I whisper.

"I don't want to hear that word," the man hisses. "Not ever again. You want to get me into trouble? Is that why you came?"

He rushes down the steps towards me and I stumble backwards, my heart tripping over itself as his face is suddenly against mine. His skin yellow, his eyes red – shot through with burst blood vessels that are running with fury.

"No!" I shake my head, frightened. "I don't want any trouble!"

"You swear!"

"I promise!"

"This way," he orders.

I scrabble after him up the steps and out of the back door – the padlock has been opened now. "They had proper meat, didn't they?" I say breathlessly as we enter a narrow alleyway. "Real meat from real animals."

"And?" he snarls.

"But how? Do people go out there? Do you?"

Silvan stops and turns to glare at me. "Are you stupid? Surely you know the answer to that."

He turns his wrists over to the white undersides, where there's no ink but the skin's coloured anyway. His own veins and arteries – blue and purple and protruding. "I can't, can I? I haven't got it. You think I'd be here if I did? I don't know what you want from me, but I'm not on your side,

108

OK? Whatever you think I am, I'm not that any more."

He moves on and my heart's racing but I keep following anyway. There's a way out of the city here and air rifles too. I'm sure of that now.

Sometimes Silvan glances round and glares at me, but I keep on after him round more twists and turns of the Warren, the walls tagged and painted with *The End Is Nigh* kind of slogans and SOS, like on our journey box. Except here it's scrawled in red paint, like blood.

At one point Silvan stops to catch his breath in front of a wall where a tree's painted. Simple, the way Bear would draw it – a brown trunk, branches splitting out and upwards, and then leaves and nuts in little cup cases.

"It's an oak," I say, catching up with him. Silvan nods and I can tell he's impressed.

The Warren might be crowded and dirty and noisy, but somehow it's alive in a way the rest of the city isn't.

The house Silvan stops at is one of the original stone ones. He stands on the doorstep and turns to confront me again. "So I take it you're coming in, oak girl, seeing as I can't seem to shake you off."

I nod my head.

There's a staircase in the hallway with an old wooden balustrade. I think we're going to go up, but Silvan carries right along the hall to the back of the house where the garden would have been. When he opens the door, I still somehow expect to see green. But it's just a shabby little room with a dirty corrugated plastic ceiling. There are plates piled high in a sink and a grimy bed in the corner, and everywhere else – pretty much everywhere – empty bottles. It stinks.

"So, oak girl, you going to tell me what you want?"

I gulp. "We need a way out. Of the city."

"We?" he asks sharply.

"M-my little brother and I," I stammer, unsure whether I've done the right thing, to come out and say it. But what choice do I have? There's no one else to go to.

He looks at me more closely. "You think you can survive out there?"

"We're resistant," I say defiantly. "To the disease."

Silvan throws back his head and laughs. "You think that's enough? You think it's that easy?" He reaches for one of the bottles and flips off the top.

"No," I snap. "Not easy. But we can't stay here. They want our blood."

Silvan looks interested. "They've tested you then?"

"My little brother. And I'll be next."

Silvan nods slowly. "A few years ago they rounded up some Warren people for tests. They found the lucky few. But they didn't feel lucky when Steel sent them out there to be her eyes and ears. Portia Steel didn't reckon on the isolation. What that can do to a person."

"What?" I ask tentatively.

Silvan grins and points to his head. "They went properly wild. Only a few ever report back now. That's what they say. And they're properly crazy, begging to return."

"Are they the people that send the meat?"

Silvan shakes his head. "No. There have always been traders out there. People passing by, seeking business with the city." He points to the floor. If you listen carefully, there's the same muffled gurgling as under the pub. "Things come in by water."

I frown. "The river? Could we get out that way? If you helped us?"

"You think I can help with that?"

"Our mum came to you once. Marian."

A blaze of red flares up on Silvan's yellow face. "No names. I don't want any names." He swigs more liquid from the brown bottle in his hand.

"We could pay you. I could bring you plants. Our grandmother's a Plant Keeper. One of the last." I pause. "There should be plants here. This was the garden once. They might make you feel better."

Silvan stares at me with actual contempt.

"You think that's what I want? To remember what things were like once? It's money I need. Cash. Gold." He holds up the bottle and takes another swig. "This is the only thing that makes me feel better now. Anyway, what do you think I am? The Pied Piper leading kids out of the city through some mountain? There is no way out. The Buffer's all you've got."

"Border Patrol—" I start.

"Go when they're not looking. If you know they want your blood, what the hell are you still doing here anyway?"

My eyes sting with tears and I reach inside my pocket for Annie Rose's rainy-day money.

I hold the curled notes out to Silvan, cross with myself because my hand is trembling. "An air rifle then."

Silvan puts up his hands and laughs. "Look, you've got the wrong idea about me, oak girl. The penalty for a gun, in here…" He takes his forefinger and cuts it across his throat. "You should know that."

"We'll need to eat," I say.

"Take all the supplies you've got. Whatever you can carry." He's rifling through a cupboard and I think he's about to give me protein balls or vitamin sticks or some other bogus city food, but he brings out a rusty metal box and places it on the table, triumphantly.

I frown. "What is it?"

"From the days of the rats, seeing as you seem to think this is Hamelin. It's a trap."

"You think we should eat rats?"

"I think you should eat whatever you can catch. If you want to survive."

"Does it work?"

Silvan shrugs and snatches the notes from my hand. Did I just exchange all our savings for a rusty box?

"I'm not sure about this," I start to say, but Silvan's rummaging through the cupboard again. Finally he brings out these little blister packs. "You should take these too. I've no use for them."

"What are they?"

"Antibiotics."

"We're resistant," I say, confused.

"Look, kid, I don't know who you are and I don't want to know, but there are degrees of resistance. Sometimes the immune system needs a kick-start. If you get bitten, which you will—"

I nod, though I feel sick inside.

"Take three tablets a day. They might help."

"Thanks," I say, not even trying to hide my disappointment as I look at the blister packs. Even if we took one tablet a day each, there wouldn't be enough for the whole journey. Not for both of us.

"I wish you luck. You and your brother. But then maybe you've already got all the luck you need, being able to escape this place."

"Did you know?" I can't help asking. "Back then. When the disease was released. Did you know you'd be shut in here too?"

Silvan nods.

"But you did it anyway?"

"Sometimes I think it was just a protest that got out of hand. I mean, we were trying to save the planet. We couldn't actually have wanted people to die, could we?" Silvan gives a long sigh. "But maybe we did. We were angry enough. One thing I do know, we never imagined it would spread so fast. It's like the disease did something to those ticks. Made them invincible. There was no stopping them. And everywhere they went the disease went with them. Across England, and then Europe, and then the world. In the end they stopped counting the dead."

He's looking at the floor and there's water in his eyes. I can hear all the crying from that old film reel back at school and I know just what he's seeing.

"You saved the Wild," I say quietly.

Silvan looks up at me. "But for how long?"

23

Etienne's there when I walk into our road. He's sat down against the wall, drumming his fingers on the pavement. He jumps up the moment he sees me. "I need to talk to you!"

"I can't. I don't have time." The trap's in my school bag, clanking on my back. I'm sure Etienne must be able to hear it.

"Please, Juniper."

"I don't have time," I repeat. "Annie Rose—"

"You have to hear this."

There's something in his voice that makes me nod. "OK. I'm listening."

Etienne looks around. "Not here. Come upstairs."

We go through the main door of our apartment block. Once there was still the old front door – painted wood with shards of multi-coloured glass spilling out from one central circular pane like sunshine. Then some kids smashed it in one night and it was replaced with this piece of PVC with no transparent bit at all.

"Where've you been anyway?" Etienne asks.

"You don't want to know," I mutter, striding up the stairs after him.

Etienne's apartment is at the top. It's the same size as ours, only his mum's study is in the small space where Bear's bedroom would be. The walls are covered in fractals, spiralling out infinitely, or lines branching out again and again hypnotically, all in shades of green. Etienne's mum says most of her fractals come from nature. "That's the real reason they're good for us. Portia Steel's never worked that out," she said once to me.

"Ms Endo's gone," Etienne says, the moment we get to his room.

"What?"

"I was at the climbing centre first thing. Mamiko was there. From school. She said they came in the night. Everyone in their block saw."

"Saw who?"

"Secret Police."

"Ms Endo? They took her away?" I gasp. The floor starts to tilt around me and there's that hand on my chest again. That iron fist.

Etienne nods. "There's more. Mamiko overheard Ms

Endo talking to her mum about you and Bear. About how she was trying to stop something happening. You're in some kind of trouble."

I stare at him. "Ms Endo was trying to help us! She was just trying to help us, Etienne!" The fist's clenching tighter, the cold fingers of steel, and I can't get enough oxygen. There's never enough oxygen in this place. No wonder, when they took away all the trees.

"Juniper!" Etienne's looking at me alarmed. "Why?"

"Because of Steel! Because she wants to take our blood. For transfusions."

"Transfusions? I don't understand!"

"So her people get our immunity. So they can go out into the Wild. Strip it all over again. That's why I needed to see Sam. That's why I had to make you take me back there." I laugh coldly. "I thought Sam could help."

"Help with what, Juniper?"

I walk over to the window. You can see right into the Palm House where a small figure is zigzagging over the tiles. Bear.

"You're leaving, aren't you," Etienne says, coming to stand next to me.

"We have to, Etienne. We're going across tonight."

"Across?"

"The Buffer," I say, not looking at him because I don't want to see the horror on his face.

117

"Juniper!" Etienne gasps. "Do you hear the shots at night? Do you hear the gunfire?"

"Yes," I say in almost a whisper.

"They say it's to scare off birds and animals. To stop them coming across. But I don't think they'd discriminate, and I don't think they'd care which way you were travelling."

I stare at the stilted metal cages that fringe the Buffer Zone at regular intervals. Each cage with its own sniper. Border Patrol.

"They don't ever stop watching. And they shoot to kill." Etienne's voice is desperate. And scared. He's scared for us.

"I'll figure it out," I say boldly, dismissive. Right now I just want him to shut up. I don't want to be told it's impossible and I definitely don't want him to use Bear against me. "Mum did it. She got across."

"It was different then."

"We don't have a choice, Etienne!" I snap. "Not if they've taken Ms Endo. Don't you see? Abbott's out to get us. Bear and I will be next. Only it won't be the Institute, it'll be worse."

Etienne nods slowly. "I'm not saying it's impossible. Nothing's impossible, but you need to know what you're doing."

"Yeah?" I say, trying to get the right tone. Like I know that already, but if he has information to share he should tell us.

"So you have a plan worked out?"

"No," I say, deciding to be honest with him. "We have some old camping gear and we have a map, but that's it."

"The map takes you to your parents?"

"Allegedly."

"And you have the resistance."

"Yeah, allegedly we have that too. The ticks won't get us. Something else can have that pleasure."

"You don't have a plan for the Buffer though?"

"We run, right? I guess we wait for dark first."

Etienne rolls his eyes. "Seriously, Juniper, you've got to do better than that."

24

Ever since Abbott threatened him with the Institute, Etienne's been planning his escape. If they ever try and send him, he'll be ready to leave. "I can't go there, Juniper, I swear. I'll run. I'll run into the Wild. I'd rather get the disease."

He gets out some papers from a drawer. White sheets scrawled over with pencil sketches.

"You never told me you drew," I say, surprised.

Etienne blushes. "I don't. Not like you, Juniper. They're just diagrams." He angles them away from me and starts rifling through them. "This is the one. Here."

It's a plan. It takes a while to work out what it is, but the Palm House is on it and from that you can work out pretty much everything else. The boundary of our city either side of our block, with all the buildings marked and the lookout stations too. Each one has a series of numbers next to it. Times. Schedules.

"Wow," I say, reeling at the detail. It's all pencil except for the lookout posts. Some are red, some are yellow, some blue. "What are the colours for?"

"They're zones," Etienne says. "It's a network. You have to understand the network." He takes me through all of it – the results of his meticulous thinking, his locked-up, clever brain, keeping itself sane.

The lookout posts are always manned, but the pool of border officials this falls to is small. Sometimes, if someone is sick, they don't bother covering their post. Or if something happens in another part of town, border officers are the first people to be called in to help. Etienne takes a clean sheet of paper and I watch his fingers sketch it out. Which alarm needs to go off, which guards this will alert and for how long. Everything that needs to happen in order to leave a stretch of Buffer unmonitored for the time it should take to cross it.

Etienne's not got the resistance but he's planned his escape anyway. That's how bad this place has become.

"How would I get the alarm to go off?"

Etienne frowns. "That's the tricky part. Sometimes there's trouble at the Warren – they pull in every guard for a mile for that, but you can't make that happen. Well, not easily. Sometimes someone breaks away on another part of the grid, but unless you've got someone willing to make a bid for freedom—"

"No," I say, terrified that that's what he's about to suggest. Some crazed sacrifice – giving himself up for us.

"But I could do something, couldn't I? Create a distraction. Get one of the security alarms to go off in one of the regime's buildings. That'd do it."

"Yeah, and I'd leave knowing you were being packed off to the Institute."

"I'm just trying to help," he says, frowning again.

"What about a fire?"

Etienne looks at me curiously. "Yeah, that would do it. If you knew how to start one."

I smile. "Well, it just so happens our camping gear contains a box of matches!"

25

"I'll help, Ju." Bear looks up at me, a deep assurance in his eyes.

"I know you will, Bear."

I'm in Bear's room, working out which of his clothes to take – the lightest and warmest. Annie Rose is in the kitchen, muttering about city rations and finding all the food we can carry.

"Are you taking Emily?" Bear asks.

I shake my head. "No, Bear. We have other stuff to carry." She could be another blanket. She could be more food.

"You're leaving her?" Bear sounds shocked.

"She's just a doll. People my age don't play with dolls."

"You do."

I roll my eyes at him. It's not playing. It isn't like that with Emily. She's my link with Mum. "There's no room for toys. It's essentials only."

"What about my Jungle?"

"Bear, you can't…" I start, but his face is breaking up. We can't leave the Jungle behind. Bear needs his toys, they're part of him. "Maybe you could bring a few," I say. "Your favourites. Lion and Tiger and Giraffe."

"And Brown Bear," he says, taking the animal down from the shelf.

"Yeah, of course. We can't leave Brown Bear, can we?"

Barney gave me that one just in time for Bear's third birthday. His namesake. The bear's the best of all the animals. The most lifelike. It's made by this old German toymaker that used to do all kinds of animals and paint them by hand.

He moves the bear along the map that's spread out on his bed, over the pale blue lines that coil round the paper like snakes.

"Bears can swim you know," he says.

"He'll love all the lakes then, see." I point to the top left of the map, where Ennerdale is. I look at the names of the blue pools now. The lagoons, the lochs, the lakes. Windermere and Elterwater and Grasmere and Wastwater. I read them out.

"Mere?" Bear asks. "Does that mean water?"

"Yes," I say. "Like the sea." It's a story word. An underwater girl who made a pact with an evil sea witch because she had fallen in love with a human boy and wanted a human soul and legs to dance with. Though I always imagined I'd do the opposite – wish for a fish tail and an ocean to swim away in.

"Was our dad a ReWilder, Ju?"

"He can't be that old, Bear! The ReWild was almost fifty years ago."

"Maybe his dad was a ReWilder then?"

I smile. "Yeah. Or his mum. Or his grandmother. I guess we'll find out all about him, when we get there."

"I bet he's a hero, Ju. Like Robin Hood. I bet everyone knows him, except us. I can't believe you forgot him."

I shrug. Bear's right, I did forget him. Just sometimes in a dream, right in the middle of it, there is someone. Someone tall with a head full of curly hair, just like Bear's, and I have to climb my way to the top of him to touch it. But if I freeze-frame or focus in on the face then he vanishes, like he was never there at all.

"What if they're not there, Ju?" Bear asks as though he's reading my mind.

"Then we'd know," I say fast.

Bear nods. The brown bear's floating down the rivers, galloping over the hills, like it's that easy.

Our parents have got to be at Ennerdale. If anything happened, Mum promised someone would send word to Annie Rose. Even if she couldn't come herself, someone would. And we've never heard anything, so they must still be there. They have to be.

There's a tap on Bear's door. I glance up, surprised. It's Etienne. "Annie Rose said I could come in. I brought something for you."

"A present for me?" Bear asks, excited, staring at this thing in Etienne's hands. A kind of box.

"For Juniper too." Etienne's eyes flick across to me.

"What is it?" Bear trills.

"It's a kind of map. For when you don't have space to spread yours out."

I laugh. Bear's bed's entirely taken up with the map and I start to fold it so Etienne can sit down. The thing he's carrying is small and circular. Etienne flicks a button on the side and it's like it wakes up. It's got a screen on it, displaying a map with a little green flashing dot.

"Where did you get it?" I ask, suspicious.

"I found it once. In the Emporium, in Miscellaneous. I don't think Barney knew what it was, and I wasn't sure, but I figured it out from some old science books. It's a GPS."

Bear and I look at him blankly.

"Global Positioning System," Etienne recites. "It shows you where you are, exactly where you are, and when you put your destination in, it shows you which direction to take to get there and how far away you are."

"How's that even possible?" Bear asks, his eyes wide.

Etienne starts explaining satellites – these orbiting bits

126

of metal out in space, pinging back signals at the speed of light.

I frown. "I didn't think satellites worked any more? They've gone off course, surely?"

Etienne scoffs. "That's what Steel says. She doesn't want us believing any of that technology works. And it's true, most of the satellites are useless now, but there are a few you can rely on. Those are the signals the GPS looks for."

"Someone's maintaining them?" I ask, dubious.

"Somewhere," Etienne says. "I guess that means some countries are doing better than us."

I nod, slowly. I don't believe the tick disease is everywhere, despite what Silvan said and what Steel tells us in her bulletins. Surely some places have recovered by now. But I'm not bothered about anywhere else right now. My question's much simpler. "Is it easy to use?"

"I've tried it out, with the obvious limitations of course. It works here OK. Once I walked all the way to the North Edge. It got me there. It's a long time since it had an update, but it has the other cities programmed in, I checked that. So you can steer clear of them."

"Can we put in Ennerdale?" Bear asks eagerly.

"You should do it, Bear," Etienne says, pushing the GPS across to him. "It works best when you put in numbers. Two coordinates. Latitude—"

"And longitude," Bear finishes. "I know from our

Campcraft book. We can get the numbers from the map. I've already seen them."

I watch as Etienne helps Bear type in a string of digits and even though it's like being handed a golden key there are tears pricking at my eyes. Because it's not our key, it's Etienne's and he's never going to get a chance to use it.

"Learn the way for me, Bear," I say, managing a smile. "I'm going to do the plant check. One last time."

26

Etienne comes out to find me. I'm in the central bit of the dome where you can only see plants and sky. The sun's already starting to fall.

"So are you ready?" he asks.

We came up with the plan together. I'll start the fire in that old warehouse. It's just an empty shell, no one's going to get hurt, but it's close to a twelve-storey residential block, so the Priority One emergency alarm will sound. Every officer in a two-mile radius will get the call to come and help evacuate the block and fight the blaze. This will include our two nearest Border Patrol officers.

Our rucksacks will be packed and ready in the Palm House. The wailing siren will drown out the noise as we smash our way through the glass. Bear and I will go where we've never been before, where no one is meant to ever set foot. We'll go across the Buffer. All the way across until we reach the Wild.

"Let me do it for you," Etienne says now. "Give me the matches and I'll set the fire. You concentrate on getting out."

I shake my head decisively. It's one thing helping us come up with the plan. It's another thing to take part in it. "I already told you. I can do it, Etienne. I don't need you."

"Let me, Juniper. In this whole adventure, it's the only thing I can do." His voice is insistent. He's not like Sam or Silvan, Etienne actually wants to be part of our escape.

"No. I don't want to be out there worrying about you. I don't want there to be anyone left here for them to blame."

"Juniper. You've barely any time left in this place. Barely any time left with Annie Rose. Are you telling me you want to spend it starting fires?"

"I couldn't forgive myself if—"

"Juniper," he says again. "It'll be campfires every night now for you and Bear. This is my one chance. Are you seriously going to deny me it?"

I laugh softly, even though I really want to cry. "You've done so much already. Especially with that GPS. Do you know how worried I've been about my map-reading?"

Etienne grins. "I should've given it to you before. You should have had it the day I found it. It was never for me. I don't have a place to type in. I'm like Colin in *The Secret Garden*. I wasn't meant for the outside."

"No. No! Don't say that. Because it's not true. Colin got out, didn't he? He went outside and you will too. I know it."

"You know it?" Etienne laughs.

"Yes, deep down inside. I know it." And somehow as I say it, it feels real. I can see him out there. I can see all of us – Etienne, Bear and I – running together across grass with flowers just like the ones on Bear's wall. "Etienne," I say suddenly, "that place at the North Edge behind the yellow tape, where I thought Sam was breeding the Sticks?"

"Yeah?"

"Well, he isn't. Not Sticks. Ticks! Ticks, Etienne! They're doing a trial for disease resistance. They're looking for participants."

Etienne nods blankly, but I see him flinch.

"You get me?" I say.

"Sam didn't tell me," he says and I hear the hurt in his voice.

"I'm telling you! You can't go back there. No one from our school can. It's too dangerous."

He nods again, but he's not quite looking at me.

"I mean it. They wouldn't care, Etienne, if you lived or died. Sam wouldn't care. You've got to stay away!"

"Sam would care," he says loyally.

"No, Etienne!"

"He would, Juniper. You don't know him like I do. After the Jack incident, Sam was the only person who understood and the North Edge was the one good thing, you know? The one thing that kept me going." His voice is breaking.

"You can't trust Sam. He's gone to their side. Maybe he didn't want to, but he did anyway. Etienne!" I take hold of his hand and shake it. He can't ever go back there. Even if Sam was trying to help him in the beginning, Etienne can't be involved in this.

Etienne looks at his fingers in mine and his face softens. "OK, Ju, seeing as you're so insistent. I won't go back."

"You swear?" I say. "Cross your heart?"

"Yes."

"Say it!"

Etienne laughs gently. "I swear, Juniper."

This gush of panic and sadness wells up inside me. "You won't need to anyway, because you're a Plant Keeper here now. You'll watch out for Annie Rose, won't you, Etienne?"

Etienne smiles. "Of course I will. I promise. I'll come down every day. You know how jealous I always was of you having the Palm House? Your very own garden. Just like Mary Lennox. Now you'll see the moors too and the hills. You're going home, Juniper Green."

"I'm not ready."

Etienne squeezes my hand. "You were always ready, Juniper, you and Bear. That's why you have to go."

27

I go back to the kitchen and make Bear help me put all our old books under the floor, where the journey things were. They'll be seen as incriminating evidence if Portia Steel's officers come looking.

"It feels like we buried a person," Bear says as we drag the chest back over the top.

"They did their job," Annie Rose says. "And maybe they will again one day, for another person."

"I don't want anyone else having *Birds of the World*," Bear says fiercely. "That's just mine."

Annie Rose smiles. We had a fight on our hands getting Bear to leave that one. "OK, Bear. I'll keep it safe for you. Your bird book isn't going anywhere."

I look round at the meagre amount of food left on the shelves. Anything she could get to fit, Annie Rose has stuffed in our bags for the journey – energy bars and fruit sticks and protein balls.

I start moving the remaining jars down from the top.

"Leave it," Annie Rose says. "I can do it, when—"

"No," I say sharply. "You can't reach them up there. You could fall." And I need something to do. My head's spinning, thinking about Etienne getting caught by Street Patrol. Getting caught and dragged away, just like Ms Endo was.

"Ju!" Bear stops me. "We missed one of the books."

I glance over. It's the book I looked up Silvan in. Bear's flicking through it curiously. "*Baby Names*! Am I in it?"

Annie Rose scoffs. "*Baby Names*! Do we still have that old thing? No, Bear, you won't be in there. Your name wasn't from any book."

Bear puffs up proudly. "What about Juniper?"

"Not Juniper either. Your names are both from real things. Real wild things. That's the book I used to pick your mum's name."

Bear finds the page for Marian. It's easy – the corner is folded over at the top and there are flowers drawn around the name.

"Marian. Wished-for child," I say, not even needing to look. I know the entry by heart.

It means rebellious too. That was the sting in the tail. Annie Rose loved her so much, but she was too wild to keep.

When the fire alarm sounds, it's piercing and

overwhelming and my stomach, which has been tied in a knot since Friday, comes loose. I run to the bathroom and throw up into the toilet.

Etienne said we should wait five minutes to give the Border Patrol guards time to leave their posts and when I come back into the kitchen, Bear's counting out the seconds. Annie Rose is nodding, prompting as he stumbles over the hundred boundary. One hundred and one. One hundred and two.

At two hundred she takes our hands in hers, and Bear and I join hands too so we're one perfect circle. Annie Rose doesn't cry. She doesn't get overly emotional. She's not like that. She knows it would distract us, weaken us. Now more than ever is a time to be strong.

Three hundred and it's time to go. Annie Rose lifts Bear's rucksack on to his back. The pans are strapped to the bottom and they jangle against each other.

"My little tin man," Annie Rose says and she kisses him softly on the head. "I hope your school shoes are up for the challenge!"

Bear looks small, stunned, unsure whether this is actually going to happen. "Can't you come too, Annie Rose?"

Annie Rose doesn't falter. She keeps her voice light, says that one day soon someone will develop a vaccine and she'll come then. Someone could come and get her, bring her to us. To Ennerdale.

She doesn't believe it. It's just a story she's telling him, to ease the goodbye, and my heart's breaking – cleaving right in two – because I know this might actually be it. The last time she pulls me close, kisses me. The last time I can hug her, my arms so tight against her thin frame, to let her know just how much she means to us.

She runs her fingers along my cheeks. "Are you ready, Juniper berry?"

"Yes."

"Your bag's not too heavy?"

"No."

"Come, then." Annie Rose pulls Bear back a safe distance and I swing Grandpa Edward's axe against the pane. I watch the glass shatter.

28

We're walking across the Buffer, Bear's hand small and hot in mine. "Shall we run, Ju?"

"No, let's just walk fast. We don't want to trip."

I hadn't thought through the terrain – the rocks and blocks of concrete that Border Patrol have strewn over everything. It's hard to get a footing. You could stumble. Turn your ankle. No doubt that's what they want, if they ever imagined anyone would be crazy enough to try and cross.

"Are we crazy, Bear?" I ask, looking down at him for some confirmation of sanity from my six-year-old brother, dutifully trotting by my side.

"I think we should run, Ju," he says, gazing back over his shoulder.

You can see the smoke funnelling up into the sky and the glow of the flames leaping up, capricious. I never saw anything like it before. I think I can feel the heat too, on the back of my neck, and flecks of ash fall down upon us like some terrible black rain. Going up like a tinderbox, that's what they used to say. It's going to take all the water the city's got to put it out.

"Will it burn down our block? Will it burn the Palm House?" Bear asks.

"No. It's just the warehouse. No one will be hurt." The smoke reaches up into my nose and my mouth, acrid. We're both coughing.

I focus on the way ahead. Each step needs picking out and we have to keep our torches right down so we're not seen. Sometimes we need to change course to detour round the higher piles of debris. The concrete blocks are more dangerous than they look, for embedded within them are nails and shards of glass. And there are coils of barbed wire, which wrap around our feet. We keep having to stop to untangle ourselves.

It's no man's land. It's one big trap.

We try and keep to the places where you can see the actual ground. Where the scattering of obstacles has become uneven and the scorched chemical earth shows.

At some point I realize there's an actual softness underfoot. That I'm sinking into something. I shouldn't stop, I shouldn't look down, but I do and my torch floods the floor with light.

Dead feathered bodies. Soft bloodied corpses. We're walking over rotting birds.

Bear screams and I clasp my fingers over his mouth to silence him. Not that anyone could hear with the sirens wailing. Maybe it's me that doesn't want to hear. It's like some awful omen. Our first sight of wild things and they're dead already.

"What's happened to them, Juniper?" Bear's voice wavers.

"They've been shot, Bear." That's what we hear at night. They're not empty warning shots. Etienne was right.

"But why were the birds here? Why didn't they stay away?" His little body is shaking. It's too much – too close, too many. I gather him up beside me to move us on, but my legs are shaking too.

You don't see dead things in the city. Occasionally, the odd insect gets through. Once we saw a dead cockroach on the way to school, sometimes there's the odd fly or spider, but creatures don't last in the city. They don't last long enough to die. If there's a breach, if one gets through, Glyphosate Patrol gets them straight away.

Here are mounds and mounds of flesh. Broken wings and small round heads with dull eyes, staring up at us.

"Don't look, Bear. Let's get to the forest. It'll be better there." I look to the horizon for the trees, but it's too dark to make out anything. I've no idea what's really ahead. No idea where I'm really leading him.

"Seagull. Pigeon," Bear says, ignoring me and shining his torch right into the carcasses. "Crow."

A murder of crows. It was in our dictionary in this strange list right at the back of the book. Collective nouns. A sloth of bears, a misbelief of painters and a murder of crows. Like the dictionary was warning me.

"Don't, Bear. Don't look."

"Starling. Magpie."

"Bear, please. Stop it!" For once he's called out their names, we can't ever unknow. And we can't ever unsee.

"Why did they come here?" Bear asks, still trying to make sense of it all.

"They're town birds, or they were once. They don't know they're not allowed." My eyes are wet and hazy as I look again to the horizon, willing my eyes to make out the treeline. "Come on! Please! Let's carry on. We have to. We have to, Bear."

The moon's overhead – a full circle of white, hanging right above us, but still not providing enough light to see. We've got too used to artificial city light.

"Bear!" I scream and I pull him on, yanking at his arm to force his legs to move. "Let's get into the forest."

PART
II

Wild

29

There's a shadow on the horizon. An uneven edge on the skyline. It's really close now.

I wish we were seeing the trees first in the daylight. It's impossible not to imagine danger when everything's so dark.

Behind us, we can hear shouts, or screams maybe, carried on the breeze. But there's no gunfire, no border alarm, just the fire siren, quieter now, but still wailing out incessantly.

We practically fall into the forest, out of breath. For a moment we pause on the threshold. Partly it's disbelief that we made it this far and partly it's fear. This is the start of the Wild, and despite everything – despite how we've longed for it, dreamed of it, sickened for it – we've been taught our entire lives in the city to be scared of it.

"We have to keep going, Bear," I say, though I'm still rooted to the spot.

"Why are you whispering?"

"Maybe there are Border Patrols this side too." But that's not really it. It's the trees looming up above us and the quiet that's suddenly around us. Like the power outages in the city, when everything turned off and for a while there was silence and you could hear your own heartbeat.

"We need to head west first. Get clear of the city," I say. Etienne's GPS is strung round my neck. The light on the screen is dim when I turn it on, but we have to save the battery and we can't be seen. The drones can search out light. Same with the torches. We'll have to ration their use.

I stare at the GPS, at the turning hourglass. It's the trees, I think, blocking the signal from the satellites. Did we seriously expect it to work? But the device is cleverer than that. Within a few seconds, a green spot lights up on the screen and around it the map comes into view. There, on the south edge of our city, our starting point.

"This way," I say, relieved that I don't have to get out the paper map. It's safe in our bags with the compass, but I'm really not sure of my ability to use it. I've never used a map before. Only ones in stories. Made-up kingdoms. None of that's going to help.

I turn back one last time. I can still see it in the distance, or maybe I'm imagining things. Maybe it's my head, painting it in – that dome of old Victorian glass. Our very own Emerald City.

The forest isn't silent. As we walk into it, it comes alive.

Everything moving, ever so slightly. There's a whisper above us and rustlings in the undergrowth, and a sudden *twit twoo* which is so textbook-owl that Bear squeezes my hand and even in the dark I can see his eyes glow.

"Tawnies," he whispers and bounds forward to look for them. There's a sharp crackle. "Ju!" he cries, panicked. "What's that?"

"It's just leaves."

"Will the guards hear?"

"No."

"What about the wolves, Ju?"

"No, but stop speaking anyway."

It doesn't take long for the glow from the city to sink away. The dark's like a liquid we could drown in.

Bear's breathing is laboured. He was amazing across the Buffer. All that way across, all the stumbles and the horror of the birds, he didn't once complain or cry. The adrenaline of the escape kept us both going, but adrenaline doesn't last forever, not in a six-year-old boy out way past his bedtime with a heavy load on his back. He doesn't say anything, but his pace has slowed, he's lagging behind. His legs are smaller than mine, his stride little.

I tug at him gently. "Come on, Bear. Keep up."

"When can we make our tent, Ju?"

"We have to get further away. From the Buffer. Here, let me carry that." I unhook his bag from his shoulders and place it on my front, even though my back's already aching with my own bigger bag and the tarpaulins in a roll beneath it, and the rat trap beneath that.

"Can we make a fire tonight?" Bear asks.

"We'll try."

"Shall I start collecting sticks?"

"Not now, Bear," I say, quietly desperate. "You have to walk faster than this."

I can't help thinking that by now some alarm has been raised. Maybe Border Patrol are already coming after us. If not, then at 9am tomorrow, when school starts on Monday morning, our desks will be empty. Our teachers will mark us absent, Abbott will call Annie Rose. She's going to pick up the phone and say we're sick. To buy us time before they come looking. I'm not sure any of us believe that will work though.

Sometimes I think I see them. Lumbering white figures lit by the moon. Border Patrol in their Hazmat suits. But it's all in my head. There's no one for miles.

When we can't go any further, we make our tent. A tree holds a branch out for us at just the right height and I drape over one of the tarpaulins and lay the other on the floor.

Bear doesn't ask about collecting sticks or making a fire. He simply gets inside his sleeping bag and falls asleep. His body can't do any more. I'm so exhausted I crawl into mine, right next to him, and shut my eyes.

30

Some bird is calling above us. This high-pitched trill, little snatches of song that stop only to start up again a moment or so later.

Bear's out of his sleeping bag already and I clamber up next to him. I want to say something but I can't find the words and anyway it doesn't matter because I know Bear's feeling it too. Anyone would. The scale of it – the trees, right up into the sky, all green and yellow and gold, and the sunlight filtering through them, dancing down on our upturned faces.

It's like the Palm House only a hundred times greener, a thousand times more fresh.

That first bird's still singing but there are different birds too, their songs weaving together. It's beautiful. But it's more than beautiful. It's alive.

"It worked," Bear says.

"We did it!"

"Not that, Ju!" Bear's half irritated. "The ReWild. I worried it was made up."

"Made up?"

"That nature hadn't grown back. That it was still all dead."

"Yes," I say softly. "It worked. Nature found a way."

"Look at the spiderwebs, Juniper! They're just like your drawings!"

I stare at them. These ornate, perfect hangings. Geometry strung between branches. Some have spiders in them – these eight-legged creatures that aren't ticks, but you're meant to be scared of anyway.

There's a spider still spinning. This incredible, graceful thing with long legs. Her web spirals out from the centre and she walks it like a circus performer. Like an acrobat.

"I wish I could tell Annie Rose about it," Bear says. "And Etienne. Why did he have the GPS if he knew he could never leave, Juniper?" His nose is crinkly.

I keep my voice flat. "He hoped things would change one day. That the disease would burn itself out or maybe scientists would make that vaccine." Or maybe if things got so bad – if it was a choice between the disease or the Institute – then Etienne would run into the Wild anyway, even though he knew he wouldn't last out here. But I don't say the last bit. Out here, the city feels like a bad dream.

There's a sudden yelp from Bear. "Ow! Ju! Something bit me." He's wandered into a clump of green straggly plants. "I think it was a snake, Juniper! It's burning."

"Burning? A snake?" I say, moving towards him into the plants, reaching out for his hand.

"Juniper!" Bear says, indignant. "Do something! What if it was a tick?"

I look at his hand again, where little round pimples are rising out of his skin, and then I look at the plants and I feel a prickling on my hands too. A strange sensation I've never felt before, halfway between an itch and a sharp pain. "It wasn't a tick, Bear!"

"A snake then. I felt it, Juniper. Why are you laughing?"

"I'm not," I say, fighting to hold back my amusement at the outrage on Bear's face. "Look, it got me too. Your snake. We're standing on it."

Bear looks down at the ground, all quiet and excited. "Where, Ju?"

I giggle. "I thought you were the naturalist. I thought you knew all this."

He pulls a face at me as he looks at the green leaves around us with their little stinging hairs. He mutters the word out loud, begrudgingly. "Nettles. See! I told you something stung me."

"Well, actually you said bit."

"It could've been an adder, Juniper, and then you

wouldn't be laughing. Or something worse!" He's wading out of the nettles furiously. "It's all right for you with your boots. I've just got my school shoes! I'm stung all over my ankles as well."

"Oh, Bear," I say sweetly, trying to keep a straight face. "Isn't there some leaf that's meant to help with nettle stings? Don't you remember, in *First Aid Naturally*…"

"The dock leaf," he says slowly, like he's talking to an idiot.

"That's right. I'll find us some."

"You wouldn't even know what they look like," Bear says, scowling at me.

"Tell me then," I coax. "Describe them."

I let Bear find them – veined leaves with pinkish stems. They always grow near nettles. That's the bit I remember – the poison and the treatment, side by side.

We sit rubbing the dock leaves on to our skin, crushing them against the rash. I don't know if they really help, but gradually the stinging ebbs away. Maybe it's having this moment to take it all in, that we made it out here, to where things grow and plants can sting.

There's a flash of movement a few metres away and Bear's up. He slips behind a tree.

"This would be the best hide-and-seek ever!" His muted voice comes back at me.

"Don't you dare!" I cry, properly shouting. "Come back!"

Bear appears from behind the tree and looks at me strangely. "I'm just here, Ju."

"I know, but…" But what do I say? That I'm worried the forest will swallow him up? He's out here, where he was always meant to be. I can't keep him on a lead.

"We should eat," I say instead.

"What have we got?" Bear says coming back, interested.

"Annie Rose made sandwiches. We should eat those, before they go stale."

"That bread's always stale anyway. It's like plastic." Bear pulls a face. "I want wild food."

"There'll be time for that. Let's eat what we have first."

There's a log, like a bench, next to where we made our tent and we sit beside each other. Nature providing, I think, like Annie Rose told us it would.

"How many miles now?" Bear asks.

"A long way. It's almost three hundred miles, remember."

"Is that too far?"

"It's just how far it is." We don't know about miles and time. We never had any distance to walk in the city. Annie Rose said adults could walk maybe fifteen to twenty miles a day, but there's no way Bear could manage that. She said maybe eight miles a day, on average. Working it out makes my head spin.

Even if we managed eight miles a day, that's more than thirty days' walking. More than a month. It will be

December by the time we get to Ennerdale. Proper winter.

I can't very well tell Bear we'll be walking for an entire month. And that's not even factoring in detours for water, or diverting round other cities, or getting lost.

Bear's stopped listening anyway. He's gulping in the air. "Sniff it, Ju! It doesn't smell clean like in the city."

I can't resist smiling. "That wasn't clean, Bear. That was disinfectant and weedkiller."

"Oh yeah," Bear says, opening his mouth wide to breathe in the forest. And suddenly, in that instant, I remember it – the smell of earth and leaves and bark. This flood of something wells up inside me and maybe there is a voice I remember and maybe it is Mum's, I don't know. But she's all that way north and she never came back for us. I've got Bear now. He's mine to take to her.

I can't think about all that. I make myself busy rolling up the tarpaulins and the sleeping bags and the space blanket. Bear's carrying the blanket but he's weirdly possessive about his rucksack and insists he puts it in by himself.

"What have you got in there?"

"Nothing!"

I give him a strange look. What has he stashed away in there? What couldn't he leave behind? It's too late now anyway. We have what we have. "Come on, Bear. We should be on our way."

We follow the arrow on the GPS along some old road.

The surface is broken up with trees, their roots bursting through the tarmac, all covered in moss and the ferns I've been drawing for years.

"Juniper!" Bear's voice is shrill. "Look!"

It's a bird, already taking to the sky, its wings fluttering, panicked. High in the trees before I see it properly – a flash of brown and blue and white.

"Why did it fly off so fast?" Bear asks.

"Maybe it never saw anything like us before."

"I think it's a jay!" Bear says. "I wish we had my book."

"You don't need it. You know this," I say quietly, envious of him. How he can notice everything and not just be looking for danger.

"And look! Look, Ju! It's a squirrel!"

It's running up the tree, fast, like it's flying too. Grey with a white belly and flecks of red on its back. Its tail, thick and coiled, moves with it like an extra limb. There are rabbits too, brown and skittish.

The footprints of before are everywhere, though it's all hidden under tangled mounds of plant life. Moss, thorns, brambles. Like when the princess pricked her finger on a spinning wheel and slept for a hundred years. Like Mary Lennox's secret garden.

At first I don't get what it all is, it's just random lines of debris, but then I start to see the shapes. The markings out. What would once have been a house. What would once have been a garden. Now the separate plots are all growing back into one. The walls are crumbling down. Even the metal is rusting away. One day it will all be powder. And somewhere, in the thickness of everything, in the depths and in the shadows, there will be the ticks.

31

"I'm still hungry, Ju. Can I have a snack bar?"

"I don't know, Bear. I think we should save them."

"We've got loads."

"We have to make them last."

He pulls a face at me.

I know what I have to do. I should have done it last night. I should have set the trap – let it work while we slept. It's not the trapping that bothers me, it's what comes next. It's the palm under the rabbit's chin, the pressing back of the neck. It's the snap. That's the bit I'm not sure I can do.

The meat we ate back in the city wasn't ever alive. Not really. It was grown in a lab somewhere.

"Let's walk for a bit, Bear," I say, stalling. "Then you can have a snack. And tonight for tea we'll catch something. Some meat. That's what you need to fill your tummy."

I thought it would feel different out here. I'd assume

another kind of identity – bolder, stronger – only I still feel just like me. Every time I see a rabbit I get this chill on the back of my neck.

It's worse because they don't seem afraid of us. Not really. They're curious, friendly even. They've forgotten what people can do.

"Can I hold the GPS, Ju?" Bear pipes up.

I shake my head.

"That's not fair! You get to do all the good stuff. I won't break it, I promise, Ju." He makes his eyes all big and tugs at my hand.

"I know that."

"Then?"

"It has to be high, to get the best signal. So it finds the best route to the satellite. Remember? Like Etienne said. And I'm taller."

Bear moans, but he kind of accepts it. My lie.

Am I worried he'll break it? Maybe. But it's more than that. I need it next to me, right up against my chest, this thing, this device that's going to lead us to Ennerdale.

Bear's ahead of me, picking up sticks, ignoring me when I say it's too early in the day to be collecting firewood.

There was this old jack-in-the-box in the Emporium. You wind the handle on the tin box and a monkey pops out at you on a spring. That's what Bear's like. In the city, his lid was closed and he was shut up in the dark. All this light and space, he's sprung right back out. He's wired.

It should make me happy and it does, but I'm worried I've lost control of him. He could spring right away from me.

I'm calling him back – we don't know the land yet, it's not safe – when I notice we're being watched.

It's the yellow eyes I see first. I think it's a fox, a big one, but it's not.

"Bear," I whisper urgently.

It's a cat. Sort of brown or golden with black spots, leopard-like, and black tufts on the tops of its ears. Its paws are big and furry, like it's wearing boots, and its neck is furry too – collared like a ruff, like long-ago queens.

"What is it, Ju?" Bear asks, stopping. "I don't recognize it."

"I don't know, Bear. Just come backwards to me. And don't turn away from it."

Never turn from a predator and run. They can't help it, you can't even blame them. It's their instinct to give chase.

Bear's still like a statue so I move instead, forwards, towards him.

I should be more scared. The cat's not taking its eyes off us. Though it could have pounced on Bear already, if it wanted to. It's not quite as tall as he is, but it's strong, you can see that. I grab a stick and hold it up like a warning – get my brother and I'll come for you.

The tufts on the cat's ears are up and there's a flick of

its little bobtail, but it doesn't move. It stands there on its long legs, watching us, watching both of us, shifting its eyes between us as if studying our connection.

I stretch an arm out for Bear to bring him closer. Together we're bigger, stronger.

"It could've come from a zoo," Bear's saying. "It could've escaped all the shooting. Some animals must have done." He's not scared at all, only curious and annoyed that he can't identify it. Like his books have failed him.

Then suddenly I know. School taught me something useful after all.

"It's a lynx. The ReWilders released some."

"A lynx." Bear says the name slowly. You didn't get them in books about British wildlife. Lynx were long gone by the time those books were written. We'd already hunted them to extinction hundreds of years before.

"They weren't meant to come over, they were outlawed, but the ReWilders brought them anyway. They brought them from Russia." They needed something – something more organic than guns, something that would still be here after the ReWild – to keep down deer and rabbits, otherwise their numbers would have exploded and with all those plant-eaters the forests could never regrow. Of course, on our Education Board syllabus, lynx cats were another example of the ReWilders' irresponsibility – letting dangerous predators loose on an overcrowded island.

"Why's it watching us, Ju?"

It's watching us intently, like it's curious. Its eyes are beautiful and outlined in black, like eyeliner, like kohl. I shrug. "Maybe it never saw a person before."

"Here, pussy, pussy." The words sound familiar in Bear's mouth, though he just learned them from stories.

"Bear!" I whisper, aghast. "It's not that sort of cat."

"It wouldn't hurt us."

"We don't know that."

"It could be our friend."

"It's wild, Bear."

Bear frowns. "Wild's good, isn't it?"

"Not always." The cat is blinking slowly but its body is completely still. Someone's got to make a move. I start to back away, pulling Bear after me. "Come on!"

"Bye bye, pussycat," Bear says. "Should we still be walking backwards, Ju?"

"I think so. Until it can't see us any more. Come on, we need to find water and then somewhere to camp, and it has to be away from anything that might eat us, OK?"

32

I've been aware of a river for miles now, from the GPS and from this sound just a few trees away. This watery murmur. But I've been scared somehow of what we might find. We can't wait any longer though and we start walking towards the water.

Before the ReWild, the rivers were running brown and orange and polluted. Chemical waste from landfill, from the clogged-up land, had found its way in. There were rivers that gave chemical burns if you touched them. There were rivers that would set alight if you struck a match. Annie Rose said that one of our most essential pieces of camping kit is the little tin of strips that test for clean water. She showed us how to use them before we left. I didn't have the heart to tell her the water from our kitchen sink made the strips turn orange, meaning unsafe to drink.

The river water doesn't look like it will show up blue on

the strips either. It's dark, murky.

"Can I do it, Ju?"

We're standing on the bank, the tin of strips in my hand. "I don't know. Maybe. But I think it's too steep here."

The incline down to the water is thick with roots and brambles. If we tripped, we could fall right in. It's hard to tell how deep it is, but we can't see the bottom and we never learned to swim. The pool in the city was too disgusting to think about. This oily lacquer clung to the surface, this scum – disinfectant and human secretions combined.

"We have to walk upstream," I say, the new word light in my mouth. Upstream. "Somewhere it's easier to get to the water. But watch out for ticks."

The plants are high here and close together. There must be ticks everywhere. This is their perfect terrain. Ticks are like vampires – they drink blood and hate the sun; they like dark damp places best. Somewhere with thick vegetation where they can wait unseen for something with warm blood to pass. Questing, that's what it's called.

"Blackberries! Like you got at the North Edge, Ju!" Bear squeals.

He's right. It's the same plant – the bramble, studded with little black fruits.

"We can be hunter-gatherers!" he says, already with juice around his mouth. Any doubts he had about eating them are long gone.

I pick too, for the rush of it on your tongue. The sweet and the sharpness together. The berries here are different to the North Edge though – they're a dull black and there are no small firm ones waiting to ripen. These are the last this plant's got. They're OK, but there's a cloudiness, like the beginning of rot.

"I could go through here, Ju." Bear's at a parting in the undergrowth. Something's been here before us. Some animal, going down to drink. Maybe that lynx cat.

"OK," I say warily. "Go steady, OK?" The ground's slippery and we have to put our hands down on to the bank to stop ourselves sliding too fast. Does the river come this high sometimes? Or perhaps it rained recently. We have no idea about weather outside the city.

I hold on to Bear's shoulders as he walks ahead, his flat soles slipping on the bank. The moment we reach the water's edge he swings round to face me. "I want to do it, Ju! You've got Etienne's GPS! It's my turn now!"

I hand over a strip slowly. "You have to hold it in the water for ten seconds, OK?"

I get this urge to shut my eyes, or look up to the sky and will the strip to show the same colour. To wait for Bear to call out the word. Blue.

I don't though. I stare at the thin rectangle in Bear's hand as it moistens, darkens. It takes a few seconds for any colour at all to show. I don't know where on the scale it would be, what the name would be on my paint palette, but it's a blue turning into green. Some kind of turquoise. It's what I always think the sea would look like.

"That's good, Bear, that's really good."

"We can drink it?"

"We can drink it."

Bear makes space for me beside him and we cup the water in our hands and pour it into our mouths. Long wet gulps of it.

It's icy and makes us shiver, but there's something else too that isn't just cold. It's fresh. Deliciously, beautifully fresh. So different to the stale city water that cycled around forever. There was some horrible statistic you had to try and forget, about how many bodies it had passed through already and how much of it was actually plastic.

The sun's a low blaze in the sky and we probably shouldn't linger, but I've got the triumph of finding water playing in my head, one of our first and most important goals. If only there was a way to send word to Annie Rose.

"There must be fish here!" Bear says, bending low over the water.

"Maybe."

"We could eat them!"

"Maybe," I say again. "If we can catch them."

"I could, Ju. And there will be some. There'll be loads!"

I smile at Bear's certainty. I hope he's right. It would mean the rivers are better now. When the ReWild happened, any fish were long gone. Annie Rose said first the rivers were full of dead, bloated fish bodies, then the bodies rotted away and you were just left with the decay. The algae that took the place of the fish, clogging up the water like a big old net.

Maybe all that made it easier to leave behind – the rivers and trees and whatever else was left by then. It wasn't beautiful any more. Then when people started getting sick and everyone saw how deadly the disease was, you can kind of see why they went along with everything. They walked into a cage and they locked the door behind them.

We haven't seen fish yet, but there are insects – long black bodies with four legs outstretched like a cross. They're balancing precariously on the surface.

"Pond skaters," Bear declares.

There's better than that too. Bear sees it first.

It's another insect, perched on a reed. It's long and thin and bright electric-blue, with four separate wings that are shiny and clear and partitioned, like that glass from our old apartment-block door.

"Dragonfly!" I say exultantly, because this one I know.

"Or damselfly, I'm not sure," Bear says.

"Dragonfly sounds better!"

The creature takes to the air, into the swirls of flies clustered over the river. Its prey. It's like a relic of a time when there really could be dragons. I think I hear its wings, beating.

I wish I didn't have to say we should move on, but what if those flies the dragonfly's catching are mosquitoes and what if the disease did transfer to them?

It's getting dark too. We have to move on so we can make camp while we can still see. I start filling our bottles, from as far out in the river as I can reach so it's as pure as you get. I'm doing it slowly, not wanting to lose this feeling, swirling my fingers through the water, when Bear screams.

"Ju! What's that?"

He knows already. I hear the fear in the pitch of his voice. And we know that sound like we know our own heartbeats. The buzzing and whirring Annie Rose said was like a fly in your ear. Only the glyphosate killed most of the flies, so an annoying buzz has only ever meant one thing to Bear and me. A surveillance drone.

It's just a couple of metres above water level. The river provides the perfect path. Bear's fumbling with his rucksack. I want to say leave it, just run, but we need everything in that bag. I hoist it on to his shoulders and grab my bag, and we tear through the brambles. Back into the trees, deeper into the forest.

I was stupid to let us dawdle by the river. Of course Border Patrol would look for us. Of course they would. Abbott will have sent word first thing. The moment he realized we weren't in school.

The river's the obvious place for them to look. They know we need water to survive. They'll have sent drones out in both directions.

I hear it behind us. The drone of it, just like its name, mirroring every move we make. Chasing us. This silver-grey orb with metallic legs. Loud. Louder. The churned-up air touches the back of my neck like fingers.

"Faster, Bear!"

It's just a machine. But you don't think about that when you're running, you just run. Fast, faster, and then some. Even if a drone can't actually hurt us, someone, somewhere, back in the city, in one of their control towers or their bunkers, is seeing everything that drone sees. They know where we are. They know we're alive and that our bags are big enough to contain supplies. Which means someone helped us. This totally contradicts what Annie Rose had been going to say. Her surprise when she found the broken glass. Her despair that she'd lost her grandchildren, because there's no way we'd survive out here with just the clothes on our backs.

"Bear, take my hand!" We have to change direction.

We swerve right and then left. This zigzag pattern through the trees. My head's swirling, dizzy, but we keep going. Right, then left, then right again.

The drone keeps after us for ages. Someone's got good

reflexes – the controller, the pilot, has practised this – and the machine flies like the dragonfly does. Fast. Precise.

But eventually I realize the sound is only in my head and when I look back I can't see it. "Stop! Let's stop a minute."

Bear collapses to the ground, his lungs heaving. I've never seen him so out of energy. "Did we lose it?"

"I think so." I have to catch my breath too. We've been running for ages – ducking under branches, jumping over roots – through the trees and the thorny scrub.

"You think it hit a tree?"

"Maybe." They'll send another though. They'll send whatever they can spare if Abbott has anything to do with it.

"Have you got the water, Ju?" Bear asks.

I pass it over, sick inside suddenly. This is the bottle I'd been refilling, the one still in my hands when we saw the drone. I left the other one on the bank.

"Where's the other?" Bear asks, seeing my face freeze up.

"We'll have to make do with this one."

"We can go back." He gets up and starts walking back the way we came.

"No! No, Bear," I say. "They'll find us. We just have to keep refilling this one. But more carefully now, and quickly, and maybe when it's dark."

"Will it be OK?"

There's only one answer I can give. "It'll rain soon. We'll catch rainwater. We'll drink that."

"I wish Etienne was here," Bear says.

"Well, he isn't, is he?" I snap. "You have to make do with me." Bear flinches. I don't know why I'm so angry all of a sudden. Maybe because I wish it too. Not that Etienne could do any of this any better. Maybe help cajole Bear, he could do that, and share the load on our backs. And be our friend, someone to talk to, help make the decisions. Etienne would have the whole route planned out. We'd know exactly where we're going and how long it should take.

Bear's eyes are shiny. I shouldn't have yelled at him – we're out here alone with no Annie Rose to console him. My stomach clenches with guilt. "Come on, Bear cub. We'll get back on track and then find somewhere to make camp."

"Can I collect sticks tonight, Ju? We can make the fire." Despite everything, he's still excited.

"I don't know, Bear," I say slowly. "I want to as well, I do, it's just with the drone nearby it'd be like sending out a signal."

"We need the fire to keep the wolves away."

The wolves came from the zoos. They escaped, or maybe their keepers let them go, because it was better than the alternative, better than what happened to all the pets, back in the city. Rufus, Jamie and Leo. Smoky, Poppy and Bo.

"We'd have heard them, Bear. We were OK last night.

Nothing came." And wolves know to stay away from people, don't they? Surely people have shown them that enough times in our long bloody hunting history? Can a species remember that? The rabbits obviously not, but wolves… Wolves are so much cleverer. That's why they're in so many of the old stories.

"You promised we'd make a fire and I'm cold, Ju."

"I know, Bear, and we will. Just not tonight."

Bear puts his face into a sulk. A scared, sad sulk.

"You can make the tent. We'll need stones to weigh it down at the edges. Let's go and find the right spot."

"It's too dark," he says flatly.

He's right, but we can't use our torches in case more drones come. We just have Etienne's GPS, which I hold out before us, a soft globe of light.

"We'll go by moonlight," I say, "like real explorers do."

"And starlight?"

"Yeah, exactly, so we have a million lights to see by. We're actually quite lucky. Let's just do a couple more miles and then we'll make camp, I promise."

We pick up our legs and keep walking. There are no drones, we'd hear them, but I look back anyway. I can't shake the feeling we're being followed.

33

The moon hangs above us, a white impossible kite on a string of stars. These tiny twinkling lights, trillions of miles away.

We're about to stop and make camp when Bear says it. Or screams it.

"Tick, Juniper! Tick!"

"Where?" I shout, brandishing a stick in my hand ridiculously, like it would do any good against an insect.

"On my neck!" He's crying. This is the one animal he knows to be scared of.

I scramble for the torch and turn it on, directing it to where Bear's little fingers point, on the side of his neck, up near his ear. It's brown or black maybe. One round body, eight legs, its face buried deep inside his skin.

"Stay still. Don't touch it."

I've gone through this scenario so many times. Even at

school they taught us how, just in case one got through. Never squeeze a tick. You take hold of it with tweezers, close to the skin, and you pull. Slow, steady, straight up.

Time matters. The longer the tick feeds, the more time there is for the disease to pass through the skin barrier. To leach through into your fluids. The microbes. The pathogens.

Only you have to do it right. If you're heavy-handed, you could crush it and then it releases even more microbes, all at once. Or the tick breaks away, but the mouthparts get left inside your skin and you've got a prime site for infection.

Even if we are resistant, we could do without having to fight off infections. And what if we're not? What if Silvan was right and the disease has mutated on past the resistance we have? Bear's only six. The youngest kids got it worst, their immune systems weren't developed enough.

"Ticks are harmless to us, aren't they, Ju? Benign? Safe?" Bear says, still playing our game, even though his voice is breaking with fear.

"Yes, but we still need to get it off."

My fingers are fat and numb as I wield the metal tweezers, trying to get the right angle as close as I can to Bear's skin, under the body of the tick and its floundering legs. Then I squeeze and pull. Slow, steady, straight up. I can feel the insect resisting, clinging on, its pincer mouth buried inside him.

You pull, but the tick has to release itself. I think it's not going to happen, that I'm going to rip a piece of Bear's skin off instead, but suddenly the tick comes away and the engorged black mite flails helplessly between the metal fingers of the tweezers. I throw the tick down and grind it into the forest floor with my boot heel.

I get the antiseptic wipes from our first-aid kit and dab gently at the red bead on Bear's neck. "It's OK, Bear cub. It's OK. It's gone now."

He looks up at me, big-eyed and grateful. "I won't get sick will I, Ju?"

I shake my head. "We just have to keep an eye on the wound. Keep it clean. Come here. I need to check the rest of you." I trace my hand along his neck and down his top, on to his shoulders, feeling for bumps on his smooth skin. We should have done this first thing this morning, although I bet that tick was from today. It was probably from the river. Anyway, there's no point spending much time looking now. It's too dark to see.

"Come on. Let's find somewhere to make camp. We've gone far enough for one day."

34

We lay our groundsheet under a tree, but don't put the top
layer on, not yet. We want to look up.

Bear's imagining creatures in the sky, drawn out in the
stars. He's got my sketchbook, the one unessential item
I allowed myself, and has his torch directed at the page.

You never saw stars in the city. Not really. There was
way too much light pollution. So many people, so tightly
packed. Someone, somewhere was always awake.

There were three more ticks – two on Bear's right ankle,
one on my shin. We found them after we made camp. We
took off clothing, one bit at a time so we didn't get cold,
and ran our fingers along our goose-pimpled skin. You
don't feel them at first, not when they bite. All the time the
tick was on my leg, for however long it was there feeding,
I didn't notice anything. As they're sucking out your blood,
they're sending painkillers into you, to deaden you to any

sensation that they're there.

That first bite, on Bear's neck, is red and sore, but it doesn't seem to be spreading, not yet. That's what you've got to watch out for – red angry weals, radiating outwards.

We've eaten the last of the sandwiches and Bear's had a snack bar too, and a few metres away, under a tree, we've laid the trap.

I can feel my energy waning. We need protein. Maybe we'll go a few miles first, in the morning, before we cook it, whatever 'it' is. Then we can make a fire and we can eat something warm that will actually fill us up.

We need to go back to the river too. I've no idea when it's going to rain, despite what I said to Bear. The sky was red tonight – bleeding across the sky, haemorrhaging – and I think that means something about the weather, only I can't remember what. I think it was some extreme, though it's just an old rhyme. Sailors or shepherds or something.

"Ju, it's the cat again," Bear whispers, but casual, so casual that I look down at the sketchbook on his lap, thinking that's what he means, that he's added the lynx to his constellations. But Bear's hand is pointing out into the darkness and when I look, I see the dim shape under the trees.

It takes a while for my eyes to make out the full picture. It's a cat, just like we saw before. It's lying down, head on its paws, watching.

"You think it followed us?" Bear asks.

"I don't know."

"But we don't have to move our camp, do we? I don't want to walk any more today. I can't!" There's a moan forming in his voice.

I don't want to walk further either. My legs and body ache, and my head aches too. It's just a cat. It's big, but not big like a lion or tiger would be big, and we've been sitting prey for ages. The cat could have got us already, if that's what it wanted.

"Let's just watch it for a while. See what it does."

"I miss the Sticks," Bear says.

"Do you, Bear?" I ask, giving him a squeeze. "They'll be OK, you know. They have a good keeper."

Bear smiles. He gave his vivarium to Etienne the night we left. "I hope Etienne takes them to the Palm House, for adventures. They like it there."

I nod. I want to say something more, that Etienne will do everything he can for the Sticks, and for Annie Rose, that we don't need to worry, but I can't. Thinking about Etienne and Annie Rose makes this lump in my throat. Plus it might not be true about Annie Rose, that we don't need to worry.

Will Steel's Border Patrol officers really accept her story – that we broke the glass on our own, that we were running from Annie Rose too? They're not stupid.

"We could give the lynx a name," Bear says hopefully. "He could be our new pet."

"There you go again, Bear," I say, raising my eyebrows. "How do you know it's a boy?"

"It's a girl?"

"I don't know, I sort of think she is." I can't explain why. It's something to do with the way she watches us.

"Shall we call her Lady Jane Grey then? She's got that collar round her neck, like kings and queens did."

"Yeah, but that name's taken. Lady Jane Grey's with Etienne. What else?"

"I don't know. Goldie? Spot? Like the pet tags in the Emporium?"

"Nah, they're too obvious." And she's better than that. She'd never be a pet, with a shiny gold medallion round her neck.

"She's a bit like a shadow," Bear says, his nose crinkling up. "Cause she follows us."

"That's good."

"Or like a ghost of the forest."

"I like that. Ghost."

"Like the Sticks," Bear says, pleased with himself.

"That's it then. I name her Ghost, in honour of our left-behind stick insects." I put on this pompous voice and Bear repeats her name after me solemnly.

"Now come on," I say, "help me with the tarpaulin.

The lynx might have a name, but she's not exactly our friend yet. I think while we're sleeping we're safer under a layer of canvas."

"Maybe Ghost will keep the wolves away."

"Maybe. That would be good."

"Our watch cat."

I look out at her – eyes still awake, still watching. That would be nice. And if she could listen for drones too – meow or something if she heard one. Warn us.

The tarpaulin keeps out the moonlight, but it doesn't keep out the cold. Nor does the groundsheet stop the damp seeping upwards into our sleeping bags.

Although the forest looks dry, when you touch it, when you sink down into it, it's not dry at all. I don't know whether it's rainwater from days ago or the leaves themselves. All the water they've ever taken in leaking out as they break down to become part of the forest floor. Their journey back to the beginning.

"I'm starving, Ju," Bear pipes up, interrupting my thoughts.

"I know," I say, thinking of the trap outside. "I hope Ghost doesn't take tomorrow's lunch."

"Me too," Bear says sleepily. "I wonder what it'll be."

"For lunch?"

"Yeah."

"Some rabbit or squirrel probably. What would be best?"

"I think a rabbit would taste nicer and you wouldn't waste as much tail as you would with a squirrel. Squirrels are all tail."

"True," I say, thinking how crazy it is. Day two and we're already fantasizing how rabbits and squirrels will taste, and hoping a wild lynx cat is somehow going to protect us.

35

"Is it broken?" Bear asks, picking up the empty metal cage in his hands.

"Careful! It could trap your fingers!"

"Why would that man give you a broken trap?"

"Maybe nothing came. Or maybe something did – it just didn't want the bait." I wouldn't blame it. The snack bar's called 'Sweet Apple' but like everything in the city it looks like plastic. It doesn't even smell of apple when you open the wrapper. Why would anything out here want to eat that?

"I'm starving, Ju! Ravenous!" Bear wails.

"I know, Bear," I say dully. Apart from expecting to wake and see our tent surrounded by drones, the trap was my first thought this morning. I was worried about what we'd find and then worried about what I needed to do.

I'd thought about all of that as I lay awake, hugging my

knees to my chest for warmth, trying to fall asleep, and then later too, in my dreams, I'd thought about it some more, and the prey had become this impossible deer that I'd not known how to kill or whether I had the heart to anyway. I hadn't thought much at all about the trap being empty.

"We have some snack bars left," I say. "I'll get you one!"

"I don't want a bar. I'm sick of bars," Bear says. Though he eats it, a Summer Strawberry, and then asks for another.

There's no ignoring the growing noise in our stomachs. It turns out that snack bars, despite the calories and protein they claim to contain, don't actually meet all your hunger requirements. And we won't even have any of them left soon, not the rate we're getting through them. The problem isn't just being out here, it's being out here and having to walk so many miles each day and stay warm. It burns up all the energy you've got.

"We could eat conkers," Bear suggests. "Like the squirrels. I've got some in my pockets."

Bear's collecting everything. He knows the trees from what he gets from them – acorns from the oak, helicopter wings from the sycamore, cones from the alder and pine, and hanging seeds like fat bunches of keys from the ash.

Conkers are his favourite, from the horse chestnut.

I can see why he wants them – these big shiny nuts that fall from a tree with leaves like handprints. It's hard not to pick the conkers up. To feel them, glossy, in the flats of your palms.

"I'm not sure you can eat conkers." The squirrels are eating them, or something is, because you find these half-chewed ones, but I don't remember ever reading anything about humans eating them. Sweet chestnuts you can eat, it's there in the name, and hazelnuts too, but we haven't seen any of those. "We could try acorns," I say hopefully. "I'm sure they're edible."

I remember something about acorns in one of the books – soaking them in hot water to get rid of the bitterness and make them easier to digest. Yet soaking involves water and we don't have enough. It's another reason to head to a river.

"I've got acorns too," Bear says, fumbling in his pockets. "But only a few. We need to find an oak tree!" He's already getting up.

"Wait. Let's pack first. We can get some on our way. We need to keep moving."

Bear's face falls. "I like it here."

"We're on a journey, Bear," I prompt gently. "To Mum, remember."

"She should have come and got us," he says, screwing up his face crossly.

"She'll be so proud when we show up. She did this journey too, remember?"

"How many more miles? Is it still more than a hundred?"

he says in a voice that makes it clear it's a deal-breaker.

I nod. "But we made a start. A really good start."

"Ghost's gone. I don't want to leave without saying goodbye."

"She could find us again, if she wanted to. She did before."

He grunts.

"Bear!" I say, pleading now, putting the straps of his bag on over his shoulders and then attaching the trap back under my rucksack so it hangs down behind me again, uselessly.

Maybe it was the lynx's fault we didn't catch anything. No rabbit or squirrel is going to come near a wild cat. Still, I circle the forest looking for the yellow eyes. For the first time last night, I thought I heard a wolf howling.

36

I run through the day's goals in my head – get water, find food, cook the acorns, make camp again, set the trap and actually catch something this time. All while walking as many miles as we can and not getting spotted by drones.

Bear appoints himself acorn-finder and gathers them as we go.

"I'm not sure how many acorns you can actually eat, Bear. That's probably enough now," I say irritably. Every time he bends down, he's making us slower. And it's not like we don't have enough to carry.

Bear kicks up the leaves with more ferocity. "I'm really hungry, Juniper."

"Ravenous? Famished?" I play, but Bear stares at me coldly.

"I want a snack bar."

"Not now, Bear. We have to eke them out. Make them last.

Look for berries instead. We can eat them as we go."

You can eat nettles too and there are lots of nettles. I'm just not sure how you eat stinging plants. It's not like you can scrunch a load up and put them in your mouth. Making nettles palatable must involve water too, to soften them and their little stinging hairs. You make them into a soup, or a tea. I think I remember that.

We see fungi – different shapes and colours, weird and kind of wonderful. If we knew what we were doing, some of them must be edible, some of them definitely are. But it's too risky, we don't have the slightest clue.

I look at them anyway, at the soft fleshy forms. I'm so hungry I'm even thinking back to Rainbow Mix with a strange longing.

"We should put acorns in the trap, Ju. Squirrels love acorns."

"Why would they come to the trap for acorns? They can get them any time they want." This is what's been going through my head. The flawed logic behind the trap. All the animals we're trying to catch, they've got food out here already, waiting to be picked up off the forest floor. Why would anything walk into a cage for some dried-out city food?

"Then we're never going to catch a thing!" Bear wails.

"We will," I say, sounding more confident than I feel. "Anyway, we should think about water first."

We make for the same river as yesterday, just further along, further north. This time we don't linger looking for a good way down, we simply part the undergrowth and head straight for the water.

There are no drone sounds, just the water, the swish of it and a splash, as if something's fallen in. Something from the trees maybe, or some water creature diving beneath the surface.

"Fish!" I whisper. I see them straight away. Dark olive shapes under the surface, glinting in the light. The water here's completely clear.

"I'll catch them!" Bear's voice shakes with excitement.

"We can't, Bear, we don't have time. The drones…"

Bear's leaning in, grabbing with his hands, but the fish scatter, disappear. The moment he pierces the surface with his hands, they're already gone.

"They saw my shadow. If we wait, they'll come back."

He's looking round for sticks. "We need something sharp. To spear them. Get the knife out!"

"Bear!" I say, frustrated.

"I think they're minnow. They're tiny, but it's OK as there are so many!"

"We can't, Bear," I say quietly.

"It won't take long."

"No, Bear!" I say firmly, taking charge. Because I have to. The drones won't have given up yet and the river is the most exposed and obvious place of all.

"Juniper!" he shouts with full fury.

"You want to hang around waiting for drones?"

"No, but—"

I don't let him finish. "We can't wait here. We need to fill the pans. Are you helping or not?"

Water gushes over the sides of the pans as we head away from the river, and Bear moans all the way about the fish, about how they were just there, waiting. How if he'd tried again he would have got one. Maybe he would, I don't know. When you're this tired and hungry it's hard to think anything very clearly.

37

Bear makes the fire. He collects the sticks and arranges them criss-cross in a pile, with dry leaves to fill in the gaps and more on top that should burn quickly. Kindling.

I let him strike the match too. He gets it first time. Bear's fingers don't tremble like mine did. Strike and there's the flame, and the leaves start to burn and we watch it spread to the wood below.

"You're good at this, Bear. You're a proper camper."

He doesn't smile. He's still cross about the fish.

The pans sit on top of the logs precariously as we set about shelling the acorns. They come out of their cups easily but you have to break open the hard casing too, to get to the softer nut inside.

I try with the knife but the acorns slip in my fingers. I can't pierce the shells – they're oddly flexible – so we end up bashing them against a stone, which was Bear's idea in the beginning. The shells break open, but the nuts inside do too, and we sit there separating out the pieces – throwing the fleshy bits into one of the pans and the shell pieces away.

The water takes ages to bubble. You couldn't call it boiling, it's just a gentle simmer. Despite the fire's good start, the flames die away quickly to this slow smoulder. We try adding more sticks and striking another match, but it only gives a couple of minutes' extra heat and we don't want to waste matches cooking a handful of nuts and nettles in the middle of the day. We're still hoping for something more substantial later on.

We munch the acorns mechanically, but then Bear spits his out. "They taste like poison, Ju."

I frown. He's right. They're as bitter as anything. "Maybe we didn't leave them long enough, or maybe the water's too cold."

The nettles are more successful. We drink the green liquid straight from the pan, the smallest one, and Bear names it Gloop, from Green Sloop. Green from the colour, and Sloop from the way you have to slurp it so you don't leave behind the soft wet leaves. They're bitter too, but not in a bad way. They must have goodness in them, surely. Green is good. Green is vitamins and iron.

Bear cheers up after the Gloop. He laughs at the green moustache around my mouth and bounds around after squirrels.

"Ghost!" he says as I'm wiping out the pans with leaves. "She found us, Ju."

I look out. It's the same cat. There's a distinctive pattern to the markings on her face – a slight unevenness from left to right.

"You think she's hungry?" Bear asks. I shake my head. The cat's staring at the fire, interested. She doesn't look hungry. She's lithe and muscular and shining.

"What do you eat, Ghost?" I say out loud. "You must eat more than nettles and acorns."

"I wish she'd catch something for us," Bear says longingly.

The trap's set again and we've left it further away this time. You hear the odd scuffle in the leaves – some mouse or rat maybe – but when we go to check the trap it's empty.

When we get up to walk, the cat follows. She keeps her distance, stopping when we stop, never getting too close. Her tread is silent, like an expert hunter's. But she's not hunting us, she can't be. Every time I look at her she blinks her yellow eyes slowly, like she's talking to us. Like she wants something from us, only I can't think what on earth that might be.

"You crazy cat," I say softly.

The sun's already dropping in the sky and it's cold, colder than ever. I think cold builds up inside you. I feel cold right down to the bone and my hands and feet hurt. I can feel the layers of flesh, hurting and freezing, freezing so much that I start to worry about frostbite. I make us stop and we put on another layer of socks on our feet and socks over our hands too, a triple layer of them. Neither of us have any spare socks left but at least, hopefully, we'll get to keep our fingers and toes.

38

It's our third night in the forest. The trap's baited with acorns, conkers and a tiny corner of snack bar. Surely something is going to want some of our spread. Even a mouse would be better than nothing. Even a rat.

Bear's shivering. I sit him as near as I can to the fire without worrying he'll go up in flames and wrap the space blanket tight around him. I've taken out more ticks from his skin. One more from his neck – I'm not sure how they get all the way up there – and two from his legs. There were two more on my legs too.

I wipe each site down and dab on the antiseptic. Weals have come up a bit from the first bites, but small faint ones, and neither of us seem to have a temperature.

For tea, it's nettle soup followed by snack bars and protein balls. We leave the acorns alone. There's an ache in the bottom of our stomachs and a bitter taste from lunchtime.

It's not a good call to make ourselves sick.

Again I wipe the pans out with leaves and put them in a clearing along with the water bottle. If it does rain they'll fill up and that's one less thing to worry about in the morning.

In the distance, a wolf is howling again. Or maybe two. If you listen, and I've been listening for ages now, it sounds like a conversation. Like they're far apart but calling out all the same, across the forest. We heard them in the city too and yet we never saw them, they never came. Though this is crazy logic. They'd have been shot if they tried to make it across the Buffer.

I look for the cat – for the yellow glow of her eyes – but there's only darkness. At some point, as the sun slipped away under the horizon, she slunk off and we haven't seen her since.

Bear's asleep now – the rise and fall in the sleeping bag has become rhythmic – but my brain won't close down, everything in it is swimming around, inky and confused.

I need to close the gap of the tent – weigh it down with stones so the cold air can't get in – but first I look out. One last time before I shut my eyes and let go.

There are no drones but the lynx isn't here either and the forest feels big and empty. There's a screech overhead. Just an owl, I figure, though it shoots through into my dreams. Makes them nightmares.

39

"Bear!"

It's morning and all the air from my lungs is pushing out his name, but it's just a tiny cry into the forest. He isn't here.

The lynx is here. The wild cat we thought might protect or attack us, one or the other. She's looking around, working everything out – our makeshift tent, the burnt-out fire, and me standing here, screaming. But no small boy. No Bear.

He could have gone to collect firewood, but why would he go so far when there are branches everywhere? He could have followed some animal or bird. He might do that then get distracted, forget the route back. Is that what happened? Did he go so far he can't hear?

I know he's not hearing my cry. If he was, he'd be yelling back to me. Bear can let rip when he wants to.

Everything's crazy in my head and I can't work it out. Slow down. Slow down. Look. There must be things that will tell me. Clues. People don't just disappear. But Bear did. He's gone. Just him and the clothes he was wearing. Even his coat is still here.

I overslept. The dark of the forest kept me sleeping and stole Bear away.

"Bear! Bear!"

I need to be methodical. Check all the routes out of the glade. Maybe he left a trail. Pebbles or crumbs. That's the best I can come up with. If there are broken twigs or indentations to follow, to track him, I can't see them. I don't know the signs. I read the wrong books and all I can think of now are the fairy tales. They were cautionary for a reason. Never go into the woods alone. Never go at night.

We came anyway, even though we knew the wolves were real. What if all the rest is real too? It's all real now he's missing. Losing Bear was always the biggest thing I had to fear.

I stumble out into the trees and then turn back to our tent, then turn in the opposite direction and do it again. Then a few degrees to the side, and repeat. Out to find him, and back, and all the time I'm calling and he's still not answering. Only the noises of the forest – the wind in the canopy, a fox like a human scream.

For some reason, despite how scared and scary I must seem right now, the lynx is still here. Sometimes she comes

194

and stands just a few steps away. If I stopped for a moment, if I crouched low, or put my hand out, I reckon she'd come right up to me. But I don't need her now. I needed her last night, or first thing this morning, or whenever it was that Bear left the tent and went out alone. So much for being our watch cat.

The sun moves up into the sky and starts falling again and I still haven't found him. The only answer to my cry is Bear's name, echoed back to me. Empty.

At some point there's a cacophony in the sky. Geese. A whole formation of them flying overhead. South.

"Bear! Bear!" My throat is raw but I go on, still circling the space where our tent is, going out into the trees and then back to the tent, where I've left a message on a flat stone. A page of my sketchbook, weighed down with pebbles. A drawing of him sat on the stone, where I so want him to be, and the words 'Wait here!'

Sometimes the lynx is here and sometimes she isn't. At one point there's a sound and I know it's Bear and I turn to him and I don't know whether I'm going to scream at him or kiss him, but it's not him at all. It's the cat again. She's traipsing over our strewn-out things, looking for a place to settle.

I pick up a stick to throw at her, furious that she's not my brother. But I don't throw it. I sit next to her, talk to her.

"Bear's missing! He's gone! We have to find him."

She doesn't understand, but somehow it's helpful to say it anyway. For the words to be out loud. It makes it real – finding him. If I say his name, he's somewhere here. Except he's not and at some point the cat starts washing herself – stretching out a leg and licking leisurely between each webbed toe.

Bear's disappeared and I hate the Wild tonight. I'm cold and I think of him colder. I'm hungry and I think of him hungrier. I'm scared and I think of him scared and crying and this is the worst thing of all. The worst thing I've ever felt.

40

I'm not in the tent, but outside it, curled at the mouth of the sleeping bag, even though I don't remember lying down at all.

There's a faint beam of early sun and the lynx is standing a few metres away, the black tufts on her ears up like antennae. Her head's turned to one side. She's listening.

I want to yell Bear's name – make him hear me – but all day yesterday I called and there was nothing. Today I have to try something else.

I leave the note in the middle of the clearing and I follow her. The cat knows where to go. I see it – not just in her ears and her glassy unblinking eyes, it's the alignment of her muscles. She's lowered her body to mirror the ground and her legs stretch out slowly, deliberately, one after another.

Maybe she's just following some rabbit or hare but I follow her anyway. And every so often a noise sounds out into the forest. Something sharp and heavy and rhythmic.

Thwack. Thwack.

It stops, but the cat keeps moving in the direction the noise came from. Sometimes she's slow. Sometimes she bounds forwards, quick, like the rabbits do. Maybe she has caught scent of one.

Every so often, the noise starts up again.

Thwack. Thwack. Thwack.

I've no idea what it is, but I know from Ghost to be quiet. Today everything's just clearer – the tangle of roots and branches – I can see better where I fit between them. The spaces I can pass through. The unseen paths. Ghost goes first and I follow after. I'm in her slipstream.

At some point she stops. It's misty and still only half light and when I first see it, it's not real at all – it's like a mirage.

A deer. A stag, I think, because of its size and its antlers, high above its head like some woodland crown.

Ghost steps back, wary, even though that's the wrong way round. Deer are her prey. Lynx catch deer. Yet this one's out of her league, even I can see that.

For a while everything stops and then the stag lets out this low noise – this growing moan, or bellow, or belch, from deep inside – and he's off, to some other adventure.

And it's absolute madness but I'm desperate, and I take it as a sign that we're going the right way. Maybe it was the stag that led Bear away. He couldn't have helped himself, following something that beautiful.

The lynx and I, we carry on moving until she stops at the edge of another clearing.

There's a stone building – some old barn, or cabin, or cottage, with a loop of smoke curling out from the chimney and a pile of broken logs outside, stacked in a little shed. The woodcutter's house.

There are two figures standing in the doorway. One big, one little.

I hurl myself forward. "Bear!"

He should be running to me, but he's holding the hand of the taller person. His hand in hers. Hers because it's a woman, not a man with an axe. She's in a long dark coat and is leaning over him protectively.

"Bear!"

The woman lets go of Bear's hand, propels him to me, and I catch him as he falls into my arms, warm and solid and scared.

"Bear! I found you!"

"We've been waiting for you to show up," the woman says and I want to hug her too, because she's here. So much more miraculous than that stag. A person, a woman, out in the Wildwood where I'd started to doubt anyone else could be.

I don't mean to stare, but I can't stop myself. Her hair's silver, like Annie Rose's, except this woman's hangs down over her face, matted with leaves and dirt. Her skin's thick and tight like leather, and she has small sharp eyes. I think of the fox in the Emporium.

"I wanted to look for you. I wanted to come back," Bear's saying breathlessly, pulling at me. Tugging at my sleeve to bring me lower, taking both my hands in his. "Juniper!"

"But it was too dark, wasn't it, when I found you last night?" the woman says kindly to Bear. "Didn't it happen just like I told you it would? That we'd light the fire first thing this morning and your sister would come. Like a moth to a flame. Our signal worked!" She's beaming at me.

I don't say that it wasn't the smoke. That it was our lynx cat.

Ghost's disappeared anyway. I look around the line of trees but she's already gone.

"I found your brother as the light was falling. Wandering around sobbing his heart right out. Without his coat as well!"

"Thank you! Thank you for finding him!" The words fall out of me.

The woman's laugh is shrill. "He made it easy. The volume he was crying at!"

I shake my head, confused. "I didn't hear anything. I was calling, calling."

The woman smiles. "Sounds are funny out here. The wind takes them away. Sounds can disappear, just like people can."

"I thought I wouldn't ever find him. I thought—" My

voice is breaking and the woman cuts in. I must sound pretty crazy.

"I've got water boiling on the fire. I can make you a hot drink and something to eat. I've not been able to get your brother to accept anything."

"Bear?" I say astonished, my relief coming out in a burst. "That's not like you. You must be famished!"

Bear shakes his head furiously.

"Well, I am," I say enthusiastically, to make up for his reticence. We should keep the woman on side. She could help us.

Bear tugs at my sleeve again. "Ju, our journey!"

"We need to rest, Bear, and eat."

"We can eat as we walk."

"We've barely got anything left. You know that. You've told me enough times!"

The woman's still smiling her bright smile.

"Ju!" Bear says. His shoulders are all high and tight, like they always were at school. He's never been good with other people. Only us and Etienne. But this woman found him. She kept him safe. And she seems so delighted to have us here. She can't see many people. I'm still reeling over the fact she's here at all.

"Juniper! Let's go. Please!" Bear hisses, still trying to pull me away. The woman's smile fades. It's obvious Bear doesn't like her.

"Bear!" I say crossly, pulling myself loose from him. "You ran off. I spent the whole of yesterday searching for you, thinking all kinds of things. I'm hungry and tired even if you're not."

Bear hangs his head and kicks his foot into the floor.

"Come in then," the woman says as though it's settled, and she ushers us both into the cottage before her.

41

There's an old stone fireplace and a fire's burning full pelt in the iron grate, and I'm drawn to it – to the warmth and the flickering flames.

There's a strange smell I don't recognize but that tugs at my stomach.

The cottage windows are small, closed. Some are boarded up. I didn't notice from outside. At one of the windows, a fat blue fly is slamming itself against the dirty pane. A bluebottle, Bear would say, if he was talking normally.

The woman catches me looking. "There's no point cleaning them. Not out here." Her voice is defensive.

"No, of course," I say quickly, smiling in case she thinks I'm disapproving.

"It's not what you're used to, in your shining city."

I shake my head because that's not what I meant. I'm not bothered about dirty windows. "You live by yourself?"

I ask, changing the subject.

The woman nods and I see her teeth through her smile, all brown and yellow. "I'll make tea."

There's an old sofa by the fire and I sink into it – I can't help it. I pull Bear down too. "Bear? What's up with you?"

"I don't want a cup of tea!" he grunts.

"I'll make one for him anyway. Then I'll sort out food. I'll have to pop out, to find something. A rabbit!" the woman says, triumphant, like she's just solved a problem. "I'll get you a rabbit!"

"You don't need to go to any trouble," I say and my eyes can't help go to the table where there are dead animals laid out in a row – rabbits and birds. That's what the smell is. And that's where the bigger buzz of flies is coming from. I can see them now. Crawling over the carcasses.

The woman's watching me. "I don't bother so much for myself, but you two don't look like you're used to being out here. Your stomachs won't be as strong as mine. You'd be better with fresh."

She goes over to the kitchen area to make the tea, still beaming every time she turns back to look at us, even though Bear's silent and sullen beside me. It's sort of surprising she doesn't ask more questions. We must be as miraculous to her as she is to us.

Though it doesn't seem like that. She just seems pleased.

Like we're neighbours who've dropped by to drink tea with her.

"Why are you here? Who are you?" I ask in a sudden rush as the woman returns with two mugs of steaming liquid.

"Violet." She places one of the mugs into my hand.

"Violet," I repeat and I smile at her. "What tea is it?"

"It's a kind of root. I can show you later. Drink now."

I take a sip, even though the rim of the mug is grimy. The tea's sweet and strange. I smile again at Violet's expectant face. "How long have you lived here?"

She pulls a strange face. Maybe I'm being rude, asking too much, but then she smiles again. "A long time. Too long. But now it's your turn. I'm curious. Where are you running off to?"

"Nowhere really." I shrug. There's something about 'running off' that irritates me and Bear's hand is in mine now. He's digging his nails into the flesh of my palm.

"You must have somewhere in mind," Violet says, bidding me to drink more of the strange tea.

I shake my head as I drink. "Just away from the city."

"Why would you want to do that?" She's still smiling brightly, in a way that makes me wonder why she's not tired already, of looking happy.

Bear's fingernails dig in tighter and I glare at him. "We just had to get away. It wasn't safe for us." I pause, not sure how to say it. "Maybe the city isn't how you remember it."

If the woman picks up on what I'm saying, she ignores it. "Drink up, both of you. I'll go out and see about that rabbit."

She picks up a worn black satchel from the table as she leaves, and takes a gun from the wall beside the fireplace. A hunter's wall – full of guns and knives. Weaponry.

"It's an air rifle?" I ask, unable to take my eyes off the gun. Watching her as she snaps it right open and takes a silver bullet from a bowl on the table. She places the little pellet in the centre of the rifle and then snaps it back straight.

The woman nods. "It'll do for a rabbit. You both look like you could do with some feeding up." She smiles at me again. "It can't have been easy. You've done well to get this far."

Tears prick at my eyes, and Violet winks at me and pockets a handful of the silver pellets. "I'll put the catch on the door so you don't lose the boy again. Get some rest, Juniper Green. You look like you need it."

The door clicks behind her.

42

"Are you not talking to me, Bear?" I ask once Violet's gone. The cottage is all crackling flames and I lean back into the softness of the sofa.

Bear screws up his face and then unscrews it right away. "We need to get out of here."

"We need to eat, Bear!" I say, frustrated. "And get warm. She can help us."

"She won't help us, Ju."

"She's out now, isn't she? Getting food? A rabbit! It's more than we've managed!"

"Ju, we have to go before she gets back." Bear's pacing the rug, not stepping off it, but looking round at the dead animals on the table and that fly still banging against the pane. He points to the knives and guns. "She's bad, Ju."

I shrug. "They're just the things you need out here. We could learn from her. All those guns, surely she could spare one? And look at this fire compared to ours! I'm properly warm for the first time since we left, Bear. She's the first person we've come across. The only one. We need help."

"I don't want her help."

I glare at him. "Yeah, well maybe we need it. I can't do everything. I can't do it alone."

Bear looks shocked. "You're not alone. There's me, and Ghost."

"You're six years old, Bear. And a wild cat isn't going to feed us. It won't show us the way to Ennerdale."

"Ju!" he cries. "Don't say that! It's secret! The woman might be listening."

I roll my eyes. "Violet's gone hunting, Bear. For our breakfast."

"There's something funny about her. Strange."

I give him a disapproving look. "She's just a bit unkempt," I say. "People used to say that about you, back in the city."

Bear sticks his tongue out. "It's not that."

"Look, she's survived out here. All this time! She knows the land, she knows what to eat. She knows how to stay alive, Bear. She's properly wild."

"Not all wild is good."

I can't help smile at him using my own words against me. "Let's at least let her feed us. There are things I want to ask her."

"Not about where we're going, Ju. You can't! You mustn't!" There's proper fear in his voice.

"I won't say the name, I'll just ask her if she's heard of any place like that."

"Why?"

I shake my head. How can I tell him what's in my head? That since we got out here, since we saw how abandoned everything is, I can't stop thinking about it. About Ennerdale. What if it's not there any more?

"Ju, please!" Bear comes up to me and tugs at my hands again. "She was different before you showed up."

"What do you mean?"

"What she said, about being worried about me, she wasn't, Ju. She really wasn't. She was mean. She kept prodding me, asking where you were."

"Because she wanted to find me, Bear. For your sake. You're six years old. Out here alone. You must have been a shock to her."

"But she didn't look shocked, Ju. It was like she was looking for me. Hunting me."

"Bear!" I exclaim, exasperated. "She doesn't hunt people. She hunts animals. Rabbits. I spent almost twenty-four hours straight looking for you. I'm exhausted! Please, Bear."

He finally shuts up and I slump back into the sofa, gazing at the fire, at the dancing flames. Hypnotized by them. Bear's still pacing and I let him. I did enough of that last night.

I'm dozing off, dreaming about the Palm House. This one plant we had, a century plant. It was an agave that Annie Rose said bloomed once in its entire life. Thirty years of nothing but leaves, then it would send up this huge great shoot with a flower on the end. Only the flower took all the energy the plant had, because right after it wilted and died.

"I didn't tell her our name was Green."

"What?" I say vacantly.

"I didn't tell her our name was Green, Juniper." Bear's voice floats out into my Palm House dream.

He's more certain now. Louder. "I didn't tell her our surname. I might have said Juniper. When I was upset. Or she might have heard me calling for you, because I called you all yesterday, but I didn't say Green. I didn't, Ju."

I sit bolt upright. "*You get some rest, Juniper Green.*" That's what Violet said as she went out.

I put my hands on Bear's shoulders. "When she was asking who you were, where you were from, it didn't slip out? You're certain about that?" I'm shaking him. It's too rough, but I'm shaking him anyway because I have to know.

"No!" Bear snaps. "I told you! She wasn't even nice to me. We didn't talk. Not like that. She just kept asking about you. Where you were. Trying to get me to remember. I didn't tell her anything about anything, Juniper. I wouldn't! I told you that, only you didn't listen."

I look at him, horror curdling in my stomach.

"Why would she know our surname, Juniper?"

But there's no time to answer. I'm already throwing open cupboards. Turning over boxes.

Everything's mostly empty so I move to the bedroom, to the little alcove off the main room, behind a pink curtain, which throws up a grey cloud of dust when I rip it aside. There's barely anything here either, except the bed with dirty sheets and an open wardrobe full of stale, crumpled clothes, most of which aren't even hanging, they've fallen to the floor.

There are no books. No pictures on the walls. No sign this woman does anything except hunt. That's what the whole cottage smells of. Dead things.

I slump down in a chair in front of a small table. There's an ornate oval mirror, dusty, with red velvet curtains either side. I've seen ones like it in the Emporium. It's a dressing table and the mirrors were always in three sections – the main one and a smaller one either side, like wings.

I tear back the curtains, but it's just my own reflection, staring back at me three ways in the dusty mirrors – my eyes hollowed out in my face, my skin smeared with dirt.

I look sick and I feel sick too – sick and sleepy. The sweet sticky tea, which Bear refused, swishes around my stomach.

There's a hairbrush on the table. I've seen things like that in the Emporium too – the cream oval base, the soft bristles. I used to think they were pretty, until Barney told me they were made from ivory – elephant tusk – and the bristles came from horses.

This one's carved with vines and the bristles are full of the woman's hair.

I trusted her because she was wild and a woman with silver hair, like Annie Rose. I trusted her because I was scared and sad and starving. Because Bear was too and I haven't done any kind of job of looking after him so far.

"Juniper!" Bear says and I turn to him. He's dragged out the clothes from the bottom of the wardrobe and is holding up sheets of stapled-together paper. He's staring at them, confused. "The address. It's in our city, I think."

I grab the papers from him. The date is in the top right-hand corner of the first sheet, like we were always taught at school. It's just three years back. And then pages and pages – words in small black type. I don't read it properly, there isn't time, but the words I need reveal themselves to me – reconnaissance, integrity of the mission, loyalty to the city. There's a name at the bottom of each sheet, like it's a contract. A signature, in elaborate calligraphy. Portia Steel.

I remember Silvan, back in the Warren. "*To be her eyes and her ears... Only a few ever report back ... they're properly crazy.*"

One of the sheets has numbers on it and other odd words. Old words. *Frequencies, bandwidth, wavelength.*

"What does it mean, Ju?" Bear asks, his nose puckered.

I have to make myself think. Fast, even though my brain's cloudy and slow.

"Can you see a radio? If she's working for Steel, if she knew about us, she must have a way of making contact with the city."

"A radio?" Bear asks, confused.

Why would he know that word? I only do because I spent so long pouring over that old dictionary back in our kitchen.

Radio. The use of electromagnetic waves for broadcasting two-way communications.

Two-way communications. That's what Violet will be doing. She'll be letting the city know that she has us. Has both of us. I walked myself right into her trap.

"It'll be a kind of box. With an aerial. An antennae. Like the drones have."

Bear frowns. "There was something like that before, on the table. She was playing with it last night – turning some dials. Talking to it, like it was a person, but it just crackled. It was broken I reckon. It's gone now."

"That must have been what was in that satchel," I say in a heavy voice. "She took it with her. Maybe there's somewhere she goes, for a better signal." Maybe she didn't dare leave Bear until she'd found me in case I broke in and rescued him. Like I should have done if I had any sense at all. Any of Bear's instincts.

"Juniper!" Bear says helplessly.

My eyes fix on his. He's waiting for me to do something. "We need to get out of here," I say.

"She locked the door!"

"The windows then."

A gunshot sounds outside the cottage and I pull Bear after me, back into the main room.

43

The moment the door opens, Bear and I throw ourselves outside. We don't give the woman time to stop us. She's got the gun in one hand and the black satchel she took with her is slung over her shoulder.

"Run, Bear! Run!" The trees. Get to the trees, we told each other. We're faster than her, smaller. We can hide. My feet are heavy on the ground but the trees are getting closer. I'm almost there.

Bear's scream stops me. He's fallen and even as I turn back for him, she's caught him. She's pulling him up from the floor.

I run towards her. "No!"

She's got a silver blade in her right hand and she's moving it to Bear's throat.

"No! No!" I cry, my voice shaking.

The woman's face is taut and focused, just like her voice.

"I'm protecting my interests. Get back inside. Now."

"No," I say, even though my heart is pummelling out of my ribcage.

"There's a warrant for you both. It's my civic duty. Portia Steel put out a call herself."

"No!" I cry. "We're not going back. Not ever."

I keep my eyes on the blade. It's dirty – encrusted with blood – but still somehow catching the light of the morning sun. "Let him go!"

"Inside!" the woman hollers.

"If you send us back, they'll kill us. Both of us!"

The woman shakes her head.

"They want our blood. They'll take yours too, if they come out here. You don't know what the city's like now." I'm yelling at her. Screaming. But I'm pleading with her too. "Please! Please! Please!" There are beads of sweat, like dewdrops, painted on Bear's face.

The woman's moving her head from side to side, wildly. "I've been promised. By Steel herself. She'll let me back in, in exchange for you two."

"Why?" I splutter. "Why would you want to go back? The city's a prison!"

"It's my home!" the woman screeches. "I didn't ask to be sent out here. You think I wanted my blood to show up positive?"

"It means you can survive. And you have. You've

survived here!"

"I'm about the only one that did. You don't know what it's like. No soul to speak to except the voices in your own head. I'm not doing another winter out here. I can't! In the cottage. Now."

"And what if I don't?"

Bear's properly sobbing now. The blade's pressing against the soft skin of his neck. There's a madness in the woman's eyes. Now she's forgotten to smile I can see it. "I will do it," she says, pressing the blade harder, and I don't doubt for a moment that she will.

I turn back to the cottage and the woman turns too, to follow after me, but something comes from the woodshed – a leaping, hurling thing, throwing itself against her. Our lynx cat. Our Ghost. Violet staggers, letting go of Bear as she hits the ground.

"Run, Bear!" I call, even as I'm hauling him up off the floor.

The woman's grabbing at my leg. Her thick calloused hand gripping tight round my ankle, like a claw. I kick out.

"Don't you dare!" she cries, incensed. "I've been promised! You're my ticket back in!"

"No!" I scream, lashing out. She's scrabbling for the gun with her other hand, but the leather strap is tangled up with the satchel.

I manage to move my leg up to her neck and start kicking

because she deserves it, because she would have used that knife on Bear, I know she would.

"Juniper!" Bear's screaming out at me from the trees, calling my name, and it's louder now and I'm terrified he'll come back and I never ever want him near that knife again.

The woman lets go of my ankle to go for the rifle, but she's still splayed out beneath me. I lift my foot up and bring it right down on to her, right into her knee, my full weight right on her, and there's a sort of snap, like that air rifle made when she broke it back to insert the silver pellets.

Then I'm off and running too. To the trees. The air rifle banging against my back as I run, the leather strap across my back.

"I'll get you! I'll get you both!" the woman screams at me, and then the cottage door bangs in the wind. A moment later a shot sounds out after us. She must have gone back for another gun.

I lurch forwards to Bear and the sweet tea pools on the forest floor at his feet. Bear looks terrified but I pull him after me and we run on. Zigzagging through the trees because now the shots really are coming.

44

We can't keep going. Or I can't. My head's spinning. Spinning fast and I need to be sick again.

The woman's still coming. She won't give up. I could see it in her eyes.

"We have to hide," I gasp. "I can't run any more."

There are twigs breaking behind us and Bear's looking up, and before I can stop him, he's climbing – disappearing high into the canopy. And I follow – even with my fear of heights, even without the climbing centre's soft, spongy floor, even though everything's moving – I clamber after him. Foot on branches, testing them for strength and then trusting them and reaching up for the next branch with my hand.

We're twice the height of Violet when we see her. She's breathing loudly and wincing as she stumbles on. Her left leg's dragging. I don't think I imagined the snap of her knee.

City bones break easily.

Not enough calcium. Not enough light.

Her eyes are working though – rolling round the forest looking for us.

We're right up against the trunk of the tree, Bear above me gripping on like a monkey. I look up at him. I can't look down anyway or else I'll fall, or vomit, or both.

It's an oak and it's lost a load of leaves already, there's not enough cover, but we shrink ourselves into it.

It's hide-and-seek, like in our Palm House. Except there's no glass around us. We smashed our way out of it. We found a ladder to the sky.

Violet fires the gun into the trees. I wince. Bear's head is bent down and our eyes stay fixed on each other. We're still, silent.

The trunk's got a strange softness and a strange kind of sound or rhythm from within, like I'm hearing its heartbeat as my whole body presses against it.

And eventually, or maybe after just a few minutes, Violet turns back to the cottage. She's cursing us – shouting out about drones and radios – but she's going back to the cottage.

"Where's all our stuff, Ju?" Bear asks nervously, once we're on solid ground and I've thrown up again into the undergrowth.

"Back at the tent."

"You left it?"

I nod. I jettisoned everything except Etienne's GPS, which hangs down inside my jumper.

"What about Ghost?"

"She ran off."

"The gunshots!" Bear shrieks.

"She ran off," I say decisively and I take out the GPS. My head's still pounding but somehow I manage to scroll back through our route. The GPS has a memory and I can work out where we camped, where Bear went missing from.

The moment we reach the clearing, I start throwing everything back in our bags. All I can think about is getting further away from that cabin.

It's Bear who sees Ghost. She's lying at the edge of a thicket. Her head's down and there's a circle of blood on her left shoulder.

Bear's creeping towards her, whispering her name. "Ghost cat, Ghost cat. We're here now. We found you. We'll look after you." His eyes are shutting slowly. Three long blinks. He's learned her language.

"Juniper!" he says quietly, urgently. "Help her!"

Ghost's bleeding. Help her.

I scramble in my rucksack. There are absorbent pads in our medical kit and I press one against the wound. It's a bleeding hole and maybe I should be delving down to look for the bullet, or maybe I should be cleaning it out, but the blood's pretty fast so I just press down. The soft pad against the lesion. To stem the flow.

It's only seconds before the pad colours bright red and I have to change it and let her bleed out again into a fresh one, and a third.

It's the first time I've touched her, touched anything this alive, this wild, and her tremble passes into my fingertips. It passes into my whole body.

I can feel her fear. Her heart beating too fast and too frantic as the blood runs out of her.

My tears drip down to wet her soft fur. "We should put something over her. To keep her warm." The tremble's in my voice now.

Bear's on it immediately. He finds our blanket – the old woollen one from home that Annie Rose stitched back together whenever we found new yarn in the Emporium. He arranges it over Ghost, talking fast. "It's good it's her shoulder, isn't it, Ju? It's not her heart. Or her head?"

I nod. What else can I do? "We can't stay here," I say, my voice dull.

"But Ghost!" Bear looks at me aghast.

"Maybe she'll follow us."

"She's hurt, Juniper! She won't be able to follow."

"The woman's got a gun, Bear. She'll come after us. She'll be coming now. Maybe she's strapping up her knee or something, but she'll come back. Or the drones will.

She's called Steel. You heard her!"

If my head was clear, if I hadn't drunk that stupid tea, I could think what to do. I'd know what to do. How did Ghost even get mixed up in this? In her world bullets shouldn't even exist. Humans shouldn't even be out here.

"Ghost saved me. She saved you too, Juniper. We can't abandon her!" Bear's yelling at me, frantic, horrified that I'm even suggesting leaving her.

Ghost has dragged herself deeper into the thicket and she's almost hidden, camouflaged against the fallen leaves. Black and brown, like the markings on her coat. That's what gives me the answer.

I take a deep breath, to pull clean air back into my body and help the nausea pass. "We have to clear the campsite, OK? There can't be any trace left, of the tent or the fire or anything. Then we hide too. We can wait for her to recover."

"Violet will see us, if she comes."

"She won't," I say. "Because that's what we'll do." I point at Ghost. I don't crawl in after her, I don't want to freak her out, but there's another thicket nearby, a tangle of bushes or shrubs, and I climb inside it on all fours. Bear passes the bags in after me.

Once our things are hidden, I scatter leaves over everything, and then I crawl back to where Bear is hidden. We've spread out one of the tarpaulins and we put the space blanket over us.

"We're like Robin Hood and his Merry Men," Bear whispers.

I smile weakly. "And Maid Marian."

"Ju!" Bear says, worried. "Are you OK? Your eyes keep shutting!"

"It was the tea, I think."

"Was it poison?"

"Nah. She wouldn't have radioed in to tell them to come and get our dead bodies, would she? I think it was just to make us sleepy. So we wouldn't escape."

"We did though, didn't we, Ju?" Bear says, proudly now.

"And I got us an air rifle."

"Huh?"

I point at the wooden rifle, which I'd shoved to the back of the thicket.

Bear gasps. "Ju! You took it!"

"These too." I dig into my pocket and bring out the silver fragments, spread across my palm. I grabbed them from the bowl on the kitchen table as we left.

"She'll be furious!"

"Yeah, well. I figured she owed us."

45

They come when we're sleeping. They come in my dreams. The low hum of them. I'm back in my bedroom, in our soft sheets, and Bear's warm against me, his breathing low and snuffly. I can hear Annie Rose snoring too, in the next room.

It's the noise that wakes me. Tears mist up my eyes when I realize where we are.

There are two of them. I see the dark shapes through the branches, whirring, whirring, like metal birds lit by their little red lights. Looping round the sky, looking for us.

I don't wake Bear. It's better he doesn't see.

When Bear wakes me, cold, without our old blanket, the drones have moved on.

It's dark and we creep out of the thicket. The blanket is still draped over the floor but the thicket is empty. Ghost is gone.

"Where is she, Juniper?" Bear cries.

"She got up."

"But where did she go?"

"To drink, maybe, or get food."

"We can wait for her though?" he asks quickly.

I swallow. "Not this time. We have to go before it gets light."

Bear shakes his head and picks up the blanket, holding it up to me, desperately. "There's blood. Ghost's still bleeding."

I look at the blanket. "It's not much and it's dry. It's good that she's up. It's a good sign. She'll find us, Bear. She always does. She didn't save us so we'd get caught again. She'd want us to be smarter than that."

"It's dark."

"That doesn't stop the owls does it? That doesn't stop the foxes? We can be nocturnal like they are."

Bear glares at me. "Not all owls, Juniper. Don't you remember anything?"

46

"I don't want a snack bar, Juniper," Bear says, staring at the empty trap. He's shivering. His hair hangs wet down his back. It's been raining all morning.

I sigh. "You have to eat. We both do."

Bear takes the bar. Of course he was going to eat it. His stomach is crying out for food, any food, just like mine is.

"I'm trying, Bear," I say weakly, sitting down next to him.

"I'm not angry with you. I'm angry with that man."

"Abbott?" I ask, confused.

"That man you went to. Silver, you said. The pirate man." I can't help but laugh at the indignation in Bear's voice. "He gave us a broken trap!"

"It might not be broken. It might be the bait."

Bear grunts.

"I've been thinking," I say, trying to sound confident. "We have to use the air rifle." I haven't tried it yet. I haven't dared, not after Ghost got shot. She's following us again on and off, but limping. She's nervous of us now. Frightened of fast movements. Frightened when we talk too loud. I'm terrified of scaring her away all over again.

I can't bear to think of losing Ghost now. It feels like she's the only thing keeping us safe.

But I can't stall any longer because Bear's right. That trap's not going to catch us anything. I don't know why I'm even still carrying it.

I've been playing with the air rifle. I think I've figured out how it works. I've bent it back, like that woman did, and inserted a silver pellet into the barrel before snapping it straight again.

"We'll find our own lunch, Bear," I say, holding it up.

Bear looks scared in a way I hadn't anticipated. I wish he wouldn't. It makes me backtrack and I think of those carcasses back on the table in the cottage. The stench of them, rotting, food for flies.

"What if the woman hears?"

"She won't, Bear. We're miles away. We lost her."

"I can do it, Ju," Bear says graciously. "I know you don't want to shoot anything."

I shrug. "You just have to out here, don't you?"

The water bottle and pans are full of water from where I left them overnight. I thought if we caught enough rain, then before we set off we'd make nettle tea. We've not had anything warm since the cottage. We've been too scared to light a fire.

I hadn't thought through what rain means though. Everything is wet. There's no dry wood left to burn.

There's a tight knot in my stomach. The rain's stopped, but water drips down on us from the trees and the ground's wet and slippery. The soles of Bear's shoes skid hopelessly along.

The clouds are dark, like they're full up with rain, and it's so cold, colder than ever – our wet clothes sodden against our skin. We're hungrier than ever too.

We look for rabbits and birds and I keep the air rifle ready, but for the first time we don't really see them. Occasionally there's a squirrel – a flash of grey in the leaves, or a bird in the canopy, but they're always gone before I realize. I wouldn't have a chance today.

Bear's given up with his acorn collection, but even they seem in short supply. Maybe the rain brought down more leaves from the trees and covered them. Only I worry that that's not it, and wouldn't the rain have brought down more nuts too? Unless there just aren't that many left to fall. We're further north and closer to winter. Even acorns won't last forever.

The squirrels know what they're doing – scurrying off with them, hoarding them for a colder, darker day than this one. That's how you survive out here.

47

When the rain starts again, it's a deluge.

We keep our heads down against the sheets of water. You can see them falling – moving across the sky, like city walls. Our coats have been breached – they weren't made for out here – and we're drenched right through to the skin. I'm terrified the GPS will get wet under my clothes and stop working.

We've been staying clear of the abandoned villages and towns since Violet's cottage. Now we actually need a building for shelter, we can't see any. It's like we walked into some primeval forest. The trees here look ancient – thick and knobbly and covered in lichen and hollows. Some have put down branches to the ground like walking sticks.

I take Bear's hand to propel us on but our feet give way under us and we slide down on to the mud. Bear starts crying and it's so loud and so sad that for a moment I don't pull us up, I just hug him tight.

"I can't do it, Ju!"

"You can. You're doing so well!"

"I'm wet and cold and my tummy hurts!"

"I know, me too, but the rain won't last forever."

"I can't, Ju!" His bottom lip is fully out and tears are streaming down his mud-smeared face, all mixed up with the rain. Muddy trails of sadness.

"But you're so strong, Bear."

"My strong got used up, Ju. The rain washed it away."

"You can," I say firmly. He can't give up. If he gives up we're done for. "Bear! Look at me!" I clasp my palms round his face – his hollowed cheeks, his red-rimmed eyes. "Don't you dare, OK! Don't you dare lose your daring. We'll find somewhere to wait the rain out. Some building. We'll light a fire. There's bound to be some old stuff we can burn."

"You said we shouldn't go near houses now."

"We'll be careful." And we don't have a choice. Our tarpaulin isn't up to this weather. Maybe we're going to have to use buildings more now.

I take a last look at the GPS, bending over it so the water doesn't hit the screen. There are a few black dots on the map, clustered together in a sweep of green. Maybe they're still there. "Look at these, Bear," I say, zooming in for him. "Woodcroft Estate."

"What is it?"

"I don't know. Some farm or village. It's not far."

I wrap the GPS in one of the waterproof pouches and hide it back inside my coat.

Bear sighs, but gets up and puts out his hand to pull me up too.

"Thanks, Bear cub," I say softly. "You know how amazing you are?"

The first buildings we see, except for old collapsed barns which the rain penetrated years before, are a row of houses. The houses are covered in vines, but they're stone underneath and weirdly alone with no trace of anything else around them except forest and scrubland. Six joined-together dwellings, each like the one before. A terrace.

We approach the first we come to. The door's still there, hanging on its hinges precariously, as if someone has already bashed it open. Though long ago – the cobwebs and ivy tell us that. A few kicks against the door and it gives way.

Inside it's surprisingly intact. Water has got in – the whole house reeks of damp – but it's not like rain is pouring in from above. There's a fireplace – a stone surround with an old iron grate, just like in Violet's cottage. There's a stone stairway too, to another floor.

Whatever possessions there were are long gone, except in one corner where a tarpaulin is covering over something. Something rigid.

I tear off the plastic sheet. If there's something awful

underneath – coffins, with the dead bodies of former inhabitants inside – I want to know immediately so we can move on.

It takes a moment to work out what they are. Thin wooden boxes. Frames. They're pictures. Paintings.

They're dusty and cobwebbed and about a hundred spiders skitter off. They're stacked against each other, but you can flick through them, from one to the next. Some of the glass is broken and some of the paintwork is damaged. Sometimes there's a layer of mould, but mostly they're OK.

They're landscape paintings. Mountains, lakes, waterfalls – in storms, in snowfall. They make me shudder to look at. If we can't cope with a rainstorm here, how will it be up in the mountains?

Bear gasps as I turn over the next picture and we come face to face with a bright blue-and-orange bird. "Kingfisher!"

I trail my fingers along the paint, for this one has no glass.

"Do you think there are any left, Ju?" Bear asks. "Out there?"

"I don't know. Maybe." Kingfishers were extinct by the time of the ReWild though, I'm sure of that. There weren't any fish left to eat. Water birds were some of the first to go.

"It's like the one you painted on my wall, Ju."

"No, Bear. It's way better than I could do."

Even as I say it, I'm feeling the frames for dryness. We're going to need something to burn. But the pictures seem so innocent and vulnerable, left behind all this time, survivors of another age.

Steel hates pictures of nature more than she hates words. Loads of old paintings were given up in the amnesty.

It wasn't a mass burning. They just did it quietly, Annie Rose said, the way they did everything. Quietly, insidiously, so no one knew to speak out. No one knew what they were losing.

We didn't need that stuff any more. That would have been Steel's argument if anyone dared ask. It was redundant. That way of life had ended and humans had moved on. Evolved. To a more modern way of life. To better things.

When you look though, through the upended pictures, our city seems uglier and crueller than ever.

48

We don't burn the pictures. We don't even burn the frames. We break up some of the crates they're packed in and arrange the wood in the grate.

It takes a while, but it's the best fire we've had. We take off our wet things to dry and I catch sight of Bear's body as he changes – his protruding ribs and hips, his flesh sunk back into him. I've been looking at him every day, checking for ticks and a temperature, but I haven't seen the whole of him like this.

"Don't, Juniper," he says, turning away when he sees me staring. Bear's never been shy of his body. Through all of the journey we've stood by while the other's gone to the loo, or we've gone right next to each other then kicked over the spot with leaves, but he doesn't want me to see how thin he is. "You're skinny too," he says defensively.

I nod slowly and hand him another set of clothes.

"Come and sit by the fire. We should do our tick bites."

We dab all the sites with antiseptic, but there are no angry weals – our blood's doing what it should. We don't need Silvan's antibiotics, we just need a proper meal again.

I stroke Bear's wet hair, trying to tease out some of the knots.

"I want to stay here, Ju," he says, leaning back against me. "It feels safe."

I nod. It's not just the thick walls and having a roof above us and being vaguely warm, it's a feeling. This place was a home once. Someone would have loved it, looked after it.

When the rain stops, we go outside and pick nettles. There are sweet chestnuts too. Finally, the prickly green cases we've been looking for. They're split open already and most are empty, but some still have the little cluster of nuts inside. You can definitely eat these. There was a song about them. A Christmas song – roasting them, on an open fire.

"Ouch!" Bear shouts, picking one up. "It's spikier than the cacti, Ju!"

I laugh. "I'll get a box. You don't want those in your pockets!"

When I come back, Ghost's there. We've not seen her all day. Bear's walking towards her. "Here, Ghost. Here, lynx cat."

She moves back, and her eyes dart across to me and to the door of the cottage. She looks nervous, or confused maybe. You can see the flames from our fire through the cottage door and smoke looping up from the chimney. She probably remembers what happened last time we went indoors. Bear tries again. "Come on, Ghost. Come on, lynx cat."

Ghost makes this odd little cry. It's not a meow, I don't think, it's a quiet kind of yelp.

"She's talking to us. She doesn't like it here, Ju."

She's sort of pacing round – turning away, but then coming back. Like she wants to just go away completely, but can't. Or won't.

"She's scared," Bear says assuredly, like he's translating her movements.

"Maybe it's the fire."

"She didn't mind the other days."

"The cottage then. She's worried about being shot again."

"She wants us to go with her."

"We don't know that. She's just freaking out. It could be at anything."

The tufts on her ears are up and her little bobtail is flicking back and forth unhappily.

"Ju!" Bear says, worried. "What should we do?"

"We have the sweet chestnuts and the nettles and the fire. We need to eat. And our stuff isn't dry yet." And she's a cat. A wildcat. We're people, we're in a house, we have fire, we have food to cook. Why would Ghost like any of that? But they're the things we need.

"I think we should go," Bear says, insistent.

"You said you liked it here."

"I don't any more. Something's up."

We're losing the light. The days run out so fast now. I haven't even had a chance to look at the GPS to recalculate our route.

But the noise Ghost is making is picking up in volume and her movements are faster. She's really frightened.

"OK," I say at last. "Let's pack up our things."

I'm still hoping to cook the nuts before we leave, but Ghost comes almost to the door. She's frantic and still making those yelps, like little stifled roars.

"You win, Ghost!" I sigh. "I'm just going to check upstairs, in case there's anything useful."

As soon as I get to the top floor, I see them through the window. Five of them – silver drones like giant ticks, hovering behind the cottage. A swarm. Waiting. Keeping just enough distance that we don't hear.

I duck down below the window ledge.

We couldn't see them at all from the front of the house and the pilots back in the city must know that. They're tracking us. They've probably been tracking us since Violet's cottage. Maybe it's not about capturing us any more. Maybe it's about finding out where we're going.

I run down the stairs.

"Bear!" I whisper loudly, already rolling things up. Our

wet clothes and sleeping bags and the tarpaulins. "There are drones. Out the back."

"They found us?"

"Maybe they never lost us. Or maybe Violet's message got through. There's five now."

"Five?" Bear gasps.

I nod. "We have to go."

The colour fades from Bear's cheeks and he starts stuffing everything into his bag. "Ghost was right?"

"Yes." I've got out one of our knives, the smaller one, and I start cutting round the back of the kingfisher painting.

"Ju?" Bear looks baffled.

I go on cutting. Releasing the bright blue-and-orange bird from its frame like I'm letting it out of a cage. Then I roll up the canvas and stuff it into the same pouch as my sketchbook.

"We're taking it?" Bear asks.

"Saving it. In case there aren't any kingfishers left. We're saving it so people can remember."

"Saving it from what?"

I'm breaking up more of the old crates and throwing them around the rest of the pictures.

"Ju?" Bear wails. "Saving it from what?"

I shake my head. We don't have time for explanations. I've got the matches in my hand and I'm already striking.

"Ju!" Bear cries, aghast. "You can't."

"They're just pictures," I say through gritted teeth. I think of Etienne, striking that match back in the city, setting the warehouse alight so Bear and I could escape.

"I don't understand," Bear says, tears trickling down his cheeks.

"Let the drones see everything burn. They'll think we're burning too. Two kids, playing with matches. Accidents happen."

"Ju!" Bear watches, terrified, as I throw the match right into the centre of the crate. One, then another, then another

The crates break open with light.

Bear looks at me like he doesn't even recognize me.

"Come on," I beckon. "We've got to move."

And he follows after me through the door, away from the blazing box and the spiralling grey smoke that twirls out from it.

All that colour in the pictures and when they burn the smoke just comes out black.

"We have to be fast and quiet, OK?" I say, trying to sound in control. "We stay under the trees for cover. We stay hidden." I can hear Ms Endo's voice in my head, all kind and clear. *Camouflage. That's what you could learn from the Sticks.*

Bear's trembling, but his eyes are big and focused. This is our chance. We have to slip away unseen.

The light on the GPS is low, a faint glimmer, just enough to see which way the arrow's pointing.

We're on the run again and we have to be as dark as the night itself. Like ghosts, sliding through it.

"Ju, I'm thirsty!" Bear whispers beside me. He's coughing. It's too dark to see the smoke, but we can smell it. It's in the air all around us. I hand the bottle to Bear and we walk on.

At some point, I take Bear's rucksack off him and strap it to my front and I hold his hand to lead him on, keep him going. Just a few more steps and then a few more after that because as tired as I am, as much as every bit of me hurts, we have to get as far away as we can while the drones have something else to watch.

There are dim shapes above our heads. Bats, I think, because the air is thick with high-pitched clicks or squeaks. Sometimes there's the screech of an owl, or the cry of a fox. You'd think it would all be scary, but somehow it's not. Everything alive is another layer of the forest around us, keeping the drones away.

We can't walk all night though and eventually we don't have a choice. We have to stop before we crash. It's just like that first night again, except we don't look for clearings now, we sleep in partings of undergrowth. I throw out the groundsheet and roll out our sleeping bags for us to collapse down into oblivion.

49

I hand Bear a snack bar and take one for myself. There's barely any city food left.

I feel the air rifle in my hands. I can't put it off any longer. I've been listening and listening for drones, but there's nothing. Did we finally lose them?

"We'll catch a rabbit today," I say. "Or one of those pigeons."

Bear looks up at me to check I mean it and I nod. We have to. We have to start providing for ourselves or else we'll starve. We're wasting away.

After we get water and there's still no sign of the drones, it's really obvious what has to happen. I've got the air rifle in my hand, unlocked, and the first time we see a rabbit, I raise it up and pull the trigger.

The pellet doesn't fire all at once like you think it should. I keep squeezing the trigger and when it finally releases, the rifle rams back into my shoulder.

"Ouch!" I yell as the air rifle drops to the floor.

"You have to be ready for the recoil," Bear says jauntily. "Don't you remember that, from the *Campcraft* book?"

"I guess not, Bear," I drawl. "Thanks for the reminder."

"You should spread your legs out more. For balance."

I stay on my feet for the next rabbit. I miss the rabbit, of course I do, but leaves fly up just near where it was before it scarpered. Which means I didn't miss by much. Ghost scarpers too – immediately, fast. Gone.

Bear looks astonished. "You did it!"

"I didn't," I say, frowning. "I missed."

"Almost though."

The wood pigeon, when we see it, is just off to the side from us, pecking through leaves methodically for grubs. I've loaded another pellet and I do it all again, legs apart this time, ready, and the pigeon miraculously keels over.

For a moment I stand there, unsure what to do. Bear leaps forward.

"You got it! You actually got it, Ju!"

There's this grey pink white bird, floppy in his hands, its head lolling. I shudder, but Bear's dancing round.

"Let's make a fire!"

"OK, but we should move on first, in case the drones are still following."

"I'll carry it though," Bear says importantly, swinging

it as he walks.

A little further on, Ghost's back, looking at the wood pigeon in Bear's hand with interest. I point her out to him.

"Oi, Ghost!" he shouts. "Paws off our pigeon! We're going to have the best lunch ever today!"

The pigeon is, literally, the best lunch we've ever tasted.

Bear makes the fire and I prepare the bird. I pluck the white feathers from its breast and cut open the skin. I break apart the ribcage to carve out two oval pieces of flesh – purple and surprisingly neat and unbloodied. The bullet must be somewhere in the head or neck, I reckon. The chunks of meat are unblemished.

We skewer them on sticks and sear them over Bear's fire and the pigeon tastes of all of it. All the flavours of the forest – rich and earthy – and the burning wood. And of survival too. That's what it tastes of most of all. It tastes like survival.

Everything is different after the pigeon. It's not just the meat in our stomachs, it's something else. I'm different. It's like a lion has woken inside me, only it's not a lion, it's our lynx cat, Ghost. There was danger and she didn't flee. She warned us. Stayed with us.

I used the gun too. I killed and Ghost still came back.

Even the way we move through the landscape feels different. At first we were on top of it, stumbling through it, fighting it to make our path. Now we're part of it. We've gone to earth, moving through it, with Ghost following after.

We're a pack, though I think it's dogs that run in packs. There was probably some word once, some cat equivalent, some lost word. Every day she allows herself closer, brushing up against us, stretching out her nose to breathe in our scent.

50

It's morning and the air we're walking through is different, all white and opaque.

Bear makes this low eerie screech.

"Don't do that!" I snap.

You got fog in the city too. They couldn't keep it away, the air there's so thick with pollution and even though I knew that's what it was – clogged-up city air – I liked it anyway because it hid everything ugly. Fog's a different matter out here.

"It's just ground cloud. It's water. Look, we can drink it." Bear opens his mouth and gapes in towards me.

I pull a face. "That's really not helping, OK?"

"You're weird," he says, running off, and in an instant he's vanished.

"Bear! Bear!" For a moment everything's silent, like the fog's taken everything away, even the sounds. I listen for

Bear's footsteps, but there's nothing. "Bear!"

A mass of fur appears beside me, brushing my fingertips.
Ghost.

"Bear!" I yell.

"Boo!" he says, suddenly right in front of me. "Wooooah!
Wooooah! I'm a ghost!" He stops when he sees my face.

I'm screaming at him now. "Never do that, OK! Don't
you ever disappear again!"

Bear's face falls. "I was just playing. Hide-and-seek, like
we've always done."

"We're not in the Palm House any more!"

He looks at me, puzzled.

"You have to stay right by me. All the time!"

"Why don't you trust me?"

"I do, but you're only—"

"Six!" he shouts in my face, before turning away.
"I know! You tell me all the time."

For a while we walk on in silence. We're on a road, one
of the big ones. A motorway. At least with the fog we don't
have to worry about being too visible and you can't deny
the road makes the journey easier. There aren't so many
trailing loops of bramble. You don't keep having to duck
down to miss tree branches.

We're walking uphill, but for some reason I don't cotton
on that we're on a bridge. A high one. We see the buildings
suddenly, all at once, looming up to the side of us and

underneath us too because we're already at the highest point of the bridge. And it's not water we're crossing – it's the city itself.

We're on this overpass with great towers either side – soaring chimneys, vast metal warehouses.

"Juniper!" Bear cries. "What shall we do?" He's rooted to the spot and it's way too near the edge. Maybe there were barriers once, but there aren't any now. The sides of the road drop away to nothing.

"Get away from the edge!" I yell.

"It's a city!" Bear cries as the shapes start to make sense to him. "Ju, we walked into a city!"

It's a city, but there was no Buffer. That means something. I pull Bear to the centre of the road. "It's not a city now."

As the fog clears a little – maybe as we've risen above it – we can see more of the buildings around us. Green, not grey. All tangled up in climbers and creepers.

"Why didn't it show up on the GPS?" Bear asks.

"Maybe none of those cities show up any more. Maybe the GPS was wiped after the ReWild."

You aren't meant to talk about the lost cities. The ones the authorities abandoned. They abandoned lots of places, but it's the big ones they want you to shut up about. The seven largest cities that were forsaken. The ones that were too big, too sprawling to contain.

"Which city is it?" Bear asks.

"I don't know. It'd be on Mum's map. I should've been looking at that too."

Beyond the chimneys for miles, for literally miles and miles, you can see buildings. Tower blocks. Houses. A huge great sprawl of them. It takes your breath away.

If you look closely there are trees too, in and among them.

"Were there really enough people to fill it?" Bear asks in astonishment.

"I suppose there must have been. Once." I think of Silvan's face, when he talked about the disease. And what I wrote in my essay – 'the beauty of the disease' – like I had any clue. Any clue what I was talking about.

Where are all the people who live here now? How many survived?

"It's a ghost city," Bear says.

"I'm not sure that's very flattering to Ghost." I turn to look at her. The one bit of gold in the tangled-up concrete and steel.

"She doesn't mind," Bear says. "She doesn't understand what we're saying. Anyway, don't you like it, Ju? There are trees."

"It's not a matter of liking, it just makes me sad. It's, you know –" I pause, trying to find the right word – "bleak."

"You said our city was bleak too."

"It was. Is. But in a different way."

"You said the ReWild was a good thing."

"It wasn't a good thing exactly," I say slowly. "Not everyone dying, but it was better than what we were heading to."

"It was the Wild or people?" Bear asks.

"No. It was the Wild or nothing."

"Because we need trees to breathe?"

"Yeah, but more than that." Even the scientific arguments, the real tangible things – that trees give out oxygen, filter the air, help control the climate. Even after all that, there's more. You just need it. The Wild. You need to know it's there.

I shake my head. "Come on, let's get off this thing, it's making me dizzy."

Bear's so intent on staring out into the city that he's crept forward again.

"Bear! Come back, you're too close."

He turns back, surprised. "I'm not." Though he comes over anyway and takes my hand. Maybe he knows I can't deal with another argument right now.

"You were," I say softly.

"You just don't like heights, Ju."

51

Even once we're off the overpass there are miles of city to trek through. We're at the perimeter. The edge lands, where it was all factories. Now it's a different kind of landscape entirely – tendrils of ivy and bindweed, blankets of moss and lichen. Some of it you wouldn't guess was ever buildings. They're just weird shapes of green, like the city's been choked up and softened at the same time.

We come to a wide span of railway lines with rusting metal trains – engines and carriages side by side and one after another, like they were gathered up for something. Something that never happened since they're all still waiting. The paint's faded now, but you can still make out the letters on one of them.

"Intercity," I read aloud.

"What does it mean, Ju?" Bear asks, staring at the word.

I shrug. "Inter means between. Between cities, I guess.

They took people from one city to another."

Most of the windows are smashed in, but the carriage interiors are less broken up than you might think. The seats are still there, some are still even padded. Not entirely – in most places the padding has been ripped out like some animal has got to it – but a few are still recognizably these big padded armchairs. And the roof's still on and that's the important bit.

"We could sleep here." I think it first, then I say it out loud. It's late in the day now and cold, really cold. The wind's getting up and the carriage would protect us from it. Plus we'd be hidden from any drones.

Once we've made the decision, it's sort of fun. Bear springs into action and starts clearing a space in the carriage, throwing out all the leaves that have gathered there. There are insects too – spiders, crane flies, beetles, woodlice. Bear carefully transports them all further up the carriage while I make the fire and start taking out our wet things. I drape them over some of the seats to dry. Bear's shoes too, which are falling apart with mud and rain and too much walking. Every time he takes them off, I'm worried I'll find actual rot on his feet.

Ghost isn't impressed with our choice of accommodation. It's too confined and she starts her agitated pacing, the toing and froing. She settles eventually though, outside, and Bear and I snuggle up in our sleeping bags, telling stories.

We make them up, getting more and more fantastical.

We're survivors of a train crash. Of Armageddon. Aliens have landed and bombed our city. It's the War of the Worlds and we're the only two people left on Earth. What do we do?

"We have to get to the sea," Bear says, with some certainty. "Find a boat. Set sail. It's bound to be better somewhere else. There are always some survivors. Or –" he says, really enthusiastic now – "this carriage could be a portal. It could take us wherever we want to go."

I laugh. "What, at the push of a button?"

"Yes, or a magic word."

"Say it then."

"Ennerdale," Bear says and we close our eyes, wishing.

52

Bear's awake, playing in a different bit of carriage. It's daylight already. I've slept later than usual, more protected from the cold than we've been for ages.

For a while I lie there, listening. Bear's pretending to be all the birds and animals we've seen or haven't seen. All the ones he's still looking for – the badger, the otter, the beaver, and more lynx.

I look for lynx all the time. I look obsessively. It's mean of me – everyone needs their own kind – but I'm relieved we haven't seen any. If we find other lynx, maybe Ghost will leave us.

"Ju," Bear says, sensing me watching him. "We could stay in our carriage today. Have a rest."

"We have to keep moving, Bear," I say automatically, already starting to fold up my sleeping bag.

Bear clasps my hand. "Please, Ju. Just one day."

I pause. "We're running out of water."

"Check the GPS," he pleads. "Maybe there's a river. There must be."

I look at Bear's little fingers, tangled through mine. His fingernails are covered in mud. Mine too.

Next is going to be the hardest stretch of all, for from here the uplands really begin. It's hills first, mountains later on. Plus it's getting colder – day by day, you can feel it and see it in the glaze of frost that's painted on everything.

There are still more than a hundred miles to go and we're covering less distance each day. Not just because we're tired – the days are running out quicker. The sun's falling earlier and earlier.

We shouldn't stop, not really, but we could do with a rest.

"OK," I say, smiling at him. "Let's stay here today, then tomorrow we'll start afresh."

We spend some time roaming through the rest of the carriages. The carriages are joined up with gangways and we can walk from one right into the next. We're freed from the weight of our rucksacks and the grind of the journey.

"We're not travellers today," Bear says happily. "We're explorers."

"Archaeologists," I add.

"What are we looking for, Ju?"

The metal has held back some of the plants and there are

old things. It's mostly just rubbish – old drinks cans and bottles, things we would recycle. I guess that's something our city does right.

"Anything useful," I reply. "Clothes or blankets. Maybe there's an old suitcase somewhere with those kinds of things." I'm checking all the glass bottles too because they'd hold water, especially if we find some with their screw tops left on.

I'm still cross with myself for leaving that big bottle on the riverbank. Even though there's been no sign of drones since the fire, I'm nervous every time we have to go for water.

Bear's scampering ahead. He's more excited about the insects than the human things. He finds a nest of ladybirds.

"Ju, they're hibernating! Look!"

They're huddled together in a corner of a seat. Bright red bugs with black spots.

"Don't wake them, Bear," I say, already wandering on ahead as he counts the dots on each beetle.

At the end of the carriage we're in is a bulging-out section of train. It's closed off and I'm wondering if there's a way to kick the door open as it's not like the cottage door – this one's thick solid plastic. Bear comes up behind me and turns the handle. The door swings right open.

"Jackpot!" I squeal.

"I can't see a suitcase," Bear says. "It's just cleaning things."

He kicks an old mop and it clatters to the floor.

"Look at those, Bear." I point to the corner, where there's a teetering stack of metal buckets. "Just think how much water they'd carry."

We clank down to the river with some of the buckets and bottles, and we clean them out, then make trips to and from the carriage. Soon we have all the water we can drink, and some left over too, to clean our teeth in and to heat so we can make an attempt at washing.

Bear's sloshing behind me back to the carriage, a bucket in either hand, even though I said he should just carry one.

"We've probably got enough now. This is the last trip." I turn back. Bear's put the buckets down and is turning something over in his fingers.

I walk back to him. "What's that?"

He shrugs. He's holding a bundle of twigs, tied up with an old piece of blue cotton.

"I found it in that tree."

Where he's pointing, the lowest tree branch comes out from the trunk and there are three wavy lines carved into the bark. An arrow points in the direction we've come from.

We both speak at the same time.

"River," Bear says.

"A signpost," I say.

I have this tingly feeling on the back of my neck. It's the

helpfulness of it. The simplicity. It's just showing where to get water.

"Maybe Ennerdale people come here!" Bear says.

"Ennerdale's still a hundred miles away, Bear. Ennerdale's got its own river. The Liza, remember?" I think of the blue line on Mum's map, flowing down from the mountains into Ennerdale Water.

"Other people then. Forest folk. Fairies?" Bear's eyes light up.

"Maybe."

"We found a magical kingdom, Juniper!"

I laugh. "Yeah, let's not get carried away. We've still got to be careful."

"We'll see the lakes soon, Ju. And then Mum and Dad!" He's pocketed the twigs and is bouncing on ahead with the buckets, swinging them, swinging them hard, so water sloshes right over the edges.

It feels like we should leave the twig bundle, but the marks are still there in the tree, if you know where to look, pointing to the river.

"Mum! Dad! We're coming! We're actually coming!" Bear sings and I only tell him once to quieten down.

I wish I could feel so happy. Sometimes it seems the closer we get, the more scared I am of what we'll find.

But Ennerdale must still be there. It has to be.

Mum knows we're coming back one day. That was always

the plan. She'll be waiting for us. And Dad. If anything had changed, someone would have got word to us. Mum promised.

Once we've made the fire, I heat a bucketful of water to wash in. It's the nicest feeling – warm water against my face.

I loved bath night back home. There wasn't enough water for separate baths, but Annie Rose always let me go first. She knew what it meant to me. That tub of hot water. There was always a lingering smell of disinfectant, some bleach-like stink in the water and in the steam that misted up the bathroom mirror, but Annie Rose had these drops that took the edge off it. Lavender oil. We've used the same bottle ever since I can remember, but because there was no hope of getting another, we made it last. Just two or three oily drops, like tiny pearls, from the old glass bottle. I swirled them in by hand and shut my eyes as I sank into the water.

We've never seen the sea, but that's where I took myself in my head. Some bright clean ocean, back when the world was this big open place you could travel across, where it was green, or blue, or yellow. Anything but grey. Anything but the city outside our windows.

Bear's never been too bothered about washing and I don't make him now because I know what he needs most is to play for a while.

He's taken his Jungle out of his rucksack.

"*Lion, Tiger, Jaguar.*

Orangutan, Gorilla, Chimpanzee."

He recites the names like they're a spell. An incantation. Like he can summon them all back. There's a switch though – today Jaguar becomes Ghost.

He lines the animals up on the carriage floor. The biggest first. The strongest. "We're going on a journey," they say to each other.

I've got my sketchbook and pencils out. They've miraculously stayed dry in their waxy pouch.

I draw the carriage first because despite the shadow of the decaying city, things feel OK here and I want to remember it. Then without really thinking about it, I draw faces. Annie Rose, standing in the Palm House where I always picture her. Ms Endo, back at school next to her table of treasures, smiling.

I draw Etienne last of all. I draw him outside our block and I make the door like it used to be. Like a great big sunshine.

Bear and I lose track of time and we forget all about hunting, but it's fine I guess to be hungry for one night. Especially when we've not been moving so far and our muscles don't need to refuel quite so much.

I'm going through our last meagre city rations, wondering how much of them we can eat, because even though we have the air rifle now I didn't take nearly enough of the silver bullets, when Bear squeals.

It's Ghost. She's brought us a rabbit. She's laid it at Bear's feet.

"Do you think she wants us to cook it for her?" Bear asks, picking it up.

"No, you loon, it's for us."

"She's feeding us?"

"Yes." I look across to Ghost. She's settling down with her own rabbit to devour. Blood all over her whiskers.

53

After we reach the city edge, we walk into the hills and it's colder every single day. Bear and I crawl into our sleeping bags the moment it gets dark, tight against each other for extra warmth. We put the space blanket around us like a shield.

Foraging is virtually impossible. The blackberries are long gone and most of the sweet chestnuts too. Even the nettles are shrinking back into the ground and now when we make Gloop it's really just hot water.

But Ghost feeds us now. Each day as the light falls out of the forest, she slinks away and finds us later, bringing something fresh.

"We're carnivores, aren't we?" Bear says. He's good with the knife, as good as I am. You learn what to cut out, what to discard. What colour of pink tastes too raw when you cook.

One day there's a whole deer. Ghost drags it over to us, and it's delicate and beautiful and still warm. Its eyes look at me as I dig the knife into its flank and I feel I should say something, offer up some kind of blessing for it. A prayer. We could feast for days from this deer, but the next morning we have to move on, and I just take a few cuts for that day and the next, which I hang with bloodied string from our rucksacks. All the rest we leave for some other animal.

Ghost doesn't mind. She doesn't even look back. This is the one thing she knows about us – we keep walking.

Sometimes we find more signs – the water ones, but others too. Notched twigs. Rags woven through branches. Carvings. There are even bones – the V-shaped ones you get in the necks of pigeons. Wishbones.

We can't figure out what any of them mean, except for the water, but somehow it still feels like we're following something. Something good.

One morning I pan out on the GPS and there it is, our first lake. We should reach it tomorrow.

"We're getting closer, Bear!" I say, allowing myself to feel excited.

"Will she be waiting?" For a moment, I don't understand what he's talking about. I think he means Ghost, but she's here already, right behind us. Then I get it.

"Mum?"

"Yes."

"I don't know. I don't think so. How would she know we're coming?"

"I suppose," Bear says thoughtfully.

"If she knew, she would've come to get us."

"I suppose," he says again.

I steer Bear on to Ennerdale instead. Just Ennerdale. Our journey's end. Our safe harbour. We have to imagine this, it's what keeps us going. One day after another, getting closer.

Bear has all these amazing what ifs. What if they live in tree houses? What if they live on the lake, on rafts so the wolves can't get to them? What if they've tamed the wolves? What if Ghost is actually an Ennerdale cat and has come to take us there?

I'm listening to him, imagining them out, all these amazing possibilities, when it happens. When my left foot descends into the most pain I've ever felt. Touches so much pain that I fall down to the ground. That I scream, louder than I've ever screamed before. Louder than you could ever scream in the city.

54

I don't know how long it takes me to come round.

There are trees above me. Branches and leaves, like I used to always dream of. I should be happy. Except there's a blinding pain. A pain so big I can't work out where it's coming from.

I'm lying down and Bear's next to me, holding my left foot, binding it tight.

"Juniper!"

He's completely pale, completely scared, but focused – binding a white ribbon bandage around my foot and ankle.

"What happened?" I ask through gritted teeth.

"It was a trap. I took your boot off," Bear says, pointing, and the abandoned boot swims into view next to me. It's torn and covered in blood, my blood, and it's all I can do to stop passing out again.

I take a deep gulp of air and focus on Bear's face. "Did you clean the wound?"

"It was bleeding a lot, Ju," Bear says, his eyes wet. "I thought I should stop the bleeding." He points to Annie Rose's little first-aid book with comic-strip-style pictures, which he's found in my rucksack. It's lying open at a page headed 'Severe Bleeding' and is covered in small bloody fingerprints. The first and most important action, in big letters and bold type, is the one we can't do – dial 999.

I gulp. "I need to get up. We can't stay here."

I try, but I collapse back down again. I can't put any weight on my foot. And I'm dizzy. Everything is moving.

The ground around me – the tapestry of leaves – is bright red, painted with my blood, and there's blood coming through the bandage too, despite Bear's efforts. And somewhere beyond that is this broken metal contraption that Bear has smashed in with a stone.

"Ju, what are we going to do?"

Ghost's here, a way off. Occasionally she makes one of those yelps again, that little nervous cry. I look around for drones, but that's not why she's crying.

I talk through my teeth, which are clasped tight with pain. "Can you get my bag off? Put it under my foot?"

Elevate the wound. You elevate the wound and apply pressure to get the bleeding to stop. I don't even need to look at the first-aid book to know that, it's one of the few things I remember. Everything else is hazy though, just

Bear's face is clear – his face and his voice too. "What now, Juniper?"

And this is what I keep telling him – elevate the wound and keep the bandages tight and I'll be OK soon.

I'll be OK because I have to be. No one knows where we are, no one has any idea, not even those stupid drones. We disappeared too well. Gave them the slip. We're dead to them already, all burnt up with that cottage.

I'll be OK because Bear needs me. I need him too. He puts my left leg up on my rucksack and wraps the foil blanket around me and puts his own bag under my head so I can rest.

I've already found the blister packets of tablets Silvan gave me. Antibiotics. We didn't need them for the ticks, but I need something for this. I'd take any medicine I had right now.

Bear holds a water bottle to my lips. "Drink, Juniper!"

"We don't have much left," I mutter. "You have some too."

"You need it. I can get more."

"You can't. You're too little."

"I'm not."

"I have to try and move soon. We can't stay here," I repeat.

Bear nods silently. There's nothing he can say. We can't stay here, but I can't move. Not yet.

That trap belonged to someone. It's rusty, old, but not fifty years old. Something that old would be powder out here by now.

Was the trap set by the same person who made the signs? Some of the twigs were looped round, like flowers. Was it to snare us in? What do they want us for?

I watch Bear as he collects sticks and leaves and arranges them expertly in front of me. Then he's off again, kicking up leaves and burying down, looking for nuts. There's a big chestnut tree a few metres away. We know them now – the long pointed oval leaves, yellow and veined; the twisted, fissured trunk and the cases of lime-green nuts beneath, spiked like little hedgehogs. Most of the nuts have gone, but Bear digs down and finds the few that the birds and squirrels haven't got to.

I watch him – the ritual of it, building the fire, opening up the prickly cases, taking the knife to carve crosses on the sweet nuts inside and then shaking them in the dry pan over small, smouldering flames.

He's a proper camper now. He was born to be out here.

I shift my position to see what weight my foot can take. I can't even think about putting my boot back on. My ankle is OK – it's my foot itself that's the problem. It's heavy and throbbing and I want to scream when I put any weight on it at all, but if I grit my teeth, bite my lip, I can walk.

55

"We need more water, Ju."

It's morning and we're walking on. Or Bear is. I'm limping beside him, dragging my left foot. It's hurting less, but not in a good way. I don't know if I'm getting used to the pain or a numbness is setting in.

The land's too steep today and after a while I collapse, exhausted. We need more water. My throat's so dry it hurts.

"I'll find a stream," Bear says, like he's reading my mind.

"No," I protest, thinking of the bloodied trap. "We have to stick together."

"You could rest."

"I couldn't rest. Not without you." We have to stay in sight of each other. We can't be further apart than that.

I stagger on to the nearest stream and then once Bear's got the water, as if on cue, Ghost appears beside us, a pigeon hanging from her jaw. I fall down, grateful, like the pigeon is a reason to rest, to let Bear sort it all out. The fire. The bird carcass. He hands me small tender strips of meat. Like I'm a little child.

The throbbing in my foot is worse now. Last night, though I desperately wanted to shut my eyes and escape from it all, I'd forced myself to take off the bandage. I did it when Bear was asleep. He'd already seen enough. I had to look though, at the deep gash, the torn, ragged flesh. I'm sure the trap's teeth made it right down to the bone. I knew I should somehow be cleaning out the wound, but when I tried it started bleeding again. I smothered it with our antiseptic balm instead and bandaged it back up.

We should be moving on. We shouldn't be in one place too long, so near water. That's been our strategy for days, to stay clear of drones, and it's worked. But my foot doesn't feel like it can take any weight at all now. When Bear points out a thicket and suggests staying here for the rest of the day, I nod, grateful.

"You're hot, Ju!" Bear says in the night, waking me.

I stare at him. "What do you mean? I'm freezing."

"You're not," he says, insistent. "You're really hot. You're sweating."

I'm about to say that that's impossible, but it's not. My body's wet with sweat and when I touch my forehead I can feel it – the heat coming off me. I'm burning up.

"Is it the disease?" Bear asks, his bottom lip wobbling.

"No." I know what it is. It's the trap – I saw the dirt and the rust. You couldn't not get an infection from that.

"You need more medicine!"

"I'll take more. Don't worry." I'm already on the maximum dose of the antibiotics, but I take more anyway. A couple of tablets, washed down by all the water we have left, then I'm pulled back down to sleep.

When it's light, Bear feeds me more tablets and water too, even though I thought we'd run out, and then somehow he gets me walking – right foot, dragging my left foot after. I feel strangely light, dangerously light, like there's nothing to weigh me down.

"My bag," I mutter. "Why are you carrying my bag? You're too little."

"I'm not, Ju," Bear says and we stumble on, and my blood, for all its disease resistance, is thick and slow and slushes around my head.

I keep having to stop. One time, after a little while, I realize Bear's gone. Gone from sight, though all the bags are still here.

It's the clatter of metal that wakes me. Bear's putting both rucksacks on, one back, one front, with the pans hanging from them. *My little tin man.* I hear Annie Rose's voice, back in our Palm House, as clear as day.

Bear's face is flushed. "I found a cave! I saw it on the GPS and I went to find it. It's just up there, Ju. Can you walk?"

"A cave?"

"A shelter," he says. "A cavern," and I know I'm meant to continue, find some new word to carry on the game, only everything is muddled and I think we've got there already because the ground is hard and rocky and it's dark.

Somewhere ahead there's an opening. The mouth of the cave. This round circle of light that's drawing me in.

56

In my head, we're still walking. The pulse of each footfall, one after another. In my head it's still going, still beating on, and Bear's voice too. *How many miles, Juniper?*

When I open my eyes, in a moment of lucidity, the scene is still the same. Stuck. We haven't moved on. The rocky ceiling, the slate floor like our kitchen back home. The dark pool of water from which Ghost drinks and the disc of light behind. We found our lair and Emily is here. My beautiful rag doll, Emily. Her dress like a meadow. How can that be? "I brought her for you," Bear says shyly. "I had her in my rucksack. She was a present. For when we got to Ennerdale. I thought you'd want her."

"I would. I do," I murmur.

Ennerdale. For when we got there.

The lucidity of all this. Is that the right word? The clarity. The clearness. The stillness.

Everything is so still. The beat has stopped. Of course we're not walking any more.

"Ju, drink. You need to drink." Bear's holding up a bottle to my lips and the liquid pours down my throat, clean and reviving. This isn't cave water. He dutifully feeds me the tablets too, and more strips of meat and little fish he says are minnow.

"I made a spear, Ju. Like I said I would. It worked."

He's so pleased and proud. I try to eat the fish because I want Bear to smile again, but really it's just the water I want.

Outside the cave, there's a tree. It's got brown leaves on but I watch them fall. Each time it gets light, I watch them fall and then one day the tree is bare. It's right down to the bone and the branches are white.

"Snow, Juniper. Like in the globe. In the Emporium." Bear's holding my hand, squeezing it tight.

"Snow?"

"I'm cold, Ju." He's crying.

I don't know what to say because I've forgotten what cold is. It feels like my whole body's on fire.

"We're like real bears. Hibernating," Bear says and I pull him up against me.

Maybe that's what we're doing. Hibernating. In our cave. Our cavern. Our den.

"Bear," I say in a sudden wakefulness. "You mustn't

forget the GPS. When you carry on." I should have let him use it. Practise.

"Don't, Ju! Don't say that."

"And the rifle. You have to keep the rifle ready. It's important."

"It's not important. I'm staying with you," Bear says fiercely and he presses his fists over his ears.

Ghost sleeps right up against us, keeping us warm. Sometimes she purrs. It's meant to mean a cat's happy, but I don't think it means happy. It's just reassurance.

Our hunting cat. She's keeping Bear alive. That was my job but I can't do it any more.

Once, long ago, long before, in a country called Italy, two baby brothers were abandoned by a river. They were left to die. A she-wolf found them. She carried them to a cave like they were her own cubs. Looked after them. Saved them. But when they grew up, they must have turned their back on her as their one desire was to build a city.

Outside our cave there are wolves. I hear them. And sometimes I see them too. Grey shadows at the entrance. "Don't go outside, Bear!" I scream, though it comes out more of a whisper.

Bear's voice is defiant. "I'm six, Ju." Six years old. Like that will save him.

Maybe the wolves wouldn't hurt us anyway. That she-wolf suckled those two babies she found. Romulus and Remus.

I think one of them died in the end. It must have been Remus because the city they built was called Rome.

Ghost will look after us. She'll keep the wolves away. It's winter that's the real predator. The season that, like all seasons, the city kept from us. The cold at its core.

It's coming, with numbing fingers and icy breath. It's reaching out for us.

We're children of the Wild and we came back to it. We offered ourselves up for the taking. I dream of two bodies of bone, still intertwined. Stripped back, stripped bare, like fine porcelain. And in the future, far, far ahead, when the disease has burned itself out and humans can come here again, maybe someone will find us. And just like in the past, when fossilized bones in a cave showed elephants and hippopotamuses once roamed through England, so too will people know there were children here. A girl and boy who never quite made it home.

57

The mouth of the cave is lit and there is a new sound. People.

"Bear, be careful!" Be careful of people most of all. They could have gone bad. They might have had to.

Even that woman, Violet, probably wasn't bad in the beginning.

Bear's not here to listen to me. He's already gone and Ghost's gone too. The cave's empty.

When Bear's back, someone is with him. A woman. She's wearing animal skin. I think it might even be lynx. She smells of the earth and her hair stretches down her back in one long plait.

But all this I notice later. When she comes into the mouth of the cave, I think she's an angel.

She places her palm on my forehead and her brow pleats as Bear lifts up the blanket and shows her my swollen, festering foot. She then nods her head and smiles at me. "Don't worry, little one. We'll make you well. We're good at this."

Bear's face is tight and worried and sort of proud too because he brought her here. And I love him so, so much.

I sink back, glad to be the little one, to have this woman here, her warm hands working to make me well.

I can smell herbs and garlic and onions and something acrid. Something unpleasant. But the woman's face and hands make me trust her. She sings as she wipes my brow and as she places a cup by my mouth and asks me to drink. Commands me.

"Come, Juniper. Your brother needs you."

Is it her voice that I'm hearing, this woman that Bear has brought to save me? Or is it Annie Rose, back in our glasshouse?

Someone calls the woman "Mama". Is it our mother? I can't ask Bear. I'm not sure what's stopped working, my brain or my voice, I just know I have to be silent. I can't form the words and my energy is needed elsewhere.

I drift. In and out of sleep and in and out of the Palm House too.

I stir when the woman touches my foot but she nods when I squirm and when my eyes close with pain. "It's good. It's good you feel it." And over again – "Shush, little one. We're here now."

The woman's voice sounds like music and she says these words over and over – shush, shush – though I don't think I'm crying. Time passes and the woman is still here, by my side.

She's not our mother. The voice calling "Mama" comes from another boy, almost my age. He comes into the mouth of the cave and brings things. Takes things away. He's always smiling and the woman calls him Cam. Sometimes Bear is with him, following him in and out like he always did with Etienne. Bear says the boy's name too. "Cam! Cam!" The name winds in and out of my head like a river.

It's not this boy I see in my dreams though. In my dreams, it's always Etienne.

It's not just hours, it's days passing. I know this because sometimes it's dark and then I wake again and it's light and, disorientated, I form Bear's name and he comes running. If he doesn't, the woman goes to the opening of the cave and calls him for me, calls him louder. His name sounds strange in her mouth. Foreign.

When Bear comes, his cheeks are red, like he's been running a long way, or if it's night, like he's just come from the fire that I can smell burning somewhere outside the cave. "Bear!"

"It's OK now, Ju! Hester and Cam and the others are looking after us. You're getting better!"

I nod. I can feel it. I'm not just clinging on, I'm waking

up, coming back to life. I've been shut up in the dark like that old jack-in-the-box, but Hester's winding the handle of the tin and with each turn the lid's lifting higher.

When I'm sat up for the first time and eating solid food – some warm thick soup with chunks of meat – Bear comes and sits beside me. He watches me eat and takes my bowl out when I've finished. When he comes back, his eyes are wet. "I thought you were dying, Ju." He can say it now because now it's not going to be true. He can see it. I'm getting better.

"You saved me," I say.

Bear bends down into the curve of my arms, cautious, afraid he'll hurt me. "You saved me," I repeat.

"Hester did that," he says, embarrassed. "She's Cam's mum. And Queenie's."

"Queenie?"

"Cam's sister. My friend."

I smile. "You saved me too. You found the cave and you brought me here. And you found Hester."

"I had to get help, Ju. I knew they were good, cause I'd heard them singing. They're the forest folk, Ju!"

"The forest folk?"

"The twig signs?" Bear says. "Don't you remember?"

"Hester's people made the signs?"

"Well, some of their people did. Forest folk, like I told you."

"Have you got the GPS, Bear? I wanted to check on the route."

His face scrunches up, red.

"Bear?"

"The battery's gone. I took the GPS to find the cave and I didn't turn it off. I thought I had, but I didn't, and now it's dead."

"Dead?" I repeat slowly. The GPS felt like a lifeline, winding out golden thread for us to follow. Maybe it was greedy of me to expect it to last all the way. "We have Mum's map," I say. "We can use that."

Bear looks relieved. "I found water too, didn't I? Proper mountain water from a waterfall!"

I hug him close. "That was the best water I ever tasted."

"Really?"

"Cross my heart."

"But don't hope to die?"

"No, I'm all done with dying."

58

The next morning, Hester leads me out into the light.

My left foot feels strange, like it's not quite part of me, but then my right foot feels strange too. I've been lying down a long time.

Outside the cave, it's totally different to the world I left. It's not green any more, it's white. Everywhere. Everything bleached and glazed and frosted. We came through the wardrobe. We walked right into Narnia.

Sunlight glints off the snow like a thousand torches and I have to put my hand over my eyes to shield them from all the light.

We're on a hillside and down in the bottom of the valley is a lake. A looking glass, reflecting back trees and sky.

I'm about to ask Bear's question – Ennerdale, how many more miles? – when this silver-grey cat emerges out of the trees and stands there, watching me.

"Ghost?" I gasp.

"It's a good name for her," Hester says.

"She's different." I recognize the markings, of course I do, but she's a whole new shade of colour.

"It's definitely your cat," Hester says. "All the days we've been here, she's barely left your side."

"She was golden."

"She's grown her winter coat," Hester says, matter-of-factly.

"She's camouflaged," Bear chirps, appearing beside me. "Didn't you notice? For the snow. The snow's pretty, isn't it, Juniper?"

He sprinkles snowflakes on to my hand. Tiny ice crystals. Snow flowers, or stars, almost violet in the light. They prick at my palm.

"Beautiful," I say, distracted, already staring back at Ghost. I call her but she retreats back under the trees. Gone. Like she's changed into her name, a real phantom of the forest. For some stupid reason, I start to cry. The ice flowers melt away in my hand.

"Ju!" Bear says, wary.

A little girl's standing a way off, her head to one side. She has dark hair winding down to her knees and pink dusty cheeks and is wearing fur, like a rabbit. She's beckoning to Bear.

"Be off with you both," Hester says, shooing him, and

283

Bear scampers after the girl without a backwards glance. He's had enough of me crying.

Hester sits me down on a rock just outside the cave, where icicles hang down from the top. She puts a fur round my shoulders and I look at it, suspicious.

"It's not lynx," she says, laughing. "Mine is. Your cat doesn't think much of me! She gives all of us a wide berth. You and Bear though, it's one of the strangest things I ever saw. Like you're her kittens."

"How long have I been ill?"

Hester's face creases. "A couple of weeks, I reckon. When your brother found us, he wasn't talking much sense, but that wound of yours, I reckon it had been festering a good few days. More. Then we've been with you seven days now."

"Two weeks?" No wonder there's snow. It must be December already. We should have been at Ennerdale by now. "Did Bear tell you?" I say reticently. "That we're on a journey?"

"Aye, he did that. Ennerdale."

"You know it?" I ask in a rush.

"I have a fair idea. It's near one of our stopping places. We go to those valleys sometimes. We collect berries from your trees."

I look at her, confused, and she winks at me. "The juniper tree. They make a nice tipple of gin."

"Have you seen anyone?" I ask, impatient. "Any people."

Hester nods slowly. "There's a village down by the lake. We've traded with them, various times. It's not a bad destination to have, Juniper."

I can hardly believe she's saying it. She's seen people there. A whole village. "It's still there? Ennerdale?"

But Hester's face has changed. Darkened, like when the sun goes behind a cloud. "This ain't the right time of year. Not to cross those mountains."

I shake my head. "We have to. To our parents. Ennerdale's our home now."

"Aye, I get that. And if it were spring or summer, or even a few weeks back, we'd take you. Show you the way. But not wintertime. Not with the coldest weather on its way. The deep freeze. You ain't seen nothing yet. Wait with us. Wait a while. Let winter do its worst and then go."

"No," I say, still shaking my head. "We've come this far. We're so close now. We've got a map that tells us the way."

Hester swipes out with her hand dismissively. "The way over the mountains changes all the time. Storms and ice."

I keep my face composed. "Our mum left the map for us. She drew the route on herself and she's been there. She's there now, waiting for us."

Hester softens. "Listen, I'll make a deal with you. We'll go west with you a little way, until I see how that foot's bearing up."

"Yes?"

"Yes," Hester says. "I can't leave you for the cat to look after." She laughs again – this soft peal of laughter. "Although she wasn't doing half bad."

"We'd be dead without her," I say loyally.

"I reckon you might be right." Hester nods gravely. "I've sent the rest of our party south with most of the horses and wagons and the kids and that. That's the direction we normally travel in wintertime. We're like migrating birds. But I reckon those of us left can at least set you on your way. Then it's up to you, Juniper Green." She looks me up and down like she's sizing me up.

"Cam and Queenie are still here," I say defensively, as laughter floats up from the lake.

Hester twinkles. "Aye, they wouldn't be having none of it when I said they should go. Queenie's taken a right shine to Bear. She's sticking to him like a burr, she is. And Cam ain't half excited about you waking up. A new audience for his tales! We don't get many outsiders."

"We're insiders, really," I say. "Or we were."

Hester nods. "Aye, you're from Portia Steel's city, Bear tells me."

I nod.

"You made a good choice, I reckon, getting out."

"It wasn't a choice."

"No," Hester says simply. I want to tell her more – tell her about Annie Rose and Etienne. How they'd have come too,

286

if they'd been able to. How we had to leave them behind. We didn't want to, but we had to. I don't say anything though. Annie Rose and Etienne and Ms Endo and the Palm House are shut away, deep inside me. It would hurt too much to even say their names.

"When do we leave?" I ask instead.

"Tomorrow. One more day for your foot to rest and for you to properly wake up, and then I reckon we've been here long enough. You'll find that out about us. We don't like to stick around."

"We tried to do that too. To keep moving."

"Sounds like you did pretty well, until that ugly great trap."

"Who do you think set it?" I ask.

Hester looks thoughtful. "Hard to say. Not us. We shoot clean, with an arrow. There are others though. People who don't fit in anywhere."

I nod. "There was a woman. She found Bear, or caught him. Caught us both. She was bad…" My voice trails off.

Hester pats my shoulder, even though I'm not even telling half the story. "It's tough out here. People go hard, just like the land in winter. It's different for us. We're meant to be out in the open."

"Who are you?" I ask, curious and embarrassed too. In case it's rude somehow. "Bear calls you the forest folk! He said you made the signs we kept seeing."

Hester laughs then, warmly. "We're travellers, my girl.

Romanies. Gypsies, you might have called us once. But forest folk will do. It has a certain ring to it!"

"I didn't think you existed, not any more. I mean, I know the words from stories. I thought the travellers had gone to live in the cities like everyone else."

"Aye," Hester says softly. "Lots did. The city authorities were fierce back then, rounding us up like we were animals. But some of us got away. We knew where to hide."

"Travellers had disease resistance?"

Hester shakes her head slowly, sad. "Not all of us. But it was never our way to be shut up. Never to see the hills or breathe the sea air again. We've been prisoners before. We know how it works out. We took our chances in the elements. Ticks or no ticks."

I watch Hester's face. It's like watching that old film reel back in assembly. Sadness turned up so loud it's unbearable.

"Lots of folk died," she goes on. "Lots of little ones and older ones too. The disease don't always come all at once, sometimes it comes slowly, wears you down. That's what happened to Cam and Queenie's mum."

"You're their mum," I cut in.

Hester snorts. "I'm far too old. Look at me!"

I look at her, gaze at her, but I still couldn't guess her age. "Cam calls you Mama."

Hester laughs again. "Plenty do. I guess it's something we all need, some time or other, someone to call Mama."

59

Hester sends Cam to come and get me. He appears in the mouth of the cave and bows, and I get this flash of Barney welcoming me into the Emporium when I was small.

I smile, embarrassed, but Cam's eyes are all twinkly, just like Hester's are. He doesn't even wait for me to get up – he puts his hand out for me to take and runs his other under my shoulders as I stand so I don't fall back.

"Thank you," I say shyly.

Cam grins. "You must be fed up of the dark. The light's been calling you, huh?"

Cam diverts past the bigger rocks and catches me when I stumble. It feels a long way to the lake but it's worth it. The fire's big and glowing, and encircled by tents – round frameworks of branches hung with brightly coloured fabric. There are horses too in and among everything – these warm, soft, breathing patchworks of white and brown and black, with long feathered hair at their feet. The people and the ponies and the bright tents, I think it's the most welcoming sight I've ever seen.

Hester's there and there's another woman too, younger than her, and two men. Cam introduces me to everyone.

The young woman is Larch. Her dark hair's tied up in a yellow scarf and she has golden hoops hanging from her ears. She smiles kindly and throws out a rug, gesturing for me to sit. Then she goes back to stirring a big cooking pot with wonderful-smelling steam wafting up from it.

The men are Danior and Manfri, though Danior says right away that I should call him Dani. He shakes my hand firmly. "We're happy you're on your feet again, Ms Green." There's a scar on his face and I try not to look at it, but it's hard not to. It cuts his whole face in two.

The other man, Manfri, nods briskly then turns away.

Bear bounds up, trailing his new friend. "This is Queenie, Ju. Like I told you about. She's their queen."

There's a cackle of laughter from Cam, and Queenie throws her hair over her shoulder and deliberately turns her back on him. She puts her hands on her hips as though waiting for me to receive her.

"Pleased to meet you, Queenie," I say. "I'd curtsey, but my foot's still healing."

"You don't need to curtsey this time," Queenie says regally, then crouches beside me on the rug. "Were there maggots in it?" she says, looking down at my foot. "Dani had maggots in his arm once. You could see them wriggling."

"Juniper didn't have maggots!" Bear says, appalled.

"Are you telling fibs again, Queenie?" Cam asks.

"No," Queenie says, sitting up straight. "It's true. There were maggots, weren't there, Dani? In your arm?"

"Queenie doesn't lie," Dani says, winking at me. "There were maggots, and flies after that! They flew right out my arm!"

Bear's green now. "Oh, don't worry," Queenie says when she sees his face. "Hester sorted it. She sorts everything. She's a miracle worker." She lowers her voice to a whisper and turns back to me. "She did think you were a goner in the beginning though, Juniper. Hester said the spirits properly wanted you."

"Queenie!" Cam laughs. "Juniper will be dancing round the fire with you soon enough."

"Will you?" Queenie beams. "Do you dance, Juniper?"

"Er, not really," I say uncomfortably. It never felt like there was much reason to dance back in the city.

Something warm and soft presses against my neck, and I jump.

Cam and Queenie are cackling with laughter.

"Dixie!" Bear says, starting to giggle too.

The black-and-white horse nudges into my shoulders,

with huge flared nostrils breathing warm air into me and the hair along her neck – her mane – tickles me. I shiver.

"She likes you," Cam says, pulling at the straps around the horse's neck. "Come, Dixie Chick. Juniper won't be used to horses."

Queenie springs on top of the pony and squeezes her legs into the black and white of Dixie's sides. She rides off, high and proud, glancing back every now and then to check Bear and I are watching.

"Not far, Queenie!" Hester calls after her. "The wolves are circling."

"Wolves?" I gasp.

"Because we've been here too long," a voice comes from across the fire. Manfri's. He's looking right at me, accusing.

Hester glares at him. "Ah, Mani, it's always the same round here this time of year, and you know it. Don't make the girl feel bad. It wasn't her fault she got caught in that trap."

Larch raps at him with a huge spoon and Manfri shrugs and turns back to what he's doing – mending something. Something leather for the horses, I think.

"So there are wolves?" I ask Cam. "We'd heard them but we haven't seen a single one. I was starting to think we'd made them up."

Cam shakes his head. "The wolves are real all right. Only they're clever. They stay clear of the bigger places. They know to leave humans alone, most of the time anyway."

Most of the time? Suddenly it comes back to me. My fever dream. The grey shapes at the entrance of our cave. How could I have forgotten? My eyes fix on Bear. "They came, didn't they, when I was sick? The wolves came!"

Bear's face scrunches up. "One did. It came in the cave. Ghost chased it off."

"Bear!" I stammer, reaching out to him.

"It was OK, Ju," Bear says quickly, though his eyes are wet all of a sudden. "I didn't mind. I knew Ghost would protect us."

"You should have lit a fire," carols Queenie, riding round the camp in circles. "Wolves are scared of fire."

"I did some of the time," Bear says, wiping at his face. "But it kept going out when I was sleeping."

"You did a grand job, Bear," Hester says firmly. "You kept Juniper safe. You should be real proud of yourself."

I pull him against me, but he pushes me away. "Ju," he whispers, his cheeks scarlet. "Queenie will think I'm a baby."

"Tell them, Cam. Tell them how you saved Dani from the wolf," Queenie's calling, and then Cam's on his feet, puffing out his chest like the birds do to keep warm. Bear turns his back on me to listen. He doesn't want to think about the cave.

Cam points his finger out round the camp. "It was a

winter just like this, the snow heavy in the hills."

"The wolves always come when there's snow," Queenie interrupts. "Cause there's less prey."

Cam nods impatiently. "We were getting ready to move south. The wolf burst from the mountainside. The biggest wolf we've seen. She jumped for Dani's face. She wanted to snap his head right off, I reckon. One giant bite." Cam snaps with his teeth and lunges forwards.

"Cause he had the meat. Isn't that right, Cam?" Queenie adds.

"That's right," Cam says. "They smell meat for miles."

I glance nervously at the cooking pot. Cam continues, acting his story out as he talks. How he flew up, bare-handed, and dragged the wolf to the floor.

"Not quite that quick, from what I remember," Dani says, tracing the gash across his face with his index finger.

I shudder, thinking of Bear back in the cave when I was sweating up with fever. Cam's still going on about punching the wolf, bare-fisted – he's clearly proud of that bit – and how the wolf went off crying like a baby. He's got a gleam in his eyes and I can't work out whether it's fear or excitement.

"You've got to fight to the death usually and make sure the dead one ain't you." He fixes me right in the eye and Hester chides him.

"Cam, give it a rest! You're scaring them."

Cam shrugs. "How they going to know how to win against a wolf if no one's ever told them?" He points his finger at us like he's a teacher in front of a class. "You've got to keep the fire going. Wolves hate fire. They don't like noise either. You've got to bang on the cooking pot, use whatever you've got. Shout and holler. Make yourself all big."

"And don't go carrying meat around, like what I was," Dani says.

"So you won't be wanting this, Dani?" Larch says, carrying out a bowl full of stew.

Dani laughs. "I think we're safe tonight with Cam on guard. He's volunteered to be wolf-watcher."

"I don't think so," Cam says, diving in front of Larch to claim the first soup. She punches him playfully in the stomach.

"Go and get the bread, will you? Guests first, remember. This bowl's for Juniper, in honour of her recovery." Larch hands it to me smiling, and Cam puts down a plate of the delicate flat bread they fry over the fire, and all thoughts of wolves go out of my head.

When everyone has finished eating, Dani gets out a wooden instrument – a collection of hollow reeds which he blows across, and this lilting, loveliest of sounds comes out. Queenie pulls Cam up and the two of them dance. Slow at first and then faster, faster, as Dani speeds up the tune, till Queenie collapses in a heap of giggles.

Larch insists on brushing out my hair as we watch. It's been in plaits ever since I left the city and it curls all the way down to my waist when she unties it. She spreads it out over my shoulders and hands me a small oval mirror with roses painted round the glass.

"You're beautiful, Juniper," she says and I blush, and Bear looks at me astonished. I always thought the curls were part of Bear's wildness. Now I've got as many as him. I don't exactly look wild in the rose mirror, I just look older. Stronger, maybe.

The dancing goes on for ages. Larch gets Manfri to join in and he spins Queenie round and round, and Bear looks on so enviously that Dani passes the pipe over to Hester so he can spin Bear too.

When the little ones tire, Larch gets up and dances in Manfri's arms, and I colour and look away because sometimes he bends down and kisses her head.

Hester's songs get slower and sadder and at some point Larch starts to sing. It's the most beautiful sound I ever heard, all sweet and haunting, although I don't know what she's singing about. She's slipped into another language entirely.

I could sit for hours, just listening, but Cam's next to me, talking a hundred miles per hour. He knows everything about the Wild, or the Wildwood as he calls it – all the places they've been, the stories and traditions, the rituals, the history.

He wants to know about our city too. He says around the other cities, the handful of other places that survived, the Buffer Zones are open. They're markets and performance spaces. There are visiting traders and acrobats and musicians.

"Not your one," Cam says, this dark excitement in his eyes. "Not Portia Steel's city. We can't get close and we wouldn't want to. We've heard all sorts. People going in, never coming out, like it's a black hole."

I don't want to talk about where we've come from, not now, when Bear and I are the happiest we've been for weeks, but Cam's leaning in, waiting. I've got to give him something. So I start talking about the Palm House and the Emporium.

"They were just the best bits," Bear pipes up. "The rest was vile. Especially school."

"Why?" Cam asks.

"Because you're always inside. Even when they say go out, you're still inside really. And the grass is plastic, and there's just a silly climbing frame to play on, and they don't even let you run fast. They say it's dangerous."

"Dangerous?" Cam scoffs.

"There wasn't space," I explain. "There was never any space. And it's all just grey and the same, everywhere you look."

"Like a prison," Bear says. "I'm never going back. Never ever!"

"I couldn't stand it," Queenie says passionately. "I wouldn't have let them lock me up! I'd have run away from Portia Steel years ago!"

Bear gazes at her like she really is a queen.

When we can't keep our eyes open any longer, Cam drags a couple of stones from the fire with a stick. He wraps them in furs and hands one to each of us and we hold them next to us like big warm hugs.

"Goodnight, city kids," Cam says, smiling.

Bear's eyelids are drooping, but he still finds the energy to stick his tongue out.

60

We set off at dawn. There are six horses, or three horses and three ponies, as Queenie corrects me. Hester and Larch ride the larger horses and they make me ride too, to keep the weight off my foot.

My face froze when Cam said I'd be riding a horse called Lightning, but he pointed to the white-bolt pattern across the back of her neck and laughed. "Her name wasn't on account of her speed. Old Lightning's the slowest we've got. Your biggest problem is going to be keeping her awake!"

Bear runs on with Queenie, whooping.

"Bear!" I scold when he winds in front of Lightning. I'm scared she's going to trample him. "You're too loud."

Hester laughs. "Let him be, Juniper."

"The drones…" I start.

"Your city's metal birds?" Hester exclaims. "They don't come this far north. Why would they?"

"They followed us."

She nods. "Aye, Bear said. I still reckon you're safe. You're far enough away."

"Don't other cities have drones too?"

Hester shrugs. "Why would they?"

"I guess," I say nodding, but if we hadn't staged that fire, the drones would have followed us, I know they would. Our city's more dangerous than Hester thinks, I'm sure of it, but what's the point in thinking about that now? There's nothing her people could do except stay clear of our city, and they're doing that already.

Ghost isn't with us. She came when we were packing. She stood on the edge of the encampment and the horses stamped and whinnied their disapproval. Manfri cursed and threw a stick at her to see her off.

"Manfri!" Hester had shouted as I got to my feet, shaky, to call her back. "She's Juniper's cat."

"She won't hurt them," I'd said angrily. "You scared her."

Manfri hadn't budged. "We had a lynx jump from a tree on to one of the foals once. The mares know predators when they see them."

"Ghost's not like that," I'd said at once, though I'd thought of the deer she caught and how I hadn't even felt sad. Only grateful and proud.

"Are you sure you're holding tight enough?" Cam asks, walking beside me, holding on to Lightning. "Your knuckles are like stones!"

I pull a face. "What if she falls on the ice? It's a long way down!"

"Trust her, Juniper. She's a mountain pony."

I smile and try to relax. There's something magic about the way Cam leads her. Something between them. Some three-way thing between the boy and the land and the horse.

Bear and Queenie weave in and out of everyone, jumping on two of the little pack ponies, Flotsam and Squall, when they tire.

Bear has proper boots now. Hester scoffed at his shoes and found an old pair of Queenie's for him before we set off. "You need proper soles out here or you'll be slipping down them mountains."

The furs help too. Ours are rabbit like Queenie's – lots of rabbit skins, all stitched together. Cam says the wind's got teeth this far north and he's right.

Hester knows when to slow and when to stop entirely so I can take a break. "You're doing well, Juniper," she says, sitting down beside me on some rocks where she's insisted I raise my foot up and rest.

I grimace. "I'm slowing everyone down."

"It's good to be slow sometimes. You see more."

"I suppose," I say, though she's right of course. After all those weeks in the cave, I see everything afresh. The way the light falls across the mountains, the dances of the birds above our heads. A lone kestrel, hanging in the air, hovering, like it doesn't need to flap its wings at all. And birds Bear says are buzzards circling over us, their wings and tail fathers spread right out like a kite.

The trees are the most amazing thing. You can trace patterns right up into the canopy. Their skin, their bark, marked with indentations – lines like ravines in the wood. Rivulets. Folds coiling into circles or spirals.

Etienne's mum would love this. The infinite variety, the shapes, the patterns. This, here, is what she was trying to replicate with her fractals. She'd never seen it for real, only in old pictures, but she understood its lure. This is what she thought would heal us.

Sometimes I think of the kids back at school. How I always thought they didn't miss this. How could they? They didn't know about it. But maybe, deep down inside somewhere, they missed it anyway.

61

"You should stay with us," Cam says, watching me ride. He's finally let go of Lightning's rope. I think this old slow horse suits me pretty well. "You'd make good nomads, you and Bear."

"Can we, Ju?" Bear asks eagerly, by my side at once.

"Bear!" I sigh. "What about Ennerdale?"

Bear looks guilty. "I don't mean… I didn't mean instead," he flounders and I have to cut in. Rescue him.

"I know you didn't mean it."

"He did," Cam says assuredly. "Why would you want to stay in one place anyway? All your life in one place? That's crazy!" He bends down so Bear can climb on to him for a piggyback. Bear stretches his arms right out like the kestrel's wings and suddenly I'm back on the pavement outside the climbing centre, with Bear an albatross on Etienne's back. Tears well in my eyes.

There was this old fairy story we had back home. *The Snow Queen*. Gerda's best friend, Kay, is taken by the evil Snow Queen and Gerda sets out to rescue him. On the way she gets distracted by a beautiful garden and forgets who she's looking for. I always loved the garden part, where every kind of flower grew but roses. The old lady who tended the garden had made the roses shrivel into the ground when Gerda came. She knew roses would remind Gerda of Kay and she wanted Gerda to stay in the garden forever.

Seeing Bear like a bird on Cam's back is like seeing roses again and remembering. Except we're not going to find Etienne or Annie Rose. We're going to a place I left almost a decade ago and parents we barely remember. Who knows what we'll find?

Ghost still hasn't shown up. The landscape's rawer now and the sides of the hills are covered in dead brown fern – bracken – and grey stones and rocks that break away and fall on to the valley floor. Cam calls it scree. Is it all this that Ghost doesn't like – the exposure, out on the hillsides, climbing between valleys? Or is it the people, the ponies, the songs?

I think Hester's people are glad Ghost has stopped following us, but I look for her. All the time I look for her on the hillsides, and backwards as we pass from one valley into the next. Have we gone too far for her to follow?

"She'll show up," Bear says, coming to stand next to me

at the edge of the night's encampment. "She always does."

"She's not been gone this long before."

"She wouldn't leave us, Ju."

I believed that too, and yet when you say it out loud, you realize how crazy it sounds. Ghost's wild. Why should she follow us? If she did feel any sense of obligation, if that's even possible, we have human friends now. They've taken over her role.

"She doesn't like them, does she?" Bear says sadly.

"It's probably the coats they wear." I don't mean for my voice to sound bitter, but it does. Even Cam's wearing lynx.

"Cam said the lynx were dead already. They don't waste dead animals."

"That's convenient," I say sarcastically. "So did they eat them too?"

Bear pulls a confused face and walks away, back into the firelight. For a while I just stand there.

"Penny for them?" a voice says beside me and I jump. It's Hester.

"Are you OK, Juniper? You look like you've seen a ghost."

"Our grandmother used to say that."

"Annie Rose? Bear's talked about her. You must miss her."

I nod, not trusting myself to speak.

"You're shivering," Hester says. "You should be by the fire with everyone else."

"I just…"

"Needed some quiet?" Hester asks.

"No!" Then I smile as Hester laughs. "Well, maybe. A little. Just to think."

"Juniper," Hester says, serious now. "It's time. We've held off as long as we can, but it's time now. We head south tomorrow."

I turn to the fire and gaze at them – Hester's little band. Her troupe. "All of you?"

"All of us, Juniper. We stick together. We go south in the winter. It's who we are."

"You don't need to explain."

"Juniper, we'd come with you if we could. You know that. But there's folks waiting for us and more snow coming. Look how low the clouds are and that light around the moon like a silver halo. They're snow signs if ever I saw them. If we get further into the mountains, getting down again will be too difficult with the wagon."

"It's fine, Hester. It's completely fine."

Hester places her hands on my shoulders. "Juniper, you and Bear fit in so well with us. Even Manfri's coming round."

I raise my eyebrows and Hester grins.

"He says we could trade some of your pictures, hire you out as a portrait painter!"

"Even though I made Queenie's nose too big and Cam

wasn't handsome enough?"

Hester cackles. I'd been tasked with drawing portraits for them all last night, and it was touching how pleased they seemed to be with my quick sketches, despite their complaints. "It's a rare gift you've got. Don't underestimate it. Come south with us, Juniper."

"We can't, Hester."

"No?"

"We're going to Ennerdale. To our parents. It's who we are. It's what we do."

Hester smiles at me and sighs. "Well, you got me there. I can't argue with that."

Back by the fire, Cam comes to sit next to me. "Hester didn't persuade you then? I told her she wouldn't."

"We didn't just want to escape the city. We wanted to go home." I swallow hard as I say this because I'm not even sure what's true. Maybe home's still a glasshouse hundreds of miles away?

"Juniper, Juniper!" Cam says. "Haven't I taught you anything?"

I smile at the mock horror in his voice. "I know, I know. Home is a thousand paths. Home is the woods and moors and valleys and streams."

"You forget the sea," Cam says. "You haven't even seen the sea yet."

Some kind of longing must show in my face because

Cam points his finger at me. "You see – the sea, the sea! I knew there would be something to tempt you!"

"No! No!" I say and I laugh and he dances round me, all light and breezy. I want to say, don't you see, I don't need anything else to tempt me. Cam and Hester and Queenie and the ponies and all of them. They've woven their magic and it's the nicest kind of magic. It's better even than that garden in *The Snow Queen* because you'd never get bored, not ever. Anytime you got tired of a place, you'd move on somewhere else.

Cam laughs. "It's OK, I get it. Ennerdale."

"Ennerdale," I repeat, softly at first, then louder, because maybe, just maybe, for a fraction of a second he did get me. Maybe I was wavering. "Ennerdale."

"Your mum," Cam coaches.

"Our mum."

"Your father. Descendant of the ReWilders."

I raise my eyebrows.

"I'm only repeating what Bear thinks!"

"I hope he's not disappointed."

Cam shrugs. "He's got to be better than my dad. He ran off. He broke the one rule."

"Sticking together?"

"Exactly!"

"And going south for winter," I can't help adding.

Cam pulls a face. "At least you've got your furs now.

And you know how to light a proper fire, thanks to me."

"Yeah. We're experts now."

"And you should take Squall, to carry your things, and Bear, when he's tired. Everyone says so," Cam blurts it out.

"No, no!" I say quickly. "We can't."

"Bear adores Squall."

"No, Cam. She's yours and Queenie's."

"We want you to have her," Cam says. "Even Queenie."

"Really?" I ask.

Cam laughs. "Well, she's coming round."

I smile. "Look, it's nice of you, but with the mountainsides and everything, we're better off on foot. I can just focus on Bear and…"

Cam reads my mind. "You want your cat back."

I flush. "Maybe when it's just Bear and I…" I stop as I realize how ridiculous I sound. Maybe when it's just the two of us. Maybe when we really need her again, Ghost will come back.

Hester's playing the pipes and the others sing, clapping hands and clicking in this warm happy chorus. Bear and Queenie cavort round the fire, dancing. We don't talk about tomorrow, but I guess Hester's told everyone by now.

Sometimes I catch one or other of them looking over at me, though when I meet their eyes they smile. There's no place round the campfire for sadness tonight.

62

I've been studying our map by torchlight. Hester's drawn on extra landmarks – odd-shaped rocks and hills and trees – to guide us. She reckons if conditions are right it's just another few days, only she swears snow's on the way.

My foot will slow us down too, she says, though it feels like it's getting better all the time now. Sometimes I forget it even hurts.

Larch has given us a little box of butter and some herbs, and promised to wrap parcels of meat and vegetables in the morning. Only I've seen inside the little wagon the ponies pull. There's barely any food left. They would all have been south two weeks ago were it not for me. They've shared their winter rations long enough.

I wake Bear before first light. He scowls as I shine the torch into the warm pile of furs he's buried in. "I'm tired, Ju."

"We have to go, Bear."

The colour drains out of his face when he realizes what I mean. "No, Ju! No!"

"Shush, you'll wake everyone!"

Bear looks around. The adults were drinking wine and singing songs way into the night. They're all still sleeping.

"But why?" Bear wails. "It's not fair!"

"Because we're on a journey."

"Queenie said we can go with them! We can stay with them for the winter, Ju! Hester's going to ask you!"

"She already did, Bear," I say flatly.

"Why are we running away then?"

"We're not running away. We're getting back on the journey. Our journey. Yours and mine. We're going to Ennerdale. To Mum and Dad."

Bear stares at me. He's got tears in his eyes, but he gets to his feet. "Why can't we say goodbye?"

I shrug. "I'm sorry, Bear. I've just had enough of goodbyes."

It doesn't take long to pack our things. I take out the picture I drew last night. It's all of them, the whole group sat round the fire, singing. I sketched me and Bear in too, so they can remember us. I put it next to where Hester's sleeping and I write two words on the bottom. Thank you.

A little body steals out of one of the tents. She's been watching us.

"You're leaving," Queenie says, accusing.

"We have to," Bear says. "We're going to find our mum and dad."

"Are you taking Squall?"

I shake my head. "No. Queenie. Squall's yours."

Queenie nods silently. She takes off her necklace – a white pebble with a hole all the way through it where a pink ribbon is threaded – and places it round Bear's neck.

"Take this. It'll keep you safe."

"Queenie," I protest. "You love that stone." She's always playing with it – sticking her little fingers through the hole, or looking through it, screwing up her eye, like the stone's a lens to a whole new world. She found it on a beach in the south of England.

"He'll need it where you're taking him," Queenie says. "I was swallowed up to my neck once in one of those valleys. There's proper sinking mud in the bogs." She puckers up her cheeks and makes this loud sucking noise.

Bear shudders.

Queenie nods solemnly at him. "Just make sure she goes first," she says, pointing at me, and she goes to hug him tight. Bear's eyes meet mine over Queenie's shoulder. She's the first friend his own age he's ever had.

63

The hills turn into mountains and the air gets colder, fiercer. Even the trees change – they're gnarled and twisted like claws.

Sometimes it feels like we're walking along corridors of stone.

"Are we going the right way, Juniper?" Bear's voice trembles. He's clasping Queenie's stone round his neck and without thinking I reach round mine for the GPS. But it's gone – dead at the bottom of my rucksack. There's just Mum's map now, and even with Hester's guide marks nothing's looking like it should.

"Yes," I say, worried I'm back in the business of lying again. Leading Bear on. Painting everything brighter than it is. But the highest mountains are still ahead and those are what we've got to get past. Ennerdale's somewhere on the other side.

It always seems like there's light on the horizon – a sort of luminescence – only it's teasing us, like the will-o'-the-wisps from the old stories, because whenever we get to where the light was, it's always gone.

The bogs are real, the ones Queenie warned us about. That's the problem with the valley floors and sometimes we scramble across the mountainsides instead.

My injured foot's weak and it keeps slipping, turning, and I feel Bear's eyes pressing on me anxiously every time I wince.

There's no one else left in these mountains. No one. You know it from the black jagged rocks and the bogs and the cold. The rawness of everything. The bleakness. No one else would be this crazy.

Bear's eyes have lost their gleam.

"Hester says they go to Ennerdale in the spring. We'll see them again, Bear," I say, desperately trying to cheer him.

Bear stares at me silently, accusing. After a while he says in a wavering voice, "Will there be other kids in Ennerdale, Ju?"

I nod. "Cam says there are. He's seen some playing."

"What if they don't like me?" The words tumble out of him and I look at him, shocked.

"Bear! Of course they'll like you! Of course they will!"

"None of the kids at school did. Not one of them. Not ever."

I stare at him. His shoulders have drooped. He's playing with Queenie's stone round his neck.

I sigh. "They just didn't understand you. And they weren't shown any better," I say, thinking of everyone in the city. How they're all shut up in the dark in their own jack-in-the-boxes too. What chance did anyone have in that place? "It'll be different in Ennerdale, Bear. I promise you."

"Why?" Bear asks.

"Because they know what it is. To be wild." I pause. "And because you're different too."

Bear raises his eyebrows.

"You're free now."

He shrugs, but maybe something lights up inside him because soon he starts bounding on ahead.

He finds us pinecones. Queenie showed him how to dislodge the little seeds inside and he hands some to me to nibble on as we go. "When will Ghost come back?"

I turn round, scanning the mountainsides for her familiar form. "I don't know, Bear."

"When it's time to bring our tea?"

"Bear!" I say, rolling my eyes. "Is food all you think about?"

The air rifle's back over my shoulder and we're looking for rabbits, only the land's still and barren. Eventually we find some mushrooms that Larch showed me were safe – wood blewits. A fairy ring of them, each with bluey-lilac gills like the thin papery sheets of a book radiating out from the central stem. We fry them up for tea with the butter and herbs.

Bear blows into the bottom of the fire and smiles proudly when the flames flare up. "I'm a dragon, Ju! Look at my fire breath." I laugh, and the heat from the fire is inside me too as I know Bear's forgiven me.

We've got hot stones warming our sleeping bags, but we stay sat by the fire for ages even though it's just the two of us. We've got used to late nights.

Bear plays with his animals and I sketch. I draw Hester, Cam, Larch and Queenie. After a while, Bear comes and snuggles next to me. "What about Ghost, Ju? You haven't drawn her yet."

"I did. Back in the cave."

"Can I see it?"

I flick back in the sketchbook. My fever had only just broken, I'd only started sitting up, but the urge to draw Ghost had been so strong. She'd been with me the whole time I was ill and I'd learned her face by heart.

64

The snow comes overnight. Hester's forecasting was right. White covers over everything, over Bear and me too, hidden under our tarpaulin.

The stones are ice-cold at the bottom of my sleeping bag. At some point in the night, Bear climbed in with me like he always used to back in the city. This time it wasn't because of bad dreams – it was to stay alive. All the words there are for cold – bitter and freezing and frosty and icy and raw – but none of them describe this feeling that's a lack of feeling altogether.

I force myself out of the sleeping bag and breathe warm air on to my fingers to make them work. I fix my mind on the little gas stove that Hester made us take. One of their precious few that they keep for emergencies.

I somehow get it going on a rock – this miraculous flame in the middle of all the snow.

"Bear, Bear!" I nudge him to get him to wake.

"It's too cold, Ju," he murmurs sleepily.

"Open your eyes, Bear! Look! The Snow Queen came. In the night."

Bear forces his eyelids open and gazes at the white world around us, the blue shadows of everything. He blinks a few times and rubs his eyes, then reaches his fingers over the stove.

"Hester saved us again," I say.

"Hester would save us from anything," Bear says fiercely.

Our water bottles are frozen solid but I melt us some snow to drink and fry up some of the mushrooms from yesterday. To defrost us from the inside.

That's when we see the wolves.

Eight of them, a whole pack, running across the mountainside, just across the valley from where we are.

Bear and I sink into the rock and the snow, right into it. We barely even breathe.

Cam's advice runs through my head – to be loud and big, to bang pans, to look strong. We don't do any of that. We just watch them. One after another, trekking through the snow like it's powdered sugar.

All the stories we've read about wolves – the dark shadows of the forest, in grandmother's clothes, puffing down pig houses and chasing children across snowy lands in the dead of winter – none of that conjured up creatures quite this beautiful. They're not just grey – they're mottled with browns and yellows and reds and white.

Only May got it. May, in the Warren, who had never seen any of the Wild.

For one awful moment one of the wolves looks in our direction. One of the younger ones. Maybe that's why it doesn't stop. Maybe it doesn't have the experience to know, to believe its yellow eyes. Or maybe Bear and I have been out here so long we're of no interest. We're part of the Wild now. We're indistinct from it.

We don't talk after the wolves have gone. We sit around Hester's tiny stove, staring silently at the flame and the winter landscape all around us. Neither of us has the energy to suggest moving on yet.

Bear's looking oddly into the twisted tree we found shelter under last night. He shakes one of the branches and snow falls into my face.

"Watch it, Bear!" I spit snow from my mouth.

"A patrin!" he cries.

"A patrin?"

He points to a bundle of twigs tied together in a white rag.

"That's what Queenie called them. She showed me how to make them while you were sick."

"A forest-folk sign," I whisper.

"I know what this one means, Ju!" Bear's voice quivers with excitement. "The white rag. It means a safe place. Ennerdale! It must be Ennerdale, Ju! It must mean we're close."

65

It's impossible to say how many times I've imagined walking into Ennerdale. In my dreams, and in my nightmares too. Sometimes there's this bustling village with wooden houses and smoke pouring from the chimneys and a crowd of people, a surge, coming forward to welcome us. Sometimes the people are hostile. The village is walled and they fire arrows. We can't get close enough to explain that we belong here, or did once. Sometimes the village is burnt to the ground or there's nothing, simply nothing, and there never was.

We reach the Liza two days after we see the wolves. We find it early in the morning and we follow the river for most of the day, through hazel, aspen, birch and oak. There are pine trees too and Bear still hasn't kicked his habit – he picks up the cones and stashes them in his already full pockets.

There's this other tree too. This bushy, spreading tree with needles and tight blue berries, dusted with snow. Bear points them out to me.

"What are they?"

"You should know, Ju!"

"Juniper?"

Bear nods and I reach out my hand. The needles are prickly and there's a sharp scent of spice. This is what Mum named me after. It really is everywhere.

There are other things that make this valley different too. Things that make you think you're entering somewhere vaguely habited. It's little things – slight trails, and places where maybe a tree or two has been cut down, not just broken up in a storm. Then we see the cows Cam told us about. Big black ones, shaggy. Like if you were to imagine a mountain cow. A cow built to survive.

Cam said they trade their wares for beef from these cows. He said it's food for kings.

"Are you scared?" Bear asks.

"A little. Are you, Bear?"

He nods and pushes his hand into mine.

As soon as we see the lake in the distance, shining, we start to see the houses. Little slate huts dotted under the trees, camouflaged against the grey crags of the valley sides, with wisps of smoke reaching up to the sky.

There's a woman at the side of the river. She's breaking

the ice with a stick and collecting it in a bucket. She's whistling and she swings the bucket as she walks.

It's the strangest sight after the bleakness of the mountain. A woman in a loose swirling skirt and a green knitted hat, with red hair flowing out of it like fire, whistling as she collects ice. She's not seen us and for some reason I can't open my mouth. Bear and I stand in silence.

But maybe we make a tiny sound, or maybe the woman feels us watching, because she turns and looks right at us. I see her profile in full. Her contours. The curve of her belly.

She puts the bucket down and walks towards us, slow at first and then faster, so fast she's running, despite the baby in her tummy. "Bear? Juniper? It is, isn't it? It's you!"

Bear runs forwards a couple of steps, before stopping, uncertain. "Mum?"

A shadow passes over the woman's freckled face.

"No, Bear," she says gently. "I'm not your mum. I'm Willow."

It should be our turn to speak, I know that, but I can't. I can't even move.

"You got here! You made it." The woman's smiling in astonishment, but there are tears swimming in her eyes.

"Is our mum here?" I ask. It's just a couple of seconds but that moment tells me everything. It's the most crushing silence I ever heard.

I know then – the woman doesn't need to say anything –

but Bear, my astute, perceptive little brother waits bright-eyed beside me for the right answer.

"She's dead, isn't she?" I shouldn't say it like that, not in front of Bear, but some things you want over with, for everyone to have already been told so you can just stop hoping. I can't stand that moment of waiting. The agony of that tiny bit of hope you still have left.

"She died, Juniper," the woman says simply and I nod, grateful that now we both know.

66

Bear sobs and falls into me, against me, and I crouch down to take him in, the weight of him, right up against me.

I keep my gaze on the woman. Willow. "When?"

"Four years ago. Just before Bear came to you. We hoped the two of you would come back some day. Come home."

I nod, although it doesn't feel like home now.

"Your father, Gael—" Willow starts.

"He's here?" I ask.

"Not right now, but he will be. Any day."

But I'm not listening. I've already turned away to Bear, to the sobbing coil of him.

Other people are appearing behind Willow – women, men, children – and I hear our names run through the crowd, and Mum's name too, a whispered refrain. I can't stand it – everyone looking on in pity as Bear sobs beside me.

All I'm thinking suddenly is Hester and Cam and Queenie. How we left them for Mum and she's been dead this whole time. No one ever sent that message. No one ever bothered to let us know.

If we'd known we would have stayed with Hester. If we'd known we wouldn't even be here. What have I done, dragging Bear all this way on a false promise? He could have stayed with his forest folk after all.

It was always Mum we most wanted. Mum would get us. She'd understand us, she'd understand everything about us, because she grew up in the city too.

Some of the kids crowd in closer to get a better look and I can feel Bear's breaths getting faster. Heaving sobs that wrack his entire body. I want to scream at them all to go away. I want to scream that our whole journey was a lie, a sham, because our mum isn't at the end of it. She's gone forever and there's no place left we can find her.

Willow ushers the others away and I gather Bear up in my arms to carry him on my hip, like I always used to, his thin legs gripping round my waist. One of the men appears next to me and puts his arms out. "I'll take him." Bear leans in to me, tighter, and I brush the man away.

Willow leads us to a few slate huts at the edge of the settlement. Old, empty ones. She directs Bear and me into the one that looks most intact. She says she'll come back later to make the beds up, but then she knows to go.

There are two simple wooden bed frames and a little chair, a child's chair, in the corner, and a few shelves on the walls, but other than that it's empty. The floor's mossy and there are spiderwebs in the corners, but after all our days in the Wild we're used to those things.

I sit down on the chair with Bear on my lap and he cries and cries. I know I should be crying too but I can't. I'm frozen, numb, like it's too big a thing to take in.

I stroke Bear's tangled hair and his cheeks, all chafed from the cold and streaked with muddy tears. He's mine now to take care of, all mine, like he always really was.

I try and think what Annie Rose would say, the words of comfort she'd reach for, but I can't think of any words at all. I think of pictures instead. I think of the stars and flowers I painted when Bear first came to us to make him feel at home.

After thinking about them for a while, I prise Bear off me so I can stand up. I go to his rucksack and take things out. His Jungle, and all the things he collected on the way as well. The conkers and acorns and pinecones and every kind of seed we saw. I start to put them on a shelf by one of the beds.

Bear watches for a little while. "What are you doing, Ju?"

"I guess this is our home now. For a while at least, till we decide if we like it. We should make it nice."

"We can stop walking now?"

"Yeah. We got here. Both of us."

Bear nods and repeats my words. "Both of us." He's still got tears in his eyes but he gets up and takes the animals from me. "It's OK, Ju. I can do them."

I watch his little hands working as he arranges the animals on the shelf. The neatness of his formation, the symmetry.

"We never did see a bear, did we?" he says as he finds a spot for his brown bear.

I shrug. "Maybe they were just an urban myth."

Bear shakes his head. "No, Ju. They'll just be further north, or hibernating. One day we'll see them."

I smile. I put Emily on one of the beds and get out my sketchbook and drawing pencils. Then even though it's kind of ridiculous for this to be a priority right now, there are these hooks high up near the ceiling of the hut and I fix up a length of string between them so I can hang up our sleeping bags to dry.

There's a tap at the door. It's Willow. She's carrying a couple of steaming bowls.

"Can I come in? I brought soup. The village is preparing a feast for you both, but feasts take time. I figured you two must be hungry now."

"Thank you." I stand aside, embarrassed at how quickly we've leaped in to make the hut ours. "Where does our dad live?" I ask tentatively.

Willow flushes. "Just a few huts that way." She pauses.

"He's in with me. We're together."

I stare at her and it takes ages to work it out. They're not just together in the same hut.

"What about your baby's dad?" Bear asks, confused.

Willow goes even redder and her eyes flick across to me.

"Bear," I say. "It's our dad's baby too. He's living with Willow now."

"What about Mum?" Bear trills, indignant.

Willow looks awkward and I feel sorry for her. "It's been four years, Bear," I say. "Mum's been gone for ages now. It doesn't mean our dad loved her any less."

Willow looks at me gratefully then turns to the shelves where we've started laying out our things. "This doesn't feel right," she blurts out. "You should come in with Gael and me for now. It'd be a squeeze, but we could start work on a hut next door to us in the spring, for when the baby's born, to give us all more room. It isn't right you being on your own."

The thought just makes me claustrophobic. We don't want to join another family. That's not what we came for.

"We're used to being on the edge," I say. Bear looks at me. I know we're both thinking of our Palm House, right on the edge of the Buffer.

Willow's shaking her head. "It feels wrong, you being out here."

"We don't mind it. We don't want to be in the way."

Willow looks sad. "Don't say that, Juniper. This is your home. Just like it was your mum's. You know you're named after this place?"

"The juniper tree? Did my mum like gin or something?"

Willow snorts with laughter. "Sometimes," she says, giggling. "But Ennerdale itself, in old Norse, the Viking language," she says, her eyes twinkling, "Ennerdale means Juniper Valley. Marian named you after this place, so it is your home and you do belong. Both of you do."

She picks up my sketchbook and starts leafing through it. All the things we drew along the way. Bear's night sky, and my picture of the train carriage, and all the leaves and insects. The people too. Those we left behind: Annie Rose, Etienne, Ms Endo. And the people we met along the way. Hester, Cam, Queenie. Larch, Dani and Manfri. It even felt sad to leave Manfri in the end.

When she reaches Ghost – the swirls of light and dark and the speckles on her jowls where her whiskers come out – Willow looks at me curiously, though all she says is, "These are really good, Juniper."

Bear snatches the sketchbook off her like he can't bear her looking at it. Willow flinches. "Don't you want to ask about your dad?" she asks gently.

I stay silent, unable to express what's inside me.

"Gael will be so proud of you both."

"Maybe," I say, keeping my face all taut.

"He made the same journey, didn't he?" Willow says. "He'll know what it feels like."

I look at her, confused. "He came from out here. It was easy for him."

Willow shakes her head slowly. "Your dad was from your city, Juniper. He came here with your mum."

"No!" I say. "Mum left the city with someone else. A boy from her school. He was called—"

"Sebastian," Willow finishes. "Only he never liked that name. He wanted something with more meaning, so he called himself Gael. It means—"

"Wild," I whisper. It was in that old baby name book, encircled with the same vines and hearts that Marian had. I always wondered why. Our dad picked a new name. He must have chosen it from that book. Maybe Mum helped him.

"Our mum and dad came here together?" I say. "We never knew."

Willow nods. "Gael hated his family. He hated them with a passion. When he left the city, he was determined never to go back, never to have any contact at all."

"His parents worked for Portia Steel," I say. That was why Mum got all the blame for them running away. That was why it was such a big deal, why Abbott never forgave our family. He got it in the neck from Steel because the precious Sebastian had been tempted away from his school.

That was why Abbott had it in for me and Bear, from the very beginning.

"Gael worried if his parents found out they had grandchildren in the city, they'd make a claim on you." Willow's voice trails off. She looks at Bear, who's crept up to me and slotted his hand in mine. "You'd like to meet your dad, wouldn't you, Bear? I know how excited he will be to see you again."

"If he's our dad, why didn't he come for us?" Bear says.

"He thought you were safer where you were, with your grandmother."

"He should have come anyway," Bear says. Willow looks to me for support but this time I stay silent.

"You'll meet him soon," Willow says in a bright tone. "I promise you will. We don't have any way of getting word to him, but it was Gael's plan to be home by winter solstice. The shortest day. It's only a few days away. Your dad's not one to break his word."

After Willow's gone, I tear the portraits out from my sketchbook and line them up on one of the shelves.

"Can I have the one of Queenie?" Bear asks.

"Of course," I say, passing it over. "Queenie's yours."

Willow's soup is going cold beside us, but I can't face it. I sit down on the chair again, exhausted, empty, and Bear climbs back on to my lap. "I'm sorry, Ju."

"Sorry?" I ask, puzzled.

"About Mum. You needed her more than I did."

"Why would you say that? I'm thirteen. I'm almost grown up. You're the one we needed her for."

"I've already got you, Ju."

He wraps his arms round my waist and places his head against my chest so he's right up against my heart.

"You're unique, Bear, you know that? The one and only."

"No one else in whole wide world?"

"And no one else in the Wild."

The Wild is the world for us. I don't think we could ever go back to the city. We'd be savages there now.

67

The villagers light fires and prepare a feast for us. We taste the beef that Cam raved about, and a huge pink fish from the lake. There are vegetables too – potatoes, kale, cabbages, leeks – in this rich steaming soup. Like our Gloop but thicker and with a load more flavour. The villagers sit round the fire on wooden benches and kids flock around the edges. Bear holds back at first, shy, but the kids don't give up. They run past him, laughing, enticing him out of the circle to play, and it doesn't take much before he's off. Running off with them.

Willow introduces me to people, tells me who everyone is and sometimes a little about their story. Who came here, who was born here, who came back.

It's hard to take in all the new names and faces but I suppose there will be time for that. We're certainly not crossing the mountains again in winter.

"Are there ReWilders here?" I ask Willow, looking around the fire at the older villages.

Willow nods. "Only a couple now. We've had a few losses lately."

"At least they got to enjoy it," I say.

Willow looks at me, confused.

"All this," I mean. "Nature's great recovery." I think of Silvan, still locked in the city.

"You're right." Willow pauses. "But it's a big legacy to have. A big thing to be responsible for. The ReWilders have their demons, all of them." Her voice is heavy and I look up at her.

"What about you?" I ask, realizing Willow hasn't told me anything about herself. I've told her pretty much everything – about why we left, about the Institute, about May and Ms Endo, and exactly how bad Portia Steel's gleaming city is now. It felt like I needed to tell someone, that someone here should know all that.

Willow smiles almost apologetically. "My mum was one of them. One of the ReWilders. I was born here."

"In Ennerdale?"

"In Ennerdale. I've spent my whole life in this valley, Juniper."

Willow talks to me about our dad, as though she has to explain things on his behalf. How things were back then. Why he travels so much. The tick disease has shifted, changed. She says maybe one day soon there will be a way to get more people out here. That's what our dad's doing. He's working with scientists in one of the northern cities to help develop a vaccine.

"With blood transfusions?" I ask sharply.

Willow looks horrified. "No, Juniper. No one here would be involved in anything like that. You're safe here."

At one point Willow disappears and I wonder if she's gone to sleep – she's been yawning a lot – but she comes back with a pile of papers. "I thought you'd want to see these."

I flick through them, spellbound. They're sketches – a tiny child, fast asleep, newborn, and then sitting up, laughing, crawling, walking. It's a girl and she has tight curls that get looser as she grows.

"Who?" I ask.

"Don't you recognize yourself?"

"Who drew them, I mean?"

Willow laughs. "I'll give you a clue. Gael certainly can't draw like this and you obviously inherited your talent from someone."

I blush.

"I've still got all your mum's paints and brushes. They're in our hut. I'll bring them across to you tomorrow."

I smile gratefully. "I look happy," I say, staring into the little girl's face.

"You were always happy, Juniper." Willow's voice is breaking up and my eyes flick across to her.

"You knew me then, didn't you? That's why you recognized us."

Willow nods. "I knew you at once. You and Bear. None of us gave up. We knew one day you'd come home."

In one of the pictures, there's a man with dark curly hair and I know him straight away. I'd know him anywhere. It's like seeing Bear all grown up.

"Dad." I touch his face and Willow smiles at me.

"Did Mum draw Bear too?" I ask.

Willow nods. "Yes, but only a couple of times. Marian was different by then. She was different after she came back from the city. After she'd taken you there. She regretted that for the rest of her days. Everyone had told her it was best, that it was for your safety. Too many little ones were dying. It was a horrible time to live through." Willow shivers, but she squeezes my hand.

"Why did she die, Willow?"

"She was just too weak. It had all got too much for her, and then the pregnancy, out here…" Willow pauses and puts her hand on her stomach.

"Why did Dad send Bear to the city?" I ask, unable to resist one final question before I let Willow go to bed.

"For you, Juniper. It was Marian's last wish that you and Bear would be together. Gael had to honour it, even though it broke his heart all over again."

68

The Ennerdale kids are playing this elaborate game of hide-and-seek in the dark. Bear's standing apart, watching.

"How's it going, Bear cub?" I ask, walking over.

Bear pulls a face. "I can't remember all their names. There are too many of them."

"But what are they like?"

"They're not as smart as Queenie, but I suppose they're OK," he says, taking my hand and leading me away from the fire.

"Where are we going?"

"To the lake."

"It's too cold!"

"We've got our rabbit skins. Please, Ju!" he says, tugging at me. "I want to see it at night."

I laugh. "OK, Bear. You lead the way."

There's this promontory that goes out into the lake,

almost like an island. It's pitch-black, inky, but our night vision is good now and tonight the sky seems more lit up than ever, even though the moon itself is thin – this new crescent of light.

Bear's picking up stones and throwing them into the water as far out as he can. "I guess we should have known," he says thoughtfully. "That's why Mum didn't come for us."

"Yeah."

"The other kids say Dad's coming any day now."

"I know."

Bear pauses. "Why would he go into a city, Ju?"

"He's working with some scientists, Willow says. To see if there's a way to bring more people into the Wild."

Bear looks shocked. "Like Steel was?"

I shake my head. "Nah. Willow promised me. This is different. This is good, Bear. And it means he's the right person to help us too."

"Help us?" Bear asks, his nose wrinkled.

"To get Annie Rose. And Etienne, if he wants to come here."

Bear looks confused. "Etienne and Annie Rose don't have the resistance."

"I know that, but I still reckon there has to be a way." If scientists are right and you can give a person immunity. There's a load of detail to be worked out, it won't be easy, but there must be a way. There has to be. They're our people and we can't just leave them behind.

Music floats out over the water, and voices too – talking, singing, laughing, just like Hester's camp. Bear looks over, his face glistening in the moonlight. "Do you think they're dancing?"

I smile, thinking back to him cavorting round the campfire with Queenie. "Shall we go and see?"

"In a minute." Bear bends down for another stone. "I bet you can't beat me."

"You sure about that?"

I reach for a pebble but there's a shriek and Bear's calling my name. "Juniper! She's back!"

Ghost. Our silver spotted lynx is stepping on to the island. She's found us, and Bear and I are running forward and she's pushing her head into our waists.

I bury my face into Ghost's fur, breathing her in, glad there's only Bear to see my tears.

Bear's whooping. "I can't believe we tamed a lynx cat, Ju! We're wilder than Ennerdale!"

Ghost breaks away from us and goes to the lake to drink. To the water, where the stars are all reflected back, the whole of the night sky like a huge canvas. Bear and I stand next to her, making our calls. Our ululations. Like war cries.

Thanks

Mum and Dad. For taking me to the trees and the sea and the mountains. The places I went as a child are so special to me, especially the Lake District, where it feels I find younger versions of myself, and all my grandparents too. Thanks for the bedtime stories, the library visits and the books you bought for me to keep as my own. Writers are readers first and foremost and I have so much to thank you for.

My wonderful sister, Emma, for finding the best books first and always passing them back to me.

Dom. From our beginning, you not only loved that I wanted to be a writer, you believed I was one. You're not always right, but on this one I'll let you have it! This whole adventure was possible because of you.

Matilda, Daisy, Freddie, Bea. Our own little tribe. You made everything new. I rediscovered the woods with you and I rediscovered children's literature too. This book is for you, but it is you too. My beautiful, crazy children, who remind me what it is to run wild.

My friends and family members, Dom's family as well as my own. I'm terrified of leaving someone out if I list you, but for everything, and each and every time you've asked about my book, thank you, all of you.

Roisin Heycock and Cara Lovelock. For reading Juniper and Bear's story in its earliest incarnation and telling me to keep going. For our late night, gin-fuelled writing groups and Friday morning book chat in Beans and Barley while our children went feral in the play area. It was the best of times, and I still haven't quite forgiven you for moving away, Cara, even though I have basically written a whole book about why leaving the city would be a good thing.

All the cats I've loved, but especially Bo, our beautiful Burmese, who died very soon after this book's conception. Ghost is for you.

SCBWI's Undiscovered Voices anthology for featuring my first few chapters in 2018. I am so grateful to everyone involved, also Alex Antscherl who critiqued my UV submission as part of Authors for Grenfell. Extra special thanks to my fellow writers and illustrators, and writer Sara Grant, who was the fairy godmother of the whole operation and got us to the ball with so much generosity and kindness.

Lizza Aiken and Julia Churchill for shortlisting my book for the inaugural Joan Aiken Future Classics Prize in 2017.

Peter Fiennes for kindly allowing me to quote from *Oak and Ash and Thorn*. I urge anyone who cares about our woodland to read this remarkable book.

The people I've connected with on Twitter – the writers, illustrators, bloggers, teachers, librarians, environmentalists. Book Twitter and Nature Twitter, I've learned so much! Extra special thanks here to the Swaggers – a dazzlingly brilliant group of children's writers debuting in 2019 and 2020. For the solidarity, the wisdom, the distraction, the GIFs.

Gillie Russell, my incredible agent, for seeing Juniper and Bear exactly as they are. I couldn't find a better ally.

Stripes for wholeheartedly embracing my world and characters and making them everything I wanted them to be. Particular thanks to: Sara Mognol for designing the absolutely perfect cover and inside imagery; Kate Forrester for realizing Sara's design so beautifully – it's a piece of art now and Juniper would be delighted; Lauren Ace and Charlie Morris; Leilah Skelton, for creative and environmentally aware marketing and publicity, and for hailing from my hometown of Doncaster and making me feel extra welcome; the hive mind editorial team that is Mattie Whitehead, Ella Whiddett and Ruth Bennett. Lastly, Katie Jennings, my extraordinary editor, who made the most incredible leaps and connections to make *Where the World Turns Wild* the very best it could be. I am frankly in awe, Katie. Thank you!

My final thanks are to you, reader. It's with you that Juniper and Bear get to go on their journey. They've been such a big part of my life for three years now and it's hard to let them go. But they've hung around long enough. Please watch over them for me – they've still got so much to learn!

About the Author

Nicola Penfold was born in Merseyside and grew up in Doncaster. She studied English at Cambridge, before completing a Computing Science Master's programme at Imperial College London. Nicola has worked in a reference library and for a health charity, but being a writer was always the job she wanted most. *Where the World Turns Wild* was shortlisted for the first Joan Aiken Future Classics Prize in 2017. It was also selected for SCBWI's 2018 Undiscovered Voices anthology. Nicola writes in the coffee shops and green spaces of North London, where she lives with her husband, four children and two cats, and escapes when she can to wilder corners of the UK for adventures.